CW00516487

ICE STATION DEATH

GUSTAVO BONDONI

SEVERED PRESS
HOBART TASMANIA

ICE STATION DEATH

Copyright © 2019 Gustavo Bondoni

WWW.SEVEREDPRESS.COM

All rights reserved. No part of this book may be reproduced or transmitted in any form or by any electronic or mechanical means, including photocopying, recording or by any information and retrieval system, without the written permission of the publisher and author, except where permitted by law. This novel is a work of fiction. Names, characters, places and incidents are the product of the author's imagination, or are used fictitiously. Any resemblance to actual events, locales or persons, living or dead, is purely coincidental.

ISBN: 978-1-925840-61-2

All rights reserved.

PROLOGUE

July, 1980

Captain Yevgeny Petrov cursed the KGB. He cursed the idiot who'd decided it would be a good idea to reach Africa by going around the far side of the world. The grey and nameless bureaucrat responsible had condemned his crew to sail across the Pacific and more than a hundred kilometers south of Tierra del Fuego.

The analysts had justified it by saying that it was the route least likely to be watched by the Americans, and that sailing around the Horn of Africa on their way to Congo might get them spotted by the South Africans which, for some reason, they considered infinitely worse than being spotted by the navies of Chile or Argentina.

He cursed the weather. Proud of being Russian born, he felt that he could take anything the planet could throw at them, but he was shocked to find that, once you got under the Antarctic Circle, the wind bit like the worst Siberian gale. Add snow and ten-meter waves, and he wished he was back in Ossora.

He particularly cursed whoever had decided that the innocuous-looking grey drums, marked only with the word 'Sverdlovsk', that they were carrying should be further disguised by loading them onto a barely seaworthy trawler built sometime in the 1950s.

His first mate, one of the few men on board who didn't work for the KGB, came onto the bridge, appearing like a spirit from the night. "We're taking on water faster than the pumps can deal with it, sir."

Petrov sighed. "Give the order to abandon ship. I don't know if the lifeboats can deal with these seas, but I'm sure this piece of junk can't. I'll try to keep us afloat as long as possible. Come and get me for the second lifeboat." There were only two covered lifeboats on board. Luckily, someone had updated them in the past couple of decades. They might survive, and he had no intention of throwing his life away to go down with this particular ship.

"Yes, sir."

The man disappeared and, for some minutes, Yevgeny had his hands full negotiating the swells. He imagined the ship groaning beneath his feet as they rose and fell at the whim of the sea. It might have been more than just his imagination, but the howling wind made it impossible for him to be certain. It would have been much safer to sail the Straits of Magellan, but that suggestion had been met with an icy refusal that left no doubt that he shouldn't ask again. These orders were not meant to be questioned.

So, in sinking between Tierra del Fuego and Antarctica, they would have to ditch too far from civilization for help to arrive until the storm abated. Ice clutched at his heart in the knowledge that his two little girls would have to grow up without a father. He hoped the State did well by them.

A new face appeared in the doorway. Vitaly Kyvat glared at him as he attempted to hold on to the frame of the door. He dripped copious amounts of water.

"Petrov," he barked. "I have cancelled your order. We are staying with the ship."

"That's madness, Kyvat. We'll die, every last one of us."

"You are a coward. Do the job you were assigned to do and stop complaining."

"This ship is going to sink."

A Makarov pistol appeared in Kyvat's hand as if by magic. "You will do your job, or I will first shoot you and then report you as a traitor to the Soviet Union. Your family will starve in the gulag. I will see to it myself."

Yevgeny gave him a curt nod and put his eyes back on the sea ahead of them. It was a hopeless task he'd been set, but he wouldn't argue. The KGB pig would make good on his promise, regardless of whether Petrov saved his life or not.

Much better to drown trying to save his family. The only comfort he had was that, if he died, so would the monster with the gun.

He miscalculated a wave and it hit them broadside, swamping the deck and causing the ship to tilt alarmingly to one side. Worse, it didn't right itself after the water receded.

The KGB man was gone, washed into the night, but that had become the least of Petrov's concerns as he wrestled with the wheel.

The controls were sluggish, even by the tub's standards. He wouldn't be able to turn into the next swell in time.

The prow disappeared beneath the dark sea again.

This time it didn't come back up.

This surprised Yevgeny. Maybe, if the ship sank slowly enough, he could get some of his men onto the lifeboats. He left the bridge and began to climb down the ladder to the deck.

In the dark night, without the prow-mounted floodlights, he never saw the next wave.

It washed him into the depths of the icy ocean and finished sinking the small ship.

CHAPTER 1

Present Day

Javier Balzano looked up at the ship with a mixture of pride and annoyance. The *ARA Almirante Irizar* was a national treasure; Argentina's only icebreaker was famous for patrolling near Antartica and rescuing the crews of disabled science vessels.

National pride notwithstanding, he didn't want to board her a week early. He'd been given only ten days' leave, and had been looking forward to spending time in Buenos Aires with his friends. He'd begged, cajoled, threatened to resign and even asked to be airlifted to the icebreaker by helicopter while the ship was in transit.

His requests had been denied. The last one had been laughed off as an insane expense for the cash-strapped Argentine Navy.

So there he was, heading up the forward gangplank. He saluted the ship's ensign and then faced the lieutenant on watch and repeated the salute. "Permission to come aboard."

The man looked up from his clipboard, surprise evident that one of the days' arrivals would honor naval tradition. When he saw the uniform, however, he quickly snapped to attention and returned the salute. "Permission granted. Welcome aboard, Colonel." He looked back at his clipboard. "The captain asked me to tell you that we've stowed your gear, and that he'd be honored if you would join him on the bridge. I'll leave your bag in your cabin."

The bridge, Balzano knew, was perched above the four-story cream-colored cube that loomed above him. To his soldier's eye, the *Irizar's* shape looked like anything but a military vehicle. Much too tall and ungainly with its weight concentrated in the front, the thing should topple into the waves. And who went about painting anything military in red and cream? Well, maybe the red hull would be invisible under the ice and the cream would blend… but still.

He trudged up the stairs. The bridge, at least, was what he imagined. Spartan, but modern, it smelled like a mix of new car and the glue used to install rubber flooring after its recent ten-year refurbishment. The view from the bridge only reinforced Javier's sense that something tall and thin shouldn't be on the water and that, as soon as they cast off, it would capsize, drowning all hands.

"Colonel Balzano," a smiling man said. "Glad you could make it."

"Captain Celmi." Javier nodded a greeting. "It wasn't by choice, let me tell you."

"I understand."

Javier knew the man would. Being a soldier in Argentina, a country with no foreign wars or overseas territories to defend, was an honorable profession, but not one that attracted fanatics or young men looking to etch their name in the history books. It was a job for family men, solid citizens who appreciated their time off.

The captain continued. "Please make yourself at home in the meantime. Ask for anything you need."

"Did anyone tell you why we're leaving in such a hurry? All they told me was that the schedule had been moved up for reasons of force majeure. Then they declined my requests not to come along. Is it a PR stunt?"

It was the conclusion he'd reached, since none other was available. The ship had been in the news about fifteen years before when it rescued the crew of a German ship stuck in the ice, but had subsequently caught fire and been drydocked for a decade amid all kinds of political bickering and finger-pointing. The fact that it was about to set sail again was major national news.

Javier didn't think the president would be above generating a little more goodwill by sending the ship out a week early on some fabricated emergency. Like all democracies in the 21st century, Argentina's ran on headlines.

Celmi smiled. "It actually looks like the real reason is legit. Belgrano II went offline a few days ago. They'd been having trouble with their uplink for months, and it finally went kaput."

Belgrano II was the southernmost of Argentina's Antarctic bases. It was the *Irizar's* final destination, after a stop in Comodoro Rivadavia for stock and supplies.

"And it couldn't wait a week?"

"Would you want to wait an extra week if you were in Antarctica without any way to contact your family… or anyone else?"

"So send the antenna in by plane."

"They're having crap weather. Supposedly, we'll be there before it clears. And before you ask, no, the ice around the base won't finish melting until mid-February, so yes, the *Irizar* is the only viable option."

"Damn." But Javier knew that any further discussion would just be griping for the hell of it—also an honored Argentine military tradition, but not one that would help at the moment. The reasons as stated were more than enough to bump up a mission that was already slated to ship out anyway. Besides, he'd always thought that griping was beneath the dignity of officers. Let the enlisted men do that. "Fair enough." He smiled. "Thanks for the welcome, and you won't hear any more complaints from me."

"Oh, don't worry about that. Just promise me that you won't talk to any of my men that way and I'll be happy to listen. But under one condition."

"What's that?"

"You have to listen to me as well. Have you got any idea what it was like getting this thing shipshape for a real mission? All we'd done out of dry dock were a few test runs with a skeleton crew. My nightmare is that we'll arrive at Antarctica to find that some welding team down below came along for the ride."

Javier chuckled. "Fair enough."

He left the bridge to see if he could find his quarters. A few minutes after he'd gotten settled in, his cell phone buzzed.

The science team he was supposed to be babysitting had arrived.

***

Camila Lopez Tirante wiped the sweat from her brow. She couldn't wait to get to Antarctica and leave the absurd heat and humidity of Buenos Aires behind. And why did they have to be on board before three o'clock? The ship was scheduled to leave at eight.

But excitement soon overcame annoyance. She was actually, finally, going.

Her own team of three geology students was already standing on the sweltering dock when she arrived. Ernesto and Martin were both Argentines, while Anderson was one of the countless Venezuelans who'd emigrated to the country in search of a better life than the socialist paradise could offer... She thought he was misguided, but then again, he was still young, with a lot to learn. All three were in their early twenties, and she'd found them at the intern program from the University of La Plata. Brilliant, hardworking kids who'd just landed the dream summer internship. On one hand, she wondered if she'd ever been that enthusiastic but, on the other, envied them. She'd had to wait until she was a well-established geologist to be able to take the trip they were about to enjoy.

Her phone buzzed. It was Clark Smith, the Australian geologist who'd begged to come along. She answered.

"Which dock did you say you were on again?" the man said.

"None of the numbered ones. The ship is moored just before the restaurants at Puerto Madero."

"Ah, yes, I see it now. Thanks."

A small grey Volkswagen with a beautiful dark-haired woman at the wheel stopped in front of them. The man sitting beside her leaned over for a long kiss before descending.

He was a tall, rangy guy with blue eyes, light brown hair and a five-day stubble broken only by a short scar that ran from his chin up his cheek on the right side of his face. He looked around and waved when he spotted Camila.

"Dr. Lopez-Tirante?" he said in strangely accented English.

"Yes. You must be Dr. Smith."

"At your service," the man replied with a smile that made Camila more than a little jealous of the young woman who'd just driven off. Although she knew that the Australian had only arrived in Buenos Aires two nights before and would likely only be there a couple of days on their way back and she immediately pegged him as the kind of guy whose heart was never really owned, only rented for a few hours at a time. For a moment, she wondered whether it would be worth it.

"We're still waiting for the Götthelm sisters. You can go find your cabin if you like."

"I'll wait with you," he replied. "I've been looking forward to meeting this team for ages." He took the time to introduce himself to the three students. That was easier said than done. Anderson, the Venezuelan, came from an upper-middle-class family and had gone to American schools in his youth, but the other two were working-class Argentines with no English language skills to speak of. Still, the outgoing Australian used the few words of Spanish he'd picked up to show that he was delighted to see them.

Camila found herself warming to the man despite her reservations about having such an obvious player on board.

Anna and Ingrid Götthelm piled out of a taxi. They hugged Camila, shook hands with Clark and the students and beamed at the sun. Anyone would have guessed they were Swedish from a mile away. Pale, with hair so blond it was almost white, tall and broad-shouldered, they looked more like Olympic swimmers than scientists.

But anyone assuming that would have been in for a shock. The sisters were probably the world's most renowned microbiologists. When they'd heard that Camila—whom they knew from a symposium on soil composition at Harvard—was mounting an Antarctic expedition, they'd signed up for it in a heartbeat. Had Camila known they were interested, she would have begged them to come. Their presence legitimized everything.

"Your equipment has been packed on board. You may want to uncrate it once we're underway. I have a feeling that Javier doesn't want us to do anything but look pretty until the ship leaves port."

"Did I hear my name?"

Javier appeared, and Camila's hackles rose immediately. She'd accepted the man's presence as a practical matter: if one wanted to get to Argentina's Antarctic bases, one needed to speak to the military. But the fact that her expedition was under this guy's command was more than she could take with good grace.

Making things worse, he was unbearably upper class. Argentine society was stratified along social lines, and many traditional families had a military background. Javier's, she suspected by the way he spoke, was one of them.

He was well-groomed, with brown hair slightly longer than she'd have expected from a soldier, and pale skin. His smile, at least, was genuine. "I apologize for making everyone run to catch the ship," he told them, "but trust me when I say that it was completely out of my hands." Even the guy's English had private school written all over it. "Now that everyone's here, we should probably get on board."

"Not yet. The American's still missing," Camila said.

"Dr. Breen? He's on board already. He arrived before I did, to supervise the loading of his equipment."

Again, Camila chafed. She'd been assured that her team's equipment would be fine and firmly discouraged from supervising the loading operation. But Breen, it appeared, was the victim of no such restrictions. Worse, he wasn't anywhere near as important as the other men and women on her team, just some undistinguished biologist from Brown that she'd had to google to learn anything about. As always, Argentina bent over backwards to make the Americans happy. But what did one expect when one voted for a rightwing government?

She followed her team up the gangway, rolled her eyes at the little ceremony performed by the Colonel when asking permission to board and followed the instructions to find her cabin.

***

Carl Breen watched a couple of marine cadets manhandle his boxes. The equipment he'd brought with him was not particularly delicate, but it was heavy, and he wanted to be sure it was securely in place before the ship sailed. If the crates moved and broke to reveal what was inside, he'd have to answer a hell of a lot of questions. It was bad enough that the Colonel in charge of the scientists had been briefed. If the rest of the crew found out, nothing would keep it from the press… and that would, once again sour the always delicate relations between the U.S. and Argentina.

Breen didn't particularly care. He was there for a reason and if some sanctimonious journalist took offense… well, that was a problem he wouldn't have to deal with.

The loading crew appeared to know what they were doing. He'd never worked with the Argentine Navy before, but found their loaders to be about the same as loaders anywhere else. They went about their business efficiently, hoping to get it done so they could goof off. To his eye, they appeared to be professionals, but not fanatical about it.

When the final crate was lashed down in an enclosed area at the back of the ship beneath the heliports, he moved towards the fo'c'sle, where he would pose for the cameras along with everyone else. It would look bad if he missed it.

He sighed.

***

Javier stood to one side and sweated. The scientists, clearly uncomfortable in the presence of massed journalists, sheltered behind him. That was exactly how Javier preferred it. If any scientific questions were asked, he could field them. He wasn't a scientist himself, but he'd read the material, and could easily spout all the official answers. The last thing anyone needed was a scientist speechifying about some obscure rock layer for fifteen minutes.

One thing that did surprise him was the fact that Breen had shown up for the event. He didn't seem like a man who'd welcome on-screen appearances… but then again, maybe appearing as a scientist in an innocuous location like Argentina might be the perfect cover for a future operation. But the Colonel wasn't fooled for a moment. The man knew less biology than Javier did: he would be lucky to be able to tell a whale from a penguin. The briefing said he was from the U.S. State Department, but the man shouted spook, and that would have been Javier's assessment even if he hadn't been briefed—extremely superficially—about the American on a 'special assignment'.

He didn't let that worry him overmuch. On a ship this size or in a nearly-deserted stretch of Antarctica, no one's activities would remain secret very long. It was always fun to watch covert operators get hot and bothered when the cook asked them how their secret listening station was coming along.

As for the press, they were focusing on the main reason for this mission: propaganda. The major outlets, more or less aligned with the government, were asking fawning questions that seemed to have been lifted right off the official press release. Every once in a while, a more pointed question would come through, especially about the viability of the expensive Argentine presence in Antarctica, but the bland answer would be accepted without follow-up.

More interesting were the opposition outlets which consisted of a couple of small socialist papers who absolutely despised the current régime. It was always fun to see what they came up with, but this time their attempts at derailing the conference were blunted by the Naval spokeswoman, a spin doctor who'd honed her craft during the presidential campaign and had been rewarded with a well-paid spot. The journalists, spewing questions straight out of 1917, didn't stand much of a chance.

They received exactly one science question, completely simplistic and having to do with whether they would be studying global warming. He fielded it quickly by saying that, though it wasn't a specific objective of the mission, it was something that the permanent Antarctic bases always looked at, and that anything found by his team that might have a relationship to those studies—particularly on the bacteriological side—would be shared both with the scientists stationed there and the wider scientific community. Heads nodded and his words were recorded by cell phones.

Finally, the press conference ended, the journalists, except for a pair who'd be sailing with the ship as far as Comodoro Rivadavia, were politely but firmly ushered off and the crew sprang into action. Javier assumed that they were battening hatches and swabbing decks… or whatever it was modern navies did before setting sail.

He approached Camila. It didn't take a genius to understand why her feathers were ruffled: he'd been put in nominal command of an expedition she'd spent the better part of a decade planning. But he needed her on his side, and not poisoning the rest of her team with her attitude. Besides, he hadn't asked for the posting and wasn't thrilled to be the babysitter for a bunch of scientists. Yes, it was a cushy job and highly visible—which meant that the higher-ups were probably preparing the ground for a future promotion—but it wasn't what he'd signed up for.

"Hi, want to get a drink?"

She looked surprised. "Is that allowed?"

The emotion replaced the semi-permanent half-scowl Camila habitually wore when speaking to him. The sudden unguarded openness looked much better, and made her look younger. He knew she was thirty-four, but always appeared to be a decade older. Her grey-streaked black hair only heightened the illusion. He felt a pang of disappointment that she hated him; her big brown eyes and open features were quite pretty when she didn't sneer.

"This is a naval vessel. I think it might be compulsory."

That actually elicited the ghost of a smile. "Lead the way."

Easier said than done. He had only the vaguest idea of where things were on the ship and no idea where the officer's bar was. He stopped a Second Lieutenant who seemed unclear on whether a mere army Colonel should be allowed into the Navy's holy of holies. But annoyed senior officers look the same in any service and the man soon revealed the location.

The guy behind the bar was more experienced and served up a whisky on the rocks for Javier and a glass of red wine for Camila without a second glance.

"So," Javier began, "What's the plan for the trip? We have five days before we get to Comodoro Rivadavia."

"I thought telling us what to do was your job."

"Yes," he said. "We can do it that way if you prefer." He let her think about that for a few moments.

"What do you mean?"

"I mean that I'm in command. So, if you like, I can tell all the scientists what they should be doing at every moment of the day. As the responsible authority, I'd be within my rights. I just don't think it would be the best way to get the most out of the impressive brainpower on board. I thought maybe, you might want to take the lead on that side of things and I can worry about the stuff I'm good at, namely keeping all of you safe and making sure the reports the army wants to see are filed in time. But it's your call."

"You'd actually let me work in peace? So far, you've been running it as your personal project."

"I had to get you on board safely and make certain all the formalities were observed. Now is the time to modify that." He held her gaze. "But only if you want to."

"Of course I want to." Suspicion crossed her features. "What's the catch?"

"No catch, except that you keep me informed of what you're planning. Also, that you check with me before sending anyone out to do something dangerous once we reach Antarctica."

"Do you mean that?"

"Yes. I want this mission to succeed. I'm not interested in getting in your way."

"I thought that was the only thing military officers were good for."

"You're thinking of the officers above me. Colonels, of course, are all brilliant and trust their people to do their jobs without ever interfering or micromanaging."

"All colonels?"

"Of course. We're quite a splendid bunch."

She finally laughed. "We'll see. What about the American?"

"Are you really interested in what he does?"

"If he's going to be doing science on my watch, yes."

Breen wasn't going to do any science. Javier knew it and he had a feeling that Camila suspected it, too. But he couldn't say it. "I'll have to check. You know how the government is about Americans. I can't promise anything."

She gave him a level look. "Fair enough, I guess. I'll be happy if you leave the rest of my team alone."

"You can count on that."

"Good."

They drank on for a while, neither wanting to break the conversation off too abruptly, but after a couple of attempts at conversation petered off awkwardly, Javier was left with the sense that either they had nothing whatsoever in common, or that Camila simply didn't want to.

CHAPTER 2

The TV blared in a corner, ignored by all. Camila had gathered the scientists—except for the insufferable Breen, of course—in one of the ship's lounges which had been reserved for them to hold a team session. There was little to discuss because all of the proposed experiments and sample-taking had been pre-approved, and any changes or additions would happen in Antarctica itself, but she'd still wanted them to get together. Experience had taught her that a group that was comfortable in each other's company would share findings and ideas, leading to additional insights and cross-pollination.

Besides, staring out at the sea and surfing the net on the ship's overloaded connection had gotten old really fast. Two days in, every scientist on board had gotten back to work either on projects related to the expedition or on their unconnected work. All of them had institutions they answered to, places that had accepted their request to take a few months off, but who had enormous trouble cutting the cord completely and were always asking for reports or information.

"Wait," Ernesto blurted out in Spanish, holding up a hand. "That's what I was telling you about before." He pointed at the TV where a reporter in a yellow poncho was bobbing up and down on a boat in a slate-grey sea.

They all turned to look.

"Oh, great, more water," Clark said, reverting to the groups' official language, English. "That should bring some much-needed variety to our lives."

"Turn it up, will you?"

Ernesto walked over to the sofa where the remote lay and turned the volume up. The reporter's words echoed off the metal walls and Camila offered a running translation to English.

"The creature has been reported by several fishing boats off the coast of Ushuaia," the woman said. "This isn't the first time a flurry of unidentified creatures have been reported in the seas in and around the Straits of Magellan, but it is the first time in nearly a hundred years that there have been so many sightings."

The screen turned to a hand-drawn sketch, in pencil, of what appeared to be a snake's head emerging from a body of water. Behind the head, something that looked like a fin broke the surface.

"In 1905 and 1906, several sightings of an unidentified sea-creature were reported to authorities in Patagonia. This drawing was made by an English sailor who was an eyewitness to one of the events."

"He should have used his iPhone," Anna joked, viewing the image critically. "He wasn't much of an artist."

"In an unusual twist," the reporter continued, "unconnected reports surfaced in Brazil, thousands of kilometers away. A nearly-identical sea creature was spotted on a beach. At that time, there were speculations, based on witness testimony, that the animals might have been plesiosaurs that somehow survived the extinction of the dinosaurs to roam modern oceans.

"Of course, in the century since those sightings, we've explored the seas much more comprehensively, and nothing of the sort has been encountered since. Until now.

"Many people are speculating that the sightings are related to the various reports of the Nahuelito creature in the Nahuel Huapi Lake in Bariloche. Eyewitnesses say that the sea creature is very similar to the one seen by countless tourists near the holiday resort.

"These images," a blurred and distant cell phone picture replaced the drawing; they showed a dark shape in the distance, "were taken just a week ago, right here in this spot. We've rented a fishing boat to see if we can get some real images of the sea monster, and we're determined to stay right here until we do. We'll keep you posted."

The image returned to the three talking heads in the studio and Ernesto turned it back down.

"We're sailing right that way," Ingrid said. "Maybe we should help them look for the monster."

"Maybe we should sail in the opposite direction," Clark said with a grin. "I hear the Bahamas are beautiful this time of year... plus, there are no sea monsters."

Anna initiated a web search on the laptop in front of her. "Here's where they got that drawing."

They all crowded around to look at the website dedicated to cryptozoology, but Anna exchanged a glance with Ingrid. "Are you thinking what I'm thinking?"

Ingrid smiled. "If you're thinking oarfish, I am."

"Bingo."

Camila tried to suppress her annoyance. The sisters weren't twins, but they often acted like they could read each other's minds... much to the irritation of anyone who happened to be around. "What," she said calmly, "is an oarfish?"

Wikipedia replaced the drawing on Anna's screen, and she showed them a picture of a group of US soldiers holding a huge flat snake. The caption called it a 23-foot-long oarfish.

"That is an oarfish," Ingrid said. "They've probably been responsible for more erroneous sea-monster sightings and sea-serpent legends than anything other than whales."

Anna toggled back to the drawing. "And if you look here, it's not all that different. The trouble is that people don't know about them because they tend to live in really deep waters and only come up when they're dying. So, sometimes they're spotted in their death throes and look a lot like that."

Clark spoke. "You biologists are always ruining everything for people. I would love for there to be real sea-monsters. The world would be a much better place."

"Well, we were heartbroken when we learned that the Earth wasn't hollow. Can you imagine the blow that represented to two girls brought up on Verne? Just awful. So consider this our revenge." But Anna's smile towards the Australian belied her words.

Clark's smile in return made Camila jealous again. And then she was angry at herself for being jealous. She reminded herself, for the millionth time, that her loneliness was temporary. She'd settle down when the right person came along. What was the use of dating a string of guys too scared to be with a woman smarter than they were.

Of course, in Clark's case, the guy was a scientist, too. That might help matters.

"Besides," Ingrid went on. "The thing that always astounds me is that, despite the proliferation of cameras on everything we carry, no one can ever get a decent picture of one of those things."

"Yeah, the only way I'd believe in something like that is to see it with my own eyes," Clark said.

"We're still a few days off from the Straits, and we won't be going through them, anyway," Camila said for no reason other than to stop the flirting that, she felt, was about to flare up.

"How long are we going to stop in Comodoro? Will we have time to explore the city?"

"We'll be there twenty-four hours. It should be more than enough to look around. I think there's a petroleum museum you can visit. I'll try to get the colonel to hire us a car for anyone who wants to go there. Other than that, the city isn't much. It's small, expensive and dusty… except for a beach to the south called Rada Tilly which is supposed to be really nice. I'm not sure we can get there, though."

"Have you been there?"

Camila shook her head. "No. I asked a couple of friends of mine who worked down there for YPF. That's the national oil company."

What Camila didn't say was that her friends had also warned her that the city had a rampant violent crime problem, and that it was best not to be out on the street after dark. Foreigners always acted like they were afraid for their lives every time they stepped on Latin American soil, even though Argentina was much safer than most countries on the planet… even the ones that pretended to be oh-so-civilized. She wasn't going to perpetuate the myth of insecurity.

***

On the day they docked in Comodoro Rivadavia, Carl Breen watched the men filing onto the *Almirante Irizar* carefully. The soldiers had to push their way through the crowds that had appeared to take an abbreviated guided tour of the famous icebreaker.

Fifteen of the men were dressed in the tan uniforms that the Argentine Army used for ceremonial occasions, but they weren't particularly impressive examples of soldiery to his eye. Some slouched, a couple ran across the gangplank in an impromptu game of tag. All of them were thin and stringy. They looked healthy enough, but not particularly well trained on the physical side. They clearly weren't commando troops… or if they were, Argentina would be in trouble if they were ever needed.

Each of them carried only a duffel bag which he assumed contained their clothes. He nodded in approval. He knew that many armies allowed their people to use wheeled luggage as it was more practical in most circumstances… but those circumstances definitely didn't include trying to manhandle tiny wheels up icy Antarctic rocks.

Two officers waited below and only strode onto the gangplank when the enlisted men were safely aboard: a second lieutenant and another colonel. It might have seemed wasteful to have a full colonel commanding such a small detachment, but Breen knew that Argentina considered the national presence in Antarctica to be of utmost strategic importance.

Three bearded civilians, none younger than fifty, rounded out the detachment.

At first glance, these guys were exactly what he'd been told they were: the replacements for the men who were rotating out of the Antarctic base, and who'd be returning—probably gratefully—to the mainland on the *Irizar*.

But he wasn't being paid to accept first glances. One of his tasks on the mission—admittedly a minor one, but one he intended to complete to the best of his ability—was to assess whether Argentina was building up a military presence in Antarctica that might go contrary to international agreements.

So far, he'd seen no evidence of that. Politically, Argentina seemed an unlikely belligerent. A stable democracy for more than thirty-five years, the few conflicts it had—mainly continuing complaints against the British regarding the Falkland Islands and disputes with Chile about moving the line a hundred meters in one direction or another along the mountain border in the Andes—had been handled through diplomatic channels ever since the Junta that launched the Falklands War was ousted in 1983.

But even more, his own gut told him that the people around him were playing it straight. He'd been given unlimited access to the entire ship. His initial tour had included the equipment bays, engine rooms and access to the helicopter bay. He'd asked to look behind a couple of closed doors, just on general principles, and his requests had been granted with a shrug… and the doors had opened into a broom cupboard and a room full of pipes.

Those were the moments he'd listened carefully. Though his hosts didn't know it, Breen spoke Spanish fluently—probably better than most of the troops on this ship, if not their officers—and could use that knowledge to overhear unguarded comments. But again, other than jokes about crazy Gringos, which he got everywhere south of the border, no one said anything suspicious.

The strongest evidence of all that things were aboveboard came from the mere fact that, after being promised the run of the ship, he'd actually been given it. No one had stopped him from going anywhere he pleased even though they had to suspect—and Colonel Balzano actually knew—that he wasn't a scientist. More telling still was that no one followed him around to see what he was doing.

Either that or the person following him was very, very good.

Occam's Razor was a good way to get yourself killed in the world of covert operations… but in this case, his instincts told him that the simplest explanation actually was the truth: the Argentine Antarctic expedition was the plain vanilla operation they said it was, even though the military was in control.

Still, Breen trusted the evidence of his eyes more than words from a foreign government. He eyed the sun. The days were long here in the deep south of Patagonia, and nightfall was still a couple of hours away.

He'd finish his evaluation then.

***

The moon was out, three quarters full, and Breen wondered why the crew had elected to stay in port. There was no need to wait for the tide. Comodoro Rivadavia was an oil port with a deep water installation that didn't require any outside assistance for ships to sail in and out any time they felt like it.

It certainly wasn't for political or PR reasons this time. They were scheduled to cast off at around six-thirty in the morning. No self-respecting news crew would be up at that time. If news didn't happen after eleven in the morning, it would go unreported.

The news actually made his own life easier. Had the ship been active and the night crew up and about, he would have had to be much more circumspect in his actions. As it was, he simply left his cabin and walked a short distance down a corridor to the stairwell, just as he would if he were out to smoke a cigarette or get some air. It wasn't even that late, just past midnight. No one would be overly suspicious if they ran into him. Many of the Argentines on board were only just finishing dinner anyway.

The wind was blowing hard, from the sea. Once over the ship, it would continue west, unimpeded, over the vast arid plains of the Patagonian desert until it finally smacked into the Andes and released the moisture it was carrying to help keep the beautiful lakes and woods at the base of the mountains verdant.

Breen wasn't concerned about any of that, but he was thankful for the chilly breeze: it would serve to keep people below decks where he wanted them. Even the smokers would come out as infrequently as possible.

The cargo hold he needed was aft, below the heliports. Sailors and loading crews from the dock had spent the day packing the space full of pallets before sealing the bay doors. Breen hoped the side door would be easy to unlock. He'd brought along a set of lockpicks and some more modern electronic equipment for the task. He'd been assigned the equipment upon leaving, but not told where it came from. He suspected that, like most of the stuff he used on his missions, the CIA was involved.

He felt the exhilaration that always accompanied the possibility of discovery. He'd originally been trained by Military Intelligence to sit in inhospitable places with a canteen and a set of binoculars and to watch enemy troop movements but, due to a certain number of unfortunate circumstances and the fact that he had features and skin color that allowed him to blend into most populations—European, Persian, Middle Eastern or Latin American—as long as he didn't need to speak, had gradually gotten roped into more and more urban situations.

Eventually, they'd begun assigning him missions like this one, where his military background served to quickly assess situations and respond if necessary, but where the primary objective was that of observation.

In other words, they'd turned the soldier into a spy. He wondered why they didn't just transfer him to one of the spook organizations and get it over with.

Breen studied the door. The lock was a simple metal key, so lockpicks, then.

The first thing to do was to test the latch to see what the movement felt like and whether he could get any information from the mechanism. He tested and the door opened outward.

It hadn't been locked.

His amazement soon turned to anger. Anger at the Argentines for ignoring even the most basic tenets of operational security—hell, of common sense in places where enlisted soldiers from the lower classes had easy access—but also at his senior officers back home for sending him here to spy on a mission that looked more and more like the utterly insignificant science expedition it was supposed to be. They were paid to be paranoid, but this was just silly.

Inside the storeroom, he looked around for cameras. If he saw one, he would simply leave and pretend he'd gone in the wrong door—the fact that it had been unlocked would lend unexpected credence to that particular claim—which would be backed up by the footage of him looking around in a confused manner and retreating back the way he came.

No cameras presented themselves. Could they really be that trusting? He actually found himself hoping that the Argentines had some invisible fiber optic lenses hidden somewhere and that he'd have to call in his immunity to keep them from locking him up.

But he doubted it.

The next step was to use his own fiber-optic camera, similar to the ones doctors used for endoscopic exploration, to look inside the bales and crates of supplies the crew had loaded. The device resembled a cable with one end thicker than the other and connected directly to his cell phone. In fact, other than the lockpicks, which would be impossible to explain to anyone who knew what they were, all of his equipment looked like consumer electronics.

Much of it wasn't… but the camera was. Anything more would have been unnecessary overkill. It was small enough to fit into small cuts in bundles and knotholes and tiny gaps in the wooden crates. If the gaps weren't big enough, one of the tools in his lockpick set was a drill just the right diameter.

A bale of what looked to be arctic jackets met his first exploration, followed by one box of food after another. Machine parts sat in a few crates near the door. His heart began to race when he saw weapons boxes and tubes in a subsequent crate but, after maneuvering the camera for a look at the stenciled words on the dark case, he was disappointed to learn that it contained ten flare guns. The tubes must be the flares.

The *Irizar* was armed, of course. It had a couple of 40mm cannons used mainly to deter illegal fishing boats if it happened to encounter them, but that was perfectly open and upfront. Likewise, the profusion of sidearms and even rifles carried by the soldiers and sailors on board. This ship wouldn't fall prey to pirates—even if any had been stupid enough to attempt to operate in frigid southern waters patrolled by both Argentina and Great Britain.

But likewise, he was confident that nothing on this ship posed a threat to another military vessel, to any of the British bases in the South Atlantic, or… to anyone other than illegal fishing boats, really.

Breen left the storeroom and walked back to his cabin, just an unconcerned passenger out for a stroll. He'd been gone for an hour. No one would have noticed.

He would confidently transmit his conclusion that the Argentine mission was exactly what they said it was: a routine operation to relieve scientists and soldiers, many of whom had spent ten cold months in Antarctica. The schedule had been moved up for the exact reasons they claimed—a broken satellite uplink which left the base incommunicado, but which wasn't a cause for immediate alarm, as the base had been functioning for more than sixty years and its crew was well-trained for the conditions… they'd survived the winter, so summer would pose few problems.

Unless his superiors had been overcome by their own paranoia and all the speculation he'd heard from them turned out to be off base, that meant that the Argentine government had no clue why he was really there, and less as to what might be going on right on their doorstep.

CHAPTER 3

The ever-present wind got steadily colder as they approached the icy south. Camila's students, employing a combination of English, Spanish and sign language, managed to explain the concept of mate, the herbal tea enjoyed by many Argentines and deemed critical to friendly get-togethers to the assorted Australians and Europeans, and they were all now seated on a pair of blankets that had been laid on a deck in the aft-most section of the ship.

Javier could never resist a mate session, the infusion calmed him, plus, he wanted to see what the foreigners would do when faced with the fact that the bombilla, the metal straining straw that went with the gourd, was not washed between rounds. After one person drank, the next was expected to do so from the same bombilla. It was always fun to see the uninitiated try it for the first time.

As soon as he sat down, Martin handed him the gourd, and he drank. "I didn't have you down as much of a mate guy," the bald student said, "but glad to have you here."

Javier chuckled. "You can't be a soldier if you don't drink mate. The men would automatically think you were a foreign spy and they'd take you somewhere out of sight and shoot you."

Everyone laughed at this. The conversation turned to lighter topics as the gourd made its way around the circle and eventually reached the first of the Swedish girls. Anna made a face, but drank. Ingrid did the same. Clark watched them both intently and when his turn came, it was almost funny to see the struggle he was dealing with. He obviously didn't want to drink from the unhygienic bombilla… but at the same time he didn't want to look like a wuss in front of Anna.

When his turn came, he faked nonchalance and simply downed the mate in one gulp… precisely the wrong way to deal with a hot drink. To his credit, he kept up the act and the gourd continued its journey.

"Do you mind if I join you?"

Everyone looked as surprised as Javier felt. Breen had kept to himself for the entire journey. Everyone had assumed that the man would continue to do his own thing.

Martin, who appeared to be the leader of this particular round of mate reacted first. "Of course. The more the merrier." He refilled the mate gourd from a grey thermos and passed it to the American.

The man sat down and drank without hesitation. He took his time and savored the mate before sighing. "Thank you. It's been years since I last had mate. It's very good, by the way," he said to Martin.

"Have you been to Argentina before?"

"Oh, no. I drank it in Syria."

"In Syria? There's no mate in Syria. It only grows in Argentina and Paraguay," Camlia said.

"Also in parts of Brazil," Javier added. He'd been on an exercise in Rio Grande do Sul, and had been surprised when his Brazilian Army hosts had told him that the trees around him were mate trees. They told him that early Jesuit settlers had established themselves in the region because mate was highly valued in Europe, to the point that it was referred to as "green gold".

"Actually, they drink a lot of mate in Syria, but it's all Argentine mate. Not that brand, though," he pointed at the open package on the blanket beside Martin. "It's a brand with a red, white and blue logo."

"Taragüí?" Martin asked immediately.

"It might be. I don't really remember. It was a few years ago."

"I wonder how that came about?"

Breen smiled, the first time Javier had seen it. "That part I remember. From what I was told, a lot of Syrians and Lebanese emigrated to South America to escape oppression by the Ottoman Empire. Then, in 1946, when Syria won its independence from France, they went back, and they took the custom of drinking mate with them."

"That makes sense," Martin said. "There are still a whole lot of them here. About ten percent of the population has at least a little blood from the region. Especially in the west of the country. San Luis and San Juan."

"But surely it's just some exotic thing, like the way we eat sushi. Maybe once a week," Camila said.

Her students looked at her strangely. They really didn't seem the type to eat sushi once a week. The two Argentines looked more the kind of people who had heard of sushi and maybe tried it once, cautiously, at the wedding reception of some rich friend. They came from families who'd been close to the poverty line all their lives, and who went for the simple things in life. They were likely the first generation of their line to go to college.

Javier saw that a lot with the soldiers around him. Many of them had chosen the military as a way to have steady employment and regular food, a real step up in the world. They were the pride and joy of families who only qualified as working-class when someone under the roof managed to find work.

The Venezuelan student, of course, was little more than a refugee. The few dollars his family managed to smuggle out of the country went towards food, books and lodgings. University, of course, was free, as were all public schools in Argentina.

Breen shook his head. "No. It's extremely well installed across the entire culture. Everyone drinks the stuff and you can buy mate in any shop, in fact…" He looked around to make certain that his audience was with him, "a Syrian lady told me that if you have a stranger in your house, the rules of hospitality demand that you give him coffee. But if your guest is a close friend or family member, then you bring out the mate."

"Wow," Ernesto said. "I would never have imagined that."

Javier admired the way the man, an object of scorn for the week since the ship had left Buenos Aires had, with one perfectly chosen anecdote and a couple of smiles, won them over completely. But the difficult question had to come up sooner or later.

"So, what were you doing in Syria?"

"There's a snake in Syria called the blunt-nosed viper, which has a venom that's used in a number of natural remedies. An American lab was studying the properties to see if they might not also have some repeatable and beneficial pharmaceutical properties, so I went with the team sent to harvest the venom. It was a slow process, and I got to meet any number of Syrians along the way. Most of them were mate drinkers." He looked sad. "Of course, the war put an end to that. Such a waste."

Javier nearly applauded the performance. His own money was on this guy being a forward artillery spotter for… he really didn't know which faction the Americans might have been assisting. Probably the Russians, since, despite rhetoric on both sides, American and Russian interests in the region were remarkably aligned… and both powers were high on the hit list of the major terrorist groups.

He kept his peace, however. No need to expose the man just as he was trying to make friends… and Javier decided to keep his misgivings about *why* the man was trying to make friends to himself as well. He would give the American the benefit of the doubt.

The trip had gone surprisingly well. Well enough that even his superiors back in Buenos Aires had decided to concentrate on other stuff and leave him alone. They'd be back on the horn as soon as the *Irizar* reached its destination, of course… but seemed to have decided that he wouldn't get into too much trouble on what was basically a working vacation.

The sky was clear. For some reason the roof of the sky appeared to be higher than it was out on the Pampas. Maybe it was the way blue reflected on the sea, or maybe it was the way a few tiny wisps of white, barely a suggestion, floated high above where clouds should be.

As the team continued to make small talk, Javier found himself watching the sea, trying to find the small ice floes the crew had said they might start seeing today. If there were any in sight, he couldn't tell them from the places where the wind had churned the top of the small waves to froth.

His anger at having been bamboozled out of his leave had faded. A cruise through the Caribbean couldn't have been more relaxing than this trip. In fact, a cruise would likely have been much more stressful, what with having to pack unnecessary items such as swimsuits and decent clothes. Plus, if he'd been on vacation, he'd have gone with either one of his friends or, if his leave went well, he could have reconnected with one of his occasional girlfriends. That would just have added to the stress. Yeah, much better to take a cruise while actually on duty.

The sea, the motion of the ship and the wind against his face all conspired to lull him into a near-catatonic state.

"Excuse me, Colonel?"

The man stood to one side, not daring to touch Javier, but the word 'colonel' had a magic effect. Years of army training and, much worse, army briefings and meetings, had trained him to react instantly whenever he heard his rank.

"Yes, sailor, how can I help you?"

"Captain Celmi asked me to bring you to the bridge."

Strange. The captain had essentially left him alone every day except during meals, where all three of the senior officers present—the captain, Javier and the commander of the troops that would remain at the base—would sit together at a table which would then be completed with junior officers chosen on a daily basis. He frowned. "Did he tell you what it was about?"

"No, sir. He just said to bring you upstairs as soon as possible."

"All right. Let's go."

The captain must have really emphasized the 'as soon as possible' part of the order because the man scooted.

"Ah, Colonel," Celmi said when Javier arrived on the bridge. "Glad you got here so quickly."

"Of course. What's happening?" There was a slight charge in the air, as if something was going on. Three men and a young woman at workstations seemed busy doing something naval.

"We're changing course. Someone at Ushuaia just received a distress signal from a Korean fishing boat."

"Legal?"

"Of course not."

Javier whistled. "They must really be in trouble. They're in Argentine waters… They know we'll impound the boat and send the crew to jail."

"Yes. Unfortunately, we're the closest armed ship which means we'll be the ones to arrest them after we rescue them. Are you armed?"

"Yes. A sidearm, but I suppose it should be enough."

"Good. If you're willing, I'd love for you to participate in the operation. The men can get nervous, and having some older and cooler heads around is always a good thing. If possible, I'd prefer to avoid having a nervous sailor pull a trigger and cause an international incident with China."

Javier sighed inwardly. After pulling him away from his leave in order to make it to the base a few days early, it figured that the Navy would decide to go off on a tangent.

The captain appeared to be a mind reader as well as a ship's captain. "Don't worry. We're only supposed to stay on site until the crew is safe and under arrest. Shouldn't add more than a few hours to the trip."

"What's the plan?"

"Well, we're expecting them to be more welcoming than these ships usually are. They did send the distress call after all, which means they're probably in some kind of serious trouble, but I still want to check it out before getting too close. We're sending up one of the Sea Kings."

The two large helicopters were hangered just ahead of the heliport. Javier was surprised to learn that the cash-strapped Argentine Navy had allotted two of them to the *Irizar*, and said so.

Celmi chuckled. "This trip is a PR event. We couldn't allow the boat to sail without its full complement of support vehicles, could we? Besides, most of the other ships big enough to stage them are in port. What else were we going to use them for?" The captain winked. "Between you and me, these were a gift from the US government. The ones we used to fly were destroyed in the fire. I think that's the main reason why the government allowed your friend the spy to sail with us. A spy for a couple of choppers. Sounds like a little too good a deal if you ask me."

Javier tended to agree with the man's assessment, but kept his mouth shut. "Where do you want me?"

"Look for Lieutenant Yoma. He'll assign you to a boarding team."

***

As always, the military practiced the doctrine of 'Hurry up and wait', so once Javier reached the boarding team he'd been assigned to, he learned that they would be reaching the stricken vessel in three hours at the earliest, so he had some time to burn.

He spent that span watching the team pull the Sea King out of its hangar and clear the decks. The big helicopter, painted grey with a vertical yellow tail stripe somehow looked just right taking off from the deck of a ship and striking out over a slate-grey ocean.

Then the wait began in earnest. Boredom didn't have time to settle in, however. They'd been seated around a small table about to break out a pack of cards to play Truco, the typical card game enjoyed by Argentines, when one of the men came in.

"The helicopter's coming back."

"Already?"

"Yes."

"Did the ship sink? Did the chopper get fired on?"

"I don't know. I just heard that it was returning without any additional passengers."

Javier knew exactly what would happen next. As a reasonably young officer who wasn't in the formal chain of command of any of the men who'd been assigned to board with him if there was trouble, he was the natural person to go fetch news.

The Argentine military, in some regards, was much less structured and formal than that of other nations… and sailors on what was usually used as nothing more military than a research vessel, even less so. They immediately asked if he could find out what was up.

Javier sighed, bowing to the inevitable. The ship was still more than an hour away and he preferred to know what he was walking into than to sit around being begged at by a bunch of sailors.

"All right," he said. "I'll see what they tell me."

The men cheered good-naturedly. They clearly weren't worried about the Korean fishermen; these boats always did the same thing. They ran until someone fired a warning shot, and then surrendered. Even the biggest factory ships used the same pattern, then paid their fines and were escorted out of Argentine waters. The smart ones stayed clear of the country in the future. Argentina was getting too good at catching them.

Javier arrived at the bridge as the pilots were beginning their debriefing, so he listened.

"We saw no one on board, sir," the naval lieutenant who'd led the exploration team was explaining. "The ship didn't look too badly damaged, all we could see were some broken windows and some smoke from amidships on the port side."

"That's a pretty typical ploy. They always go belowdecks when they run."

"This one wasn't running. The ship appears to be locked in a turn that describes a big circle. We watched them for a few minutes and all they did was simply go around and around."

"You didn't send anyone down?"

"I thought it better not to. If they're waiting below to ambush us, why give them a chance?"

"I agree. No need to rush. If they make a run for it, they're screwed. Now that we've made visual contact, we can get air support if necessary."

"I don't think they're going to run, sir."

"We'll see. I hope not. We really, really don't need another international incident. The Chinese are still mad about the boat we sank last time. They don't like small navies getting uppity." He dismissed everyone.

Javier returned to his men. "Not much to tell, men. The chopper didn't see anyone on deck and flew back. They don't think the ship is going to run… and if they do, they gave me the impression that they're scrambling airplanes to sink her before she reaches international waters."

"Do you think we'll board?"

"Yeah. I do. She's not going to run."

Now the silence got a bit more tense. It was one thing to joke around when a civilian ship was still a couple of hours away and would do the typical runner… and quite another to be approaching a ship that might be lying in wait.

They played a couple of hands of truco, but no one's heart was in it. Everyone kept glancing out the forward-facing window, trying to catch a glimpse of their quarry.

Finally, a cadet who wouldn't be joining the boarding crew jumped up. "There," he said.

They crowded around to look, but the speck in the distance could have been anything.

But the man's young eyes hadn't deceived him. The speck slowly resolved itself into a ship, white with rusty streaks down the side, probably refuse from the catch. It appeared to be even longer than the icebreaker, but much lower. Torn nets straggled beside it, blown by the wind and waves.

The helicopter's description had been spot on. The ship was under power, but still gave the impression of drifting aimlessly.

"Yeah, definitely a poacher."

With that identification, the excitement level increased. There were few things Argentina's Navy liked more than to catch someone in the act of stealing from the rich fisheries on the continental shelf.

Javier didn't share their enthusiasm. Something about that ship made him nervous. Maybe it was the way the loose netting fluttered in the wind, or maybe it was the sheer lack of life on deck. Whatever it was, he felt a shiver run up his back as he looked over the sea at the empty decks.

A naval lieutenant popped his head into their staging room. "All right, men, it's time."

Two of the *Irizar's* lifeboats were powered, and Javier's team was on the second. The crew of the first was more heavily armed and contained the only four men aboard with marine infantry experience. If anything went wrong, they would be the ones to deal with any resistance.

The second boatload of men would come aboard once the deck was clear and help with what might become a cabin-by-cabin search of the ship. Meanwhile, the *Irizar* would cover them with her 40mm guns.

Javier watched the team from the first boat send grappling ladders up the side and climb aboard. It was a tense few moments, but soon, the marines waved down to the rest of the crew to come aboard. The sailor in command of Javier's lifeboat eased forward.

They climbed aboard, Javier leading the way.

He shuddered. The deck was as empty as they'd expected, dirty and unkempt.

The rust-colored streaks to the side, he now saw, were the end of long trails of what looked like blood.

CHAPTER 4

Javier walked across the deck of the fishing vessel. The metal had once been painted white and had also, at some time, possessed non-skid surfacing. Age and disinterest had cured it of that. In many places, it was rubbed through to the bare metal.

"What do you think that is?" Javier said, pointing out the reddish streaks to one of the sailors who'd come aboard with him.

The man studied it and shrugged. "I've never been on a factory ship like this one before, but on a regular fishing boat, those are the marks where the discarded catch gets pushed off the ship. Guts and heads and bits that aren't used as well as the non-commercial species."

Javier nodded. It made sense, and he began to get his breathing under control. The marks had seemed like blood to him and for some reason that had startled him more than a soldier should be at the sight of gore. Of course, that's probably exactly what they were, but his imagination had made them look like human blood, not the effluents of fish.

"We've secured the bridge," the naval officer in charge of the lead team told him. "It doesn't look like there's anyone there, and the place is pretty torn up. Once we get the crew off, someone with a lot more salvage knowledge than we have is going to need to do a lot of work to get this one back on course. It will likely empty its bunkers before anyone gets it facing forward. Also, we found some blood on the floor." He shrugged. "Right now, we're working on the assumption that the crew had a falling out amongst themselves, so be very careful when you search the ship."

"How do you want to do it?"

"I left a man on the bridge, but we think most people are going to be hiding below decks. I think the best thing would be for you to take the processing plant in the bow, and we'll take engine room and pump rooms in the aft. We think if anyone's hiding, they'll be hiding there, so best to have the marines present. We've already checked the cabins. They're empty."

Javier headed towards the bow. A covered metal stairway led downwards, and creaked under his weight. All of his men had flashlights, but the factory floor was illuminated, albeit not overly bright.

He stopped at the foot of the stairs and looked around. Bins lined one side of the wall and fed into some kind of machine. By its configuration, Javier guessed that it was likely a press, to turn the right kind of fish into compact bars. Both bins and machine were painted a dull industrial green.

Opposite them was a conveyor belt about two feet wide that ran the length of the room. Another belt ran above head-height and dumped its contents in a small room off to the side.

Javier imagined this room must normally have been cramped and bustling as men jockeyed in the confined spaces to sort the catch coming from above and place it onto the right conveyor or bin. The noise of the belts and the heat of the machines would have made it an oppressive place to work.

He wondered how people could stand to live and work in these conditions. One of the reasons he'd become a soldier and not a sailor—against family tradition—was that he hated the cramped, tiny spaces of the Navy. Give him an open field any day, even if he had to run ten kilometers in it.

Everything was as still as the grave. Deep shadows lurked where the light failed to penetrate, under conveyor trusses and between machines and pipes. A solid layer of grime covered the floor below the belts.

It looked completely mundane, if a bit disgusting. He certainly wouldn't want to eat a fish product that had been initially processed in this place. The sheer dinginess began to calm his anxiety. This wasn't a place for an ambush. This was a place to process fish.

Nevertheless, a sense of something wrong, something essential that was missing, nagged at him. It was right there, like an image at the edge of his vision or a word at the tip of his tongue. It was an obvious thing, but he couldn't quite put his finger on it. He knew he'd feel like an idiot when he finally nailed it down. All he really knew was that whatever was causing the feeling, it wasn't letting him relax and concentrate on the task at hand.

Thinking about it, he'd had a variation of the feeling since he boarded the *Irizar*. Not only was there something obvious missing on this ship, the entire mission had something wrong with it… and he also couldn't figure that out. He put it down to nerves.

He called: "It looks clear, come on down."

If an army of enraged sailors had been waiting with fish cleavers, the factory would have been the ideal place for them. Nooks and crannies, dark spaces between pieces of equipment, and locked cupboards abounded. The general feel made Javier think of an industrial kitchen in a submarine.

They searched the main room, and found nothing. No people, no clues… and no fish.

"Looks like they weren't having much luck this trip."

"They probably had their problem as soon as they crossed into the Argentine area. Not much point in fishing anywhere but over the continental shelf. The yields are much higher here."

The soldier smirked. "Yeah, if the Coast Guard doesn't sink you."

"Of course."

Smaller rooms tucked into the space available inside the hull opened up at odd angles. Javier assumed that each space had a specific use, but they all looked the same to him: cramped, full of pipes and painted over in the same stupid green, too bright to be military, too subdued to be attractive.

His men, the edge completely rubbed from their fear by the simple fact that nothing had happened since they boarded, chattered. Javier let them: if anyone was waiting around the next bend, they already knew they were coming; silence wouldn't be much additional help. And telling them to concentrate on the job at hand wouldn't do much good either, he imagined. These weren't really fighting troops—they'd been trained, but that only went so far after a few years where any fighting was done by the guys who controlled the ship's cannon and your enemies were cowed civilian sailors who'd likely just been shot at with said guns.

"It doesn't look like there was a fight here. And the ship's intact."

"So what happened to all the Koreans? Did they suddenly decide to jump into the sea?"

"I wouldn't laugh at that. If they did, they probably had a good reason. What's on this ship that would make them prefer to drown or freeze in the South Atlantic rather than face it?"

A short silence descended on the men after that. Sailors were a superstitious breed—life at the mercy of the most savage of elements made certain of that. Even though they were silent, Javier could almost imagine what they were thinking. Ghost ships. Vampires. Spirits. Curses. Things that threatened both the body and the soul.

He chuckled. Every army platoon had its token believer in the occult, the man who kept trying to stop them from walking under ladders or talking about the merest possibility of having something bad happen to them. The one who refused to stay in room 175 of a clinic one time because the digits, when added up, equaled thirteen. But even those guys seemed paragons of stability when compared to the sailors he'd been around.

The next room held some kind of big tank. Probably a boiler vat of some sort, but Javier really couldn't tell. The only thing about it that called attention to itself was the fact that it was a pristine white color, and looked out of place in the grimy green room. It must be some new piece of equipment allowing the owners of the vessel to lower costs or make more money somehow, probably by processing fish heads. He shuddered.

Then it hit him.

"Wait." He held up his hand.

His troops stopped.

"Do you notice something about this place?"

"It's a factory?" one of the sailors said tentatively.

"Right, a fish factory. Now, if I told you we were going into a place where fish were crushed and cut and stored and fell onto the floor, what's the first thing you'd say?"

"That you should watch out for the smell," one laughed.

"Exactly."

The men shifted as they realized what he was aiming at. While the ship was grimy and well-used, with ancient dirt coating the underside of everything, it only smelled faintly… and not particularly of fish. What should have been an overwhelming presence, a nearly physical entity… wasn't.

That was what had been bugging him, the sense that something was off. He'd entered the factory space braced for the smell of decomposing fish, even if only unconsciously. When it hadn't hit them, the feeling of wrongness persisted. The relief of not having to smell the fish had overcome any alarm bells that might have been going off in his head.

"Be careful," he told his men, "I want you to work in teams of two. You come with me," he pointed at the sailor who'd answered the question. "You two, stay by the door to the stairs. No one gets out, and no one comes in without me knowing it."

The banter disappeared completely. He wondered if he was overreacting, but then silenced his doubts. Better to overreact and live to tell the tale. There was something off about this ship, they'd known that. On land, he would never have charged in with his troops making jokes… but on land, places that felt off were usually riddled with drug smugglers' tunnels—and often with the smugglers themselves. This was a much more subtle business.

They now advanced with sidearms drawn and a companion covered each person in charge of checking out a room from the door. The shadowy light hadn't changed… but now that he was certain that it held a sinister secret, it felt darker to him.

They checked another room. As far as Javier could tell, it was the last in the bow sector; an empty storeroom with light grey walls and four boxes sitting inside. The boxes contained plastic sheeting, probably for one of the industrial processes.

They were about to turn away when one of the men stopped and looked at the base of the back wall.

"Colonel, have a look at this," the man whispered.

They squatted near the floor and Javier looked down. A faint indication of light emerged from behind the metal. "A door?"

"Probably, or a false wall."

Javier nodded. "See if you can figure out how to open it."

They worked quietly, on the assumption that if anyone was behind the wall, they wouldn't want to be found. It was actually a common trick for illegal fishing ships to have secret areas on board. They usually used them to smuggle illegal immigrants, but it wasn't unheard of to find drugs inside. Secret chambers were often fitted by master welders, then painted and covered with the same kind of grime as the rest of the place. They could be nearly impossible to spot unless you knew exactly what to look for.

On one memorable occasion, after a ship had been captured and towed to port, the supposedly empty craft suddenly started its engines and attempted to make a break for the open ocean. Only quick thinking by the captain of a Coast Guard vessel stopped them. On boarding, it was discovered that five men had hidden away in a concealed drug vault.

"Here," the sailor whispered. He pointed at a raised area in the wall, a rounded rivet at head height that didn't appear to be serving any structural purpose, and whose paint had been rubbed to the metal.

Javier pointed to two of the men. "Cover me," he whispered, and pressed the button.

A click echoed in the storeroom and the panel ahead of them shifted to expose a well-lit crack.

With a final look back to see whether his sailors were paying attention, Javier slammed his shoulder into the door, quickly took his bearings on the other side and rolled to the right, behind a tall, long table. It wouldn't provide much cover, but until anyone inside realized they could simply shoot under the table, he might have enough time to take stock.

The room was white and brightly lit. It appeared to occupy the entire extreme front portion of the ship. It was long and tapered at the end, forming the unmistakable wedge of the ship's prow, where some kind of high-tech equipment, much more modern-looking than the rest of the room's content, was connected by wires to the hull. It looked like a room from a completely different ship.

Two long white tables—laboratory tables, complete with high stools—ran along the sides of the room, ending in a V-shape at the end. Each table had two stainless sinks in them, and the pipes below were of steel as well. Glass-fronted cabinets stood behind them in the wider part of the room until space ran out at the front. The cabinets held nothing but an assortment of glass labware.

This room did smell: it smelled of paint and glue and gave the feeling that it had never been used before. Beside the door through which he'd entered, Javier saw a gun rack. It held six shotguns, all of which were present and locked down by a metal bar and a big padlock.

Other than that, it appeared empty. "Clear," he called back. And then stopped to listen. "No, wait. I think I hear something. Hold position near the door."

The sound was like an animal, panting and whining somewhere in the room. It sounded like a large animal. There was a rustle.

He looked under the tables, but saw nothing.

There was no choice; he had to go deeper. He wondered if the crew had owned a pet dog and entered carefully. Dogs could be quite territorial and aggressive, especially on ships where the crew might have mistreated them. He'd feel pretty silly getting hurt by a dog.

A few feet inside the room and it was quite clear that nothing was hiding under the tables. The angle where the two sides of the hull joined together to form the prow, likewise, was visibly empty. That left the nooks between the cupboards.

He tried to understand which of those the sound might be coming from and, once he convinced himself that he had the right one, Javier scooted carefully over to just out of sight from the place he'd selected as the most likely hiding spot… and then rolled in front of it, gun drawn.

Something screamed and he jumped backwards.

Out of the corner of his eye, he saw his troops take a few steps forward and held up his hand. "No! Wait!"

They stopped.

His mind finished processing what he'd seen: the sound, the violent swirling hair, the wide, bloodshot eyes. He placed his gun on the ground and crawled forward. "Hello?" he said in English, which he assumed a Korean crew would be much more likely to understand than if he spoke to them in Spanish.

Javier eased himself around the corner of the cabinet and into view. Frightened eyes looked back at him.

They belonged to a woman with pale skin and black, shoulder-length hair. Her eyes were the ice blue of deep mountain glaciers… and she certainly didn't look Korean.

Javier held out his hands to show he was unarmed and approached very slowly. She cowered back into the corner formed by the wall and the cabinet and made incoherent yelping sounds.

Then he saw the blood. She was wearing a blue jacket that was torn around one arm and stained completely black. The woman hugged that arm to her side. "Juan, call the *Irizar* and tell them to send a doctor right now. Tell them to send the helicopter. I think this woman needs more help than we're going to be able to give her."

Having said that, he turned back to her. "Just calm down," he said in what he hoped was a soothing voice. "You're going to be all right."

His eyes looked to the ground beneath her. A rivulet of bright red was running from a pool next to her foot.

"Can you get out of there?"

He didn't want to move her, but he did want her out of that corner, preferably lying on her back where he could hold the wounded arm above the level of her heart. So he inched closer.

The woman continued to scream at him, eyes wide, obviously in an uncontrollable panic. Her screams formed words, but not words he could understand. Maybe, he thought, she was Korean after all.

He put a hand on her shoulder. The woman pulled away but there was no space for her to retreat to and he soon had a firm enough grip to be able to ease her out. When she realized what he was doing, she struggled briefly and then went unexpectedly slack. He had to hold her head to keep it from hitting the deck.

He was worried, but the fact that she'd fallen unconscious at least made it possible to pull her out of the corner and to get her onto the floor. Fortunately, this room appeared to be much cleaner than that of the factory space.

"Does anyone have a knife?" he asked the sailors who were now crowding around to see the injured woman, all thoughts of ghost ships and sea curses forgotten.

One of the men produced a commando blade. What he thought he might achieve by carrying it on the raid, however, was a question for another time. Javier used it to slice into the woman's jacket and carefully peel away the fabric from the skin. The sleeve of her sweater and a shirt beneath suffered the same fate.

"Oh my God," Javier said.

One of the men behind him rushed off, and the sounds of retching could be heard from the factory. Javier couldn't blame him.

The woman was badly hurt. A piece of flesh as long as his hand had been torn away, leaving muscle and gristle exposed. A splintered bone speared out at an unnatural angle.

She was holding something in her hand. Whatever it was was covered in blood and torn cloth, but when he tried to pull it away, she refused to surrender it. He gave up, preferring not to hurt her in an unnecessary struggle.

He abandoned his plan of keeping the arm above her head and let it lie next to her in a position that seemed least likely to cause any further harm, placing it carefully over the discarded cloth. That was filthy with gore, but at least it was her own blood. He certainly didn't want to risk any infection by laying the exposed flesh on the floor.

"You. Go see if anyone brought bandages and if there's a stretcher on the boats that brought us here."

Then, all he could do was wait. They told him later that the doctor had reached them in under ten minutes… but it seemed like days to him as he held the hand of the woman's uninjured arm, cold as if she were already dead, occasionally checked her for a pulse and watched her bleed.

The doctor did arrive, and he was all business. He took one look and ordered everyone out except Javier, who he told to keep her hand still and two sailors who he told to shut up and stand against the wall. Then he applied a gauze bandage from a sterile package and a tourniquet and used a modified splint to hold her arm in place.

"You two, take her legs," he ordered the men. The doctor himself grasped her shoulders and they lifted her just enough to get her onto a stretcher. "Now move. I need to get her into the surgery on the ship as soon as possible. I should be able to save her arm, but I don't want that tourniquet on for any long period of time."

They rushed through the passages they'd so carefully explored on the way in and then jumped onto the chopper. The doctor and Javier seated themselves next to her.

"Will she be all right?" Javier said.

"I think so. But it depends on a lot of factors I don't know yet. I couldn't get a great look at her wound. But that's not the thing that worries me most."

"What is that?"

"The wound looks like a bite mark. Did you find what bit her?"

Javier shook his head. He'd thought it was some kind of shrapnel wound… but now that it had been pointed out, the shape of the injury could only be a bite mark.

"I didn't think so. Had to be something pretty big though."

CHAPTER 5

Breen fumed as he watched the abandoned fishing vessel disappear into the distance, left to drift until the salvage team arrived. He'd found out about the woman and the hidden lab too late to do anything about it, and now it would take a message from the White House to get the Argentine government to allow an American observer on board with the recovery crew—more likely to be a team from Argentine intelligence than from a shipyard bent on profit, at least initially—that were due to arrive in a few hours.

At least he'd been on site to report the incident. As coincidences went, it was a pretty positive one. Had this happened at any other time, the U.S. would likely never have learned of it. Argentina, of course, was probably convinced that the hidden lab was nothing more important than a drug kitchen.

He would do nothing to disabuse them of the idea. He'd been told enough about the situation to be able to speculate on what the "Koreans" were doing.

The woman who'd been rescued was another matter, though. He'd taken her photo as she was being brought into the ship's infirmary, and had sent it to Fort Belvoir, Military Intelligence headquarters, for identification. He expected it to be a couple of days. Whoever this woman might be… she was probably not on America's radar. He suspected the Russians, and the Russians had gotten much better at hiding their agents lately. After years of bumbling, including the famous British poisoning affair, they were reaching Cold War levels of efficiency in that regard.

But, as he stared out over the sea just a couple of hours later, he was surprised to find a message from home with a name and a suite of photographs of the woman looking decidedly better than she had when they wheeled her into surgery.

Natasha Voldoyeva, 33 years old, zoologist, University of Oxford. Born in St. Petersburg. No known ties to military or SVR operations.

"Yeah?" he said under his breath as he opened the file with a longer biographical summary. "It looks like she's got a few ties after all. I'd say up to her neck." Just another example of the newfound Russian covert effectiveness.

The trace on the ship had drawn a blank. Though sailing under the South Korean flag, the vessel's name tracked back to a holding company in Hong Kong. His contact at HQ told him that they'd pinged the CIA at

Langley to see whether they had anything on the company… but unless they'd been caught being naughty before, and therefore landed on someone's watch list, it was likely that some digging would need to be done, and that would take some time.

He drifted towards the medical sector, trying to make it look like he was out for an innocent walk and certain that no one would buy that ruse. He'd passed the two operating rooms—a legacy of the Falklands War, when the *Irizar* had been used as a hospital ship—during the initial tour of the ship and been impressed by the modern equipment inside. His briefing about Argentina had said that, though the country was still developing as measured by most economic indicators, it had a long tradition of medical excellence.

For Natasha's sake, he hoped they were right: she'd been bloody and unresponsive as they wheeled her from the chopper.

He arrived at the door of the operating room to find Javier pacing the corridor outside.

"Any news?" Breen said.

"The doctor assured me that she'd survive, but other than that, I have no clue. For all I know, they've cut her arm off."

Breen digested this. "You look like it matters to you."

"You didn't see her. She was scared, Carl. More scared than I've ever seen anyone. We tried to calm her down… but it almost looked like she didn't even realize we were human. If she hadn't passed out, we would have had to drag her back kicking and screaming."

Breen grunted. He'd seen that reaction before, usually in the heat of battle in the shadow of some godsforsaken mountain in Pakistan where surrender wasn't an option. Those had been hardened soldiers. A civilian woman as this zoologist appeared to be—despite her obvious employment by some agency or other—might have had that reaction from some relatively innocuous cause. Her injuries, however, suggested otherwise and his gut agreed. There was something big going on.

Javier looked at him suspiciously. "And what brings you here?"

"Curiosity, mainly. The woman didn't look Korean to me. She looks Russian, and if the Russians are operating something in these waters, especially something that can cause an entire crew to disappear with signs of violence, my government is interested in it. In fact, I'm pretty confident that someone knew about this, and it's one of the reasons they sent me on the *Irizar* instead of airlifting me to the base directly."

That was complete bullshit, of course. He'd been put on the *Irizar* because the boys in Washington wanted to watch the Argentines to see how much they actually knew. The main action was supposed to be on

Antarctica, but the possibility of listening in on his hosts' conversations in the process of getting there was simply too good an opportunity to pass up. From his briefing, it was clear that the Russian connection in the case was more than forty years old, they'd had ample time to establish terrestrial operations and no one expected to find them operating in these waters... and yet, there they were. If Argentina knew why, it would be extremely valuable intelligence.

Telling Javier that he was watching Russians would remove some of the suspicions the man might have about why he'd been shipped instead of airlifted. Anything that made the Argentines a bit more malleable might come in handy later.

For his own part, the Colonel looked surprised at the frank admission. He nodded once. "We're surprised too. Argentina's not a drug producing country, and we really don't have that much of a consumer base either, but we have been used as a transport hub. No one looks at people coming from Argentina quite as closely as they do Colombians or Mexicans. A floating lab might be something someone would try... although I think it's a losing bet; the Navy can be a bit trigger happy."

Breen chuckled. The sinking of an illegal Chinese fishing ship by the Argentines was the stuff of legend. While everyone else on the planet was trying to placate the Asian giant, the yahoos in the local Coast Guard had decided to fill a vessel that refused to heed its commands to halt with holes, presumably to see what would happen or to keep their cannons from rusting. Only the fact that no one had been killed in the incident had prevented it from becoming a serious diplomatic shitstorm.

The time had come when the appearance of honesty would serve him best. Against every fiber of his being, he confided in the Argentine—after all, he seemed to be keeping his promises about not blowing his cover and giving him the run of the ship. "I don't think it's about drugs, Colonel. If this is what I think it is, it's something that's been dragged along since the Cold War."

"What is it?"

"I can't tell you that. But it's definitely tied to my main reason for being here. I need to ask a favor. Do you think you can allow me to speak to the woman?"

"In due course..."

"I mean soon. It might be important."

Javier hesitated. "Let's see how she's doing. If the doctor says it's all right..."

Breen nodded. He did believe it might be important. Perhaps not critical to the Argentines or even to most world governments, but the woman and the ship might shed light on certain Soviet activities in the 1970s that included a weapons program that the Russians had kept under the strictest veil of secrecy… and which some people in Washington suspected was still ongoing.

On the other hand, if he pressed too hard, Javier might start asking questions.

They waited, and waited some more. An hour and a half later, the doctor emerged and pulled down his surgical mask. His face was haggard. He spotted Javier. "We're done. The woman is going to have a nasty scar… but she should get nearly all the movement in that arm back. She was lucky the major artery wasn't severed. It was a close thing. She would have bled out before you got there."

"Good work, doctor," Javier said. "How long before we can speak to her?"

"She's already awake. But you won't be able to get much out of her. She doesn't speak any Spanish, or any English for that matter."

Breen thought that strange for a woman who'd graduated from Oxford with high marks, but he kept his mouth shut.

"Where is she from?"

"One of my nurses, Hilda, had a Russian grandmother. She said her words sounded Russian," the doctor gave him a shrug. "So I guess we'll need to look for someone in the crew who speaks the language."

The conversation had been going on in Spanish, his knowledge of which Breen had been endeavoring to keep secret. But the opportunity was much too good to squander. "I speak some Russian," he said. "I can try."

The doctor looked at Javier for guidance, and the colonel shrugged. "Lucky break, isn't it?"

"Always be prepared," Breen replied.

They filed in behind the doctor, past the operating room where blood-stained blue sheets gave mute witness to the drama that had unfolded within to a hall with beige painted walls where a rolling hospital stretcher bed held the woman from the ship. She was still as pale as when the men had found her, but her eyes were alert and the panic had subsided. She smiled wanly at the doctor as he approached.

Breen exulted. Up close, it was clear that he had the correct woman. The photos from Military Intelligence looked exactly like the girl on the bed. "Hello," he said in Russian.

The woman looked up sharply. "You speak my language?"

"And some others," Breen said with a smile.

"Is that Russian?" the doctor asked.

"Yes."

"Good. Ask her if she's allergic to any medicines or antibiotics."

Breen did. "She says she isn't."

"Ask her if she knows her blood type."

"O positive."

"Good."

"Let her know that her arm is going to be all right, but that she's going to have a nasty scar. I'm supposed to fix sailors that fall off cranes, not people mauled by tigers. Also, ask her what the hell bit her."

Breen informed her of the condition of her arm, which appeared to make her reasonably happy, but when he asked about the animal, her eyes went wide and she refused to speak further. She just sat on the bed, shaking her head. At length, she began to cry.

Faced with her agitation, the doctor threw them out. "I'll call you if I need you," he told Breen.

The colonel stepped in. "Call me any time he's talking to her," he said.

Breen smiled. The Argentines might be trusting souls, but they weren't stupid.

***

To Javier's surprise, the doctor knocked on his door a few minutes later. He was carrying something in a cloth bag. The man had taken a shower and changed into his uniform, and the haggard look was gone from his features.

"I thought you should see this." He held up the bag. "I didn't think you'd necessarily want to share it with the American."

"What's in there?"

"The thing our patient was holding in her hand. You told me you couldn't pry it away, so I took it while she was under sedation. I cut the cloth off and cleaned it up."

The doctor pulled down the bag. Inside was a squat round metal container packed in ice. He unscrewed the top and let Javier look inside.

It contained a clenched human fist, torn off raggedly at the wrist. Pale white skin and blond hair growing from the pores; a large hand, a man's hand.

Javier swallowed. "Cover that up. And don't let anyone get near her unless I'm present. I've already discussed it with the Captain. Do you have any idea what did that?"

"No more than you do. A piece of large machinery, maybe. Do you think she fed the crew into the processing plant?"

"Alone? She doesn't look big enough to have overpowered everyone… but the truth is I don't know. The salvage crew up from Ushuaia should be able to give us a better picture of what's in there."

The doctor walked away, grisly prize safely covered once again and Javier sighed. He had written half of the report he'd have to send in already… but he knew that he was about to kiss his on-ship holiday goodbye. It was time to get back to work.

***

"You've been picking at your food all through dinner," Camila said, pushing the unoccupied chair away from the two-person table Javier had selected and sitting down on it uninvited. Anyone would have been able to tell that the Colonel wanted to be alone with his thoughts. She wouldn't be particularly welcome, but she suspected he'd be too much of a gentleman to object.

"Thanks for noticing," Javier replied.

"I'd never neglect our fearless leader."

That earned her a sour look. "I thought we were past that."

"We are. I wouldn't be here if we weren't. I really was watching you, and I really am worried. You've been staring out that window for an hour. I mean the Weddell Sea is fascinating when you first come in and realize that the little white mountains out there are pretty much the same as the icebergs that sank the Titanic, but after a while, every iceberg looks the same… and this is supposed to be an icebreaker after all. It shouldn't sink."

"That's what they said about the Titanic," he replied with a lopsided grin.

She laughed in spite of herself. This guy represented most of what was wrong with Argentine society. He was where he was because of his family, not his ability… but he still seemed like a good guy. She really should push aside her natural disgust and give him a chance. As her grandmother always said, exceptions confirmed the rule. "Seriously, what's the matter? Was it the Korean ship and the injured woman?"

"That has to do with it, although I'm really more worried about the rest of the crew than the one we actually rescued. As far as we could tell, all the lifeboats were still on board, so yes, I'm worried about them. There aren't many places for the crew of a ship to go in these waters, especially since the lifeboats were all still aboard, as far as we could tell." He looked away as if there was something more he wanted to say but checked himself at the last moment. "But even more than that, there's something bugging me about the fact that Base Belgrano hasn't made any contact with us. Yes, I get the fact that their satellite uplink is down. But shouldn't someone on the base have had a backup satellite phone? I mean, it seems like a basic precaution to take if you're going to Antarctica, doesn't it?"

Camila laughed.

He looked irritated. "What?"

"Is that what you're thinking? Satellite phones?"

"Well, yes. I mean we have twenty of them on board this ship… why not on the base? I know there's satellite service down there. Argentina has a bird to relay messages, and I imagine everyone else with a base in Antarctica probably has their own as well. No idea how it works, but I assume they're available for emergencies."

"You're not really getting the nature of backup plans. When technology fails, your backup should be something just as effective but foolproof."

"So… flares?"

"Don't be silly. Radio."

He looked shocked. "Of course. How could I be so stupid? It's been bugging me since we left. I'm just so accustomed to no one using radio anymore, except on an actual field of battle or on maneuvers. If they don't have the juice to reach Ushuaia or Buenos Aires, all they need to do is to call in to any of the nearby stations—ours or anyone else's—and they would relay the message to us."

There was a long pause. Camila studied him and, after a while, came to a conclusion. "You're telling the truth, aren't you?"

He looked surprised. "Of course, why wouldn't I?"

"Because you're supposed to work for the government. I… well, we've all been discussing this. All the scientists, I mean. Well, not Breen; the real ones. We thought you were covering up some awful secret so we wouldn't demand to go back home. We'd come to the conclusion that the base had been hit by some disease and we were here to ship the survivors back out… and to pretend it never happened."

"I don't think anyone would do that. I actually think it's more likely that the radio's been broken for years and no one sent them a replacement because the Kirchners stole all the money for it."

She almost allowed herself to be drawn off topic. The Kirchners were a husband and wife who'd been presidents of Argentina over the course of twelve years. The rampant corruption in their regime, and the barefaced stealing of billions of dollars had allowed the right to win the previous elections. She hated the fact that they were corrupt on a scale never seen before in Latin America, but the sheer smugness of the people who used it as a way to attack everything on the left raised her hackles to the point where she wanted to defend them despite knowing just how criminal they'd been. It was a close thing, but she managed to bite back her reply.

She swallowed back her reply. "So, Occam's Razor?"

"What does that mean?"

"That the simplest explanation is likely the truth."

"Until I saw that ship, I would have said so. But now? I'm not sure." He held up a finger. "A base in Antarctica suddenly goes offline." Another finger. "Then, right at the same time, the crew of a Korean fishing boat disappears," a third, "and the only survivor we pull off the boat isn't a Korean man, not even a man at all, which is how these ships are usually crewed, but a Russian woman."

"Really?"

"Yeah. Not much point in trying to keep that a secret. A lot of people saw her. No one would mistake her for an Asian of any sort."

Again, despite the openness about the woman, Camila got the feeling that he was holding something back. She chided herself for being paranoid and letting her prejudices get the better of her.

"Isn't that a bit much for it to be coincidence? I'm thinking there might be something going on."

"You think the Russians attacked our base? Why would they do that?" she asked.

"I have no idea. But to be completely honest, I also have no clue what we might be sailing into."

"You really know how to comfort a girl." She joined him in looking out the window at the slate-grey sea dotted with ship-killing pieces of ice. "At least one thing is certain: we'll know for sure tomorrow."

CHAPTER 6

Ice. Lots of it, gleaming in the sunshine, reflecting into her eyes. Camila located her sunglasses in one of the pockets of her jacket and popped them on. She stared out over the expanse.

It was a plain of stark beauty. She knew the frozen crust hid all kinds of life, from the smallest krill to the whales that ruled the sea. But it was an invisible kingdom, impossible to surmise from above.

"They say it's only three kilometers to the mainland," Ernesto said. "I certainly can't see it. All I see is that water over there. We should just have sailed in."

"The captain says that the water is too shallow over there and that it covers a couple of nasty ridges. He maintains that the only safe approach is through the ice," she replied. Then she grinned, the excitement of knowing that Antarctica was just an hour or two away, even if they decided to leave the ship and hike, was the most exciting thing she'd ever felt. "But I think he just wanted an excuse to play with his icebreaker."

"That open water over there is supposed to be right next to the base."

"I know. The plan is to unload over the ice as close as we can get to land and then use the base's bulldozer to drag the luggage the final few hundred meters."

"Do you think they'd let us walk?"

It was a fine day, if very cold—what did she expect, it was Antarctica after all, not Tahiti—and Ernesto's idea sounded good to her, but she assumed there would be some impossible-to-ignore protocol involved with the changing of the guard at the Antarctic base. She shrugged. "I'll ask. In fact, here comes the person I should ask right now."

Javier was smiling so broadly that his teeth were a real danger of blinding her even more than the reflection on the snow.

"Someone's happy," she remarked.

"And so are you," Javier replied without missing a beat. "They just told me that the winds are calm enough that the helicopter can fly civilians."

"So?" Camila asked, trying to keep outwardly cool despite her rising excitement.

"So the captain has decided that, as honored guests, the science team will be allowed to fly into the base and perform the official turnover ceremony."

"Really?" She certainly hadn't been expecting that. She believed her team was seen more as a nuisance than as honored guests where the honor actually meant something. "What do we have to do?"

"I gathered that there isn't really a ceremony per se. We just have to walk up to them and say 'congratulations, you've been relieved. Our ship's over there—you can go back home!', and we automatically become their favorite people. Oh, and we need to give them this." He opened a bag to show a bunch of candy bars.

"Snickers?"

"Apparently, it's become a bit of a ritual. From what I was told, if we don't have the chocolate, they are within their rights to throw us into the sea for the penguins to eat."

"You're much too big for the penguins to eat," she said.

The men were rolling out the other chopper, and the banter subsided as she rushed madly to get her team together.

Everyone was in his or her cabin except for Clark Smith and Anna Götthelm. Ingrid, however, smiled impishly when asked about her sister. "There's a small space with an amazing view of the sea behind the second lifeboat. They like it there. But," she smirked, "Make sure you make a lot of noise. Otherwise, you might see something you would have rather not seen."

"Ugh." Then she smiled back at Ingrid. "Although they are both rather attractive people. Maybe I'll go in quietly and watch for a while. Should help ward off the Antarctic chill."

Ingrid made a face. "Whatever floats your boat."

Camila played it straight. She spotted the nook—an ideal hiding spot, well hidden from view—and called out to her two missing scientists. They emerged, flushed and blushing. Clark couldn't quite keep himself from scowling, while Anna looked embarrassed.

They soon forgot their discomfiture, though. As soon as they learned the reason for the untimely interruption, they darted off to grab a few things in their cabins.

"Just a backpack," Camila called after them. "We can come get the rest of our stuff when the *Irizar* arrives."

Last of all, she located Breen, who gave her one of his false little smiles and told her that he was staying on the ship. She shrugged and told him to suit himself, secretly pleased that the agent of imperialism wouldn't be coming.

Minutes later, they were airborne, and Camila wasn't certain if she was more excited to be living a lifelong dream or to be taking her first trip on a helicopter. Initially, the ride was what held her attention… and especially the incredible noise the machine made.

Javier and Clark were the only members of the crew who appeared to take the chopper ride in stride. She assumed that military types were always flying around everywhere, and maybe Australian universities had more money than their Argentine counterparts. For whatever reason, they were both impassively facing forward while the women oohed and aahed and pointed out ice floes and Antarctic landmarks memorized from a map.

In moments, they were over the open stretch of water, and she could see the rocks of the coast poking out under the snow cover. She was surprised when a group of red buildings came into view on a small hill near the open water. "Look!" she cried. "Is that the base?"

"Of course it's the base. What else would it be out here?"

"It's just that I thought it would be further from the water."

"Actually, it would have been last year. There was a big glacier that separated off from the shelf—it was in all the papers. All the mappers had assumed there was rock down there, but it was actually just ice."

"Well, now it's a seaside base."

"Still a few hundred meters away from the coast, but closer than before."

They circled the base once, giving the science team a good look. The complex was much bigger than she'd expected. Aside from the big red cube in the center, there were several other buildings, some squat rectangular shapes, others long half-pipes of metal. A large Argentine flag fluttered in the wind.

Two tracked snowplows—one with a bulldozer mounted on the front—and two covered vans, also tracked, were dotted around the base. A sort of wooden sled with runners was on its side near one of the vans.

"There's the source of our problems," Javier said, pointing to a fallen latticework structure. "The main antenna mast is down."

"So are the rest," Clark pointed out.

"That must have been some storm."

"Yeah. The buildings don't look too badly damaged, though. That hangar over there was crushed, but the rectangular ones look OK."

"Would the wind crush a hangar?"

"The winds here in Antarctica can get pretty nasty," Camila told them. She was surprised they didn't already know this. When she learned that her petition had been granted, she went online and read everything she could about the white content. The very first thing she looked at was the weather—after all, the first thing one needs to know when going to a new place was what clothes to bring along—and she soon discovered that Antarctic winds had been known, albeit infrequently, to hit speeds of nearly three hundred kilometers an hour. Yeah, something being blown about at that speed could crush a hangar or anything else you might put in its path.

The wind wasn't blowing on that day though, and the pilot brought the chopper down to a soft landing about forty meters away from the nearest building. She assumed there was some kind of concrete helipad there, but it was invisible under the snow.

They dropped onto the snow. Camila found herself tensing as if, just because they were standing on Antarctic soil, the temperature should have dropped well below what it was on the ship. But no, the temperature was the same; in fact, she didn't even think it was cold enough to freeze water out, not by a long shot. She estimated it must have been near ten degrees centigrade.

"Where is everybody?" Javier asked.

Camila shrugged. "Probably inside."

"That's strange. They should have heard the helicopter coming from miles away. Why aren't they out here to get their chocolate? And besides, there should be someone outside." For a moment, he looked like her image of a professional soldier, formed by a hundred Hollywood movies. His tan coat and steely eyes were probably a front, though.

Regardless of his play-acting, the base did look desolate, so they headed to the big red cube, the closest structure. Camila knew that wasn't a building, but a casing housing astronomical instruments. A few steps beyond that, the rest of the buildings huddled together. The ruined hangar was nearest, but they bypassed that one and headed towards the observatory. This was a rectangular building—also red, like all the others—perched on the side of the small hill.

The door was open—a terrible breach of energy protocol, Camila imagined, although not as critical in summer as it would be in the cold, dark season—so they walked inside, into a short, dim hallway.

"Merry Christmas," the chopper pilot shouted. "Special delivery from the mainland. Who's up for some chocolate?"

No one answered.

"Oh, God, not again," Javier said. He tried to make it sound like a joke, but it was clear from his face that he was truly worried.

They advanced to the end of the hall, where the door to an office stood open.

"What happened here?" Camila said. The room looked like it had been savaged by a tornado. Pages torn from spiral-bound notebooks carpeted the floor. A shattered coffee cup lay on a brown-stained comforter. Three chairs lay on their sides.

"Is this blood?" Ernesto asked. He was pointing to a rust colored mark on the floor where some viscous liquid had dried on the carpeted floor.

The pilot looked down at it and shrugged. "If it is, someone is in bad shape. Maybe everyone's in the infirmary. That would explain why no one was there to meet us."

The infirmary was located inside one of the other rectangular buildings, directly up the hill from the observatory and next to the living quarters. They turned the corner and approached the door, the whole group moving together. It made for uncomfortable going in the snow, but suddenly no one wanted to be left behind or get separated. Nine of them—Javier, the scientists and the pilot—made their way slowly.

Javier, leading the way, stopped dead in his tracks.

The door, a solid wooden affair, had been torn off its hinges and lay splintered on the ground halfway down the hall.

Javier rushed inside and looked around. It was clear that this place was built on a different plan: there was a small room just inside the doorway, and the door in the far wall of that one led into a much larger chamber. Camila saw beds in the second room.

It was an infirmary, but where the *Irizar* boasted high-tech beds with automated movement and perfect ergonomic adjustments, the six beds in this room were made of pipes welded together and painted military green. No luxury or high-tech medicine, just a comfortable place to recover from minor injuries.

Or it would have been had it not, like the door, been trashed. One bed lay on its side, most of the rest had been pushed out of any semblance of order. Mattresses and sheets were torn to ribbons; one mattress had actually been torn in half, foam rubber splaying out.

And this time there was no doubt whatsoever: the dark red stains on every surface, absorbed indelibly into all the fabric could only be blood. Camila got the impression that she was looking at the site of a massacre.

Martin, one of the students, took one look at the stained sheets and ran out of the building. Sounds of retching followed the rest of the group as they went deeper.

The next space was the operating room. This, too, resembled something straight out of the nineteen fifties. Whatever the cost of having a presence in Antarctica, the Argentine government had evidently defrayed it partially by not updating the medical center… ever.

Camila felt fury rising again. She knew that only units with a high concentration of officers or places that appeared on the news frequently had access to decent health care. No one worried about the common soldiers from the base of society's pyramid.

In the operating room, it was hard to tell whether the blood had come from some violent action or whether it was the product of an operation. The red splashes were concentrated around the operating table. Blue sheets were stained and tousled, but only a few drops had made it to the floor.

Javier quickly checked the room and pronounced it clear. He turned back to them: "Let's get back outside. I want to check the rest of the buildings quickly and return to the *Irizar*. I'd like to come back with a bunch of marines and some guns."

Camila shook her head at his typical male response. Even she could tell that whoever or whatever had done this wasn't around now. The base felt as if it had been deserted for days if not weeks. She suspected that all of this had happened when they went off the air. There was no need to go charging in like kindergarteners. There was a logical explanation for what had happened here, and the answer would be found by thinking about it, not by playing cowboys and indians. But she doubted the military minds around her would agree.

Her mind was working at full speed to try to think of who would want to do something like this. She knew of at least two groups who were strongly opposed to a human presence in the virgin wastes of Antarctica, but suspected that neither would have the resources necessary to carry out an attack on a base… but for anyone who did, Belgrano II was probably the ideal candidate: isolated from the rest of the Antarctic community and run by one of the least security-conscious countries with a presence on the continent.

They huddled together outside.

"We'll quickly look over the other buildings and then get back," Javier said. He turned to the pilot. "Can you restart the chopper?"

The man nodded. "Yeah, I left the copilot with orders to keep the engine warm. Get back as soon as you can." He hurried off around the observatory towards the helicopter.

The other buildings were empty of life as well. The barracks were empty but undamaged. The equipment hangar was perfectly intact, nothing seemed out of place. A pair of technical huts were likewise untouched.

They left the crushed hangar for last. The doors were locked, but there was no real need to use them because the semi-cylindrical roof had been torn open almost all the way to the ground. They walked in through the torn roof.

"This was the food storage. Look."

Javier was right. Cans, boxes, and even cuts of meat were strewn all over the floor. What had once been crates neatly stacked on pallets now looked like an explosion in a supermarket.

"This wasn't done by the wind." Ernesto pointed to half a cow carcass lying on the ground. Large chunks were missing.

"That looks like it was bitten."

Javier kicked it. "I don't think so. Something would have had to be fantastically strong to bite into that. It's frozen solid."

"Guys, look at this," Ingrid said. "I don't think this was the wind either." She was pointing at the roof, or what was left of the roof.

Beside the large hole that exposed the interior of the hangar, three parallel lines had torn through the metal.

Ernesto studied them critically. "Those look just like the claw marks on the poster for a horror movie," he said.

No one contradicted him, and they shuffled their feet in silence.

At that moment the pilot returned, huffing and red. His service pistol was gripped in one white-knuckled fist. "My copilot's gone! And the helicopter is trashed."

Without thinking, they ran in the direction of the helicopter, slipping and sliding down the slope. The aircraft appeared to be perfectly all right from a distance, but when they got closer, Camila saw that one of the landing struts was bent, and the nose was making contact with the snow.

The cabin was worse. Instruments had been ripped out of the panel, wiring covered the floor, but the most shocking was the fact that the massive copilot's seat had been torn out of its mountings. It lay ten meters away from the helicopter. Dark liquid patches covered the chair, and bright red dots adorned the snow around it. The snow itself was churned up… and two long furrows in the pristine white headed in the direction of the sea.

One of the holes plowed in the snow was sprinkled with blood.

They stood in silence until something in her subconscious, something she'd been putting off, bubbled to the surface.

Suddenly, an icy fist grabbed Camila's heart. "Where's Martin?"

CHAPTER 7

Breen waited beside the door. The doctor had given him strict orders that Natasha wasn't to be disturbed until after she'd had her lunch. He had an equally adamant communication from Fort Belvoir telling him that he needed to get the relevant information as soon as possible. They suspected that the Argentines would cut off his access to the Russian woman soon.

He'd sent a quick message back to his handlers. It was short and to the point:

What the hell is going on down here?

He was still awaiting a response, but there were a bunch of questions he'd wanted to add to the initial request, like who was calling the shots. He'd been with Military Intelligence for a good chunk of his career, and the missions he'd been on were usually somewhat related to operations—black or white—happening in the field. This one, on the other hand, smelled like Langley. This was the kind of weird duty that always came up whenever the CIA got involved. The spooks liked nothing more than to pull strings without letting the puppets suspect what might be going on.

His brief had said that he was supposed to watch out for Russian activity in the extreme south seas, but mainly around Antarctica. Well, the Russians had fallen into his lap in a nearly comical coincidence, but he still had no clue as to the scope of their presence; it was possible that the fishing boat and whatever had been found inside—the Argentines were being coy about it—represented the full extent of the operation. It was also possible that the Russians had built a Bond-villain-like base underneath the Antarctic ice from which they would do dastardly deeds. With the growth of China and the proliferation of threats from the Middle East, no one had been watching Russia as closely as they should have.

The only specific instruction he'd received was that he was to report any indication of biological or chemical weapons. He'd certainly seen no sign of that so far. All he had was a badly mauled zoologist, so unless the biological weapons program consisted of creating some kind of mutant shark, there was little to report.

He sighed. He wouldn't put it past Langley to send him after mutant sharks.

While he waited for the woman to eat, he stood at a window in an empty room in the clinic and looked out at the ice. The ship was advancing excruciatingly slowly. Every once in a while a sharp crack, reminiscent of a gunshot, would echo over the icy wastes as the solid surface snapped under the onslaught of the sharp prow.

Suddenly, the ship vibrated like a struck bell. Breen had to catch himself against the wall to keep himself from being pitched to the floor.

"What the hell was that?" he asked, but there was no one in earshot.

He ran down out onto the deck and located a staggering Lieutenant who was attempting to run in his direction. "What happened?" he asked in Spanish.

"I'm going to try to find out now. It sounded like we hit something."

"A rock?"

"There aren't any rocks down there according to our sonar."

The sound came again, louder, if anything. Someone on the bridge must have been listening because the thrumming of the engines, nearly imperceptible, but always *there*, stopped suddenly. A few moments later, they started up again and Breen felt a small tug… in the opposite direction. The ship was reversing up the channel it had cleared in the ice.

He followed the officer up the stairs. The captain was telling the sonar operator in no uncertain terms that he wanted to know what the hell they'd hit, and he wanted to know right now. The woman was pale as a sheet. Breen and the other officer stood to one side as she double-checked her readings.

"I'm sorry sir, there's nothing showing."

The captain snorted in disgust. "Well, we hit something. I want to know what, where and how big it is. Damn this ice. It makes it impossible to see anything." Then he looked around and saw he had an audience. He chuckled ruefully. "I guess this is what I get for lobbying to take command of an icebreaker.

"Ah, Hanssen," he said to the officer who'd climbed up with Breen. "Just the man I needed to see. Please grab a crew and see if we have any damage. We should be all right because the prow is pretty thick, but I want to be damned sure."

"Yessir." The young officer disappeared.

"And Mr. Breen, don't worry. We won't be sinking any time soon, although this might delay us a little. We need to find a way around this invisible barrier." He made to turn to speak to the poor girl on the sonar, but then something occurred to him. "You can watch from here. It should be pretty interesting… icebreakers usually don't go backwards for any number of good reasons… but it appears our instruments need space to work."

Breen didn't need to be asked twice. The view was excellent, like looking down from a seven-story building onto a glacier. The ice was dirty grey on the surface, with patches of brilliant white interspersed at intervals, but the broken ice behind them also had bits of blue in it, like the pictures he'd seen of ice in mountain glaciers.

He'd expected the ice they were ploughing through to be a solid mass, but from here, it was clear that it wasn't. They were breaking a thin—albeit several feet thick in places—layer on the top of the sea, and there were spots where the water came through in oval puddles. From this high, it was very evident that the ice sheet they were navigating was floating on the sea, not attached to the land.

As the ship reversed, an open patch of water grew in front of it. Tiny sheets of ice flowed back into the vacated space as Breen watched. He'd always thought that icebreakers tore through thick walls of ice, but now that he thought about it, the thin crust was a much more realistic proposition.

He could see a female sailor was looking down the railing, over the prow, apparently trying to see whether any damage might have occurred above the water line.

Breen was turning back to speak to the captain when, out of the corner of his eye, something black about the size of a car darted from the water and made contact with the prow. The entire ship shook and, when Breen looked again, the sailor was gone and the railings were bent.

"What the fuck?" It came out before he had a chance to think. "Captain, I think you should come over here."

"Did you see what hit us?"

"Yes. Well not in detail, but I saw the movement, and if you look at that railing, you'll see the effect without my help."

The captain rushed over.

"Holy shit. I wasn't expecting to be hit by anything above the surface. Do you have any idea of what it might have been?"

"All I know is that it came out of the water and then it went back in. And it was big."

"A submarine?"

Breen shrugged. "If it was, it had some kind of above-the-surface extension claw which took down one of your crew."

"Are you sure?"

"She was standing right next to the railing. She's not there now."

"Captain," the woman at the sonar desk said. "I got something, but now it's gone."

"Where was it?"

"Crossed the bow from left to right and went down. It might have gone under us. No wait, I've got a signal coming back up."

A huge wave broke impossibly from the open sea between the *Irizar* and the ice. It was followed by… Breen couldn't believe his eyes.

It looked like an alligator's head. Except it was the size of a minivan. It was perched on an impossibly long and thin neck that shouldn't have been able to support the head, much less power it from side to side vigorously.

Then the sound arrived. It was half lion's roar, half pig's grunt and all volume, loud even through the hermetically sealed windows. A pair of clawed feet gripped the railings on the deck in the prow. The legs were clearly made for walking on land… but the monstrous feet were webbed.

The ship rocked as the creature tried to pull itself aboard, and then the sway in the other direction as the claws lost purchase and its sheer weight sent it tumbling back into the water.

"Forward!" the captain shouted. "Pull us forward. Try to crush it!"

"Crush what?" the man on the throttle asked. Unlike the captain and Breen, he didn't have a clear view to the front.

That hesitation proved fatal; just moments after it disappeared under the surface, the creature launched itself back onto the foredeck. The entire ship tilted forward under the weight of the colossus. Breen was certain the nose would sink and send them all to the bottom.

Then his reflexes, honed in countless hours of training and on more than one informal battlefield, kicked in. He realized the creature's head was shooting towards the bridge and dove for the stairwell an instant before glass sprayed all over the interior like shrapnel from a mortar. The metal bulkhead buckled and shifted nearly two meters.

The creature's snout didn't make it through the wall, but that made little difference. Huge claws finished tearing out the remains of the wall and then ripped into the bridge. The captain was cut in half.

From where he stood, Breen had a direct view of the woman at the sonar panel. She'd somehow managed to stay on her seat as the bridge rocked from the blows. Her face changed to shocked horror when the captain flew apart in a spray of blood. She was close enough to get soaked by droplets.

She looked down at her scarlet uniform, a look of profound incomprehension on her features.

Then it was Breen's turn to gasp as the next swipe removed the girl's head from her shoulders. It arced across the bridge and thudded against the far wall, leaving her body seated at her console as if nothing had happened.

A couple of heartbeats later, she slumped forward onto her desk, blood from a still-beating heart gushing over the instruments.

He'd seen enough. Time to go somewhere safer. He rushed down the stairs trying to make as little noise and hoping, against all evidence, that the metal walls down which the stairwell had been built would withstand the onslaught.

The flights flew by until he reached the exterior deck. Breen wasn't certain why he'd stopped there—the smartest thing to do was probably to bury himself in the deepest part of the ship, surrounded by as much metal as possible, and make the bastard work for it.

But when he reached the main deck, he heard loud cracks. Was the boat moving through the ice?

No. Four sailors had found guns somewhere, the ubiquitous FAL rifles that the Argentine military liked so much—and had spent so many resources upgrading and modding over the years—and had begun to shoot at the monstrosity that was now eating the morsels it had been able to pry from the bridge.

He almost laughed. Infantry rifles against that thing? It was a quarter of the size of the ship. If it had been his call, he would have called in an airstrike, probably using nuclear ordnance, just to be on the safe side.

But these guys were attacking the thing with assault rifles and actually advancing. He wanted to tell them they were moving in the wrong direction, and that what they really wanted to do was to hide behind the huge beige cube in the middle of the ship.

Instead, his training took over again and he ran in their direction. "Where can I get a gun?" he asked.

"Over there."

A wooden locker on the deck held FALs and ammunition. He chuckled and pulled one out, surprised to see it came complete with a loaded magazine. The Argentines had fooled him into thinking the ship was lightly defended… he wondered what else was hidden in plain sight.

He tried to fire a controlled burst, but the gun was one of the fully automatic Argentine versions which was difficult to control—the FAL had always been at the limit of its design capabilities with the 7.62 round, a characteristic that was only made worse by the fully automatic mode. That made no difference, however. The men had a target they would be hard pressed to miss.

His fears that they wouldn't even be able to penetrate the lizard's skin proved unfounded. Blood did spatter, and the thing roared in pain, and standing there firing the kicking gun was one of the most satisfying things he could remember doing… but he still felt the rounds were too small to do any real damage.

To his surprise, it began to retreat. As the sailors concentrated their fire around its head, the creature began to wave its long arms around as if swatting flies. Eventually, in confusion, it dove back over the side.

The sailors cheered, but Breen wondered how long the reprieve would last.

"Do you guys mind if I keep this thing?" he asked them.

"Be our guest," the nearest one replied with a nod of thanks for Breen followed by a cold glare at the rest of the ship. "You've earned it, unlike everyone else."

Breen nodded back. He had a new respect for Argentine sailors… or at least for these four.

They didn't even seem surprised that a scientist was able to pick up a random infantry rifle and use it competently. Either they thought everyone in the U.S. was a gun nut… or his cover was blown sky high. He suspected the latter.

He also suspected there were more important things to worry about.

***

Three minutes later, he was arguing with the doctor.

"I don't give a damn what your patient needs," Breen said and he shouldered past. "We just got attacked by something, and that woman knows what it is, or at least has a much better idea than we do."

The doctor spluttered. "I'm going to talk to the captain about this."

"Oh yeah? Which half?"

"What?"

Breen ignored him. "Go find one of those lieutenants, I assume one of them is in command now. Tell him the captain is dead, the bridge is history and there's something big after us. Also, tell him to recommend the four sailors who saved our asses for medals. I'll call you if I need you back."

Natasha was sitting in bed, a tray suspended over her legs by a kind of wheeled C-shaped trolley whose bottom half was under the bed and whose top half supported the tray. He'd spent enough time in hospital to be familiar with most of the common equipment. He had little difficulty pulling the tray from under the bed.

"What happened?" she said. "I heard the noise, felt the ship moving. Did we hit something?"

He could tell she was scared. More scared than the mere prospect of hitting something should have made her. After all, even if the ship sank, they could walk to the base easily over the ice.

"I think you know what happened. It was a monster, a big one."

She shook her head. "I don't know."

"You do. And you also speak English, probably better than I do. If you don't tell us what you know, more people are going to die. And this time it will be your fault."

"I can't... they told me..."

"They're all gone." Breen let that sink in. "No one knows you're here. Hell, no one even knows you're alive. And if you don't tell us what we need to know, we won't be able to save you."

"No. My family..."

"Nothing will happen to them."

"I don't know anything."

"Of course you do. You're in a secret intelligence operation pretending to be a Korean fishing boat, except you aren't Korean, that wasn't a fishing boat and everyone else disappeared. You obviously know something." Breen lost his patience. "Did you create that monster?"

"What? How could you even..."

Gotcha. "So you do know what it is?"

Natasha sighed. He was glad she wasn't a soldier or some kind of fanatic. Those could take days to break. She, on the other hand, appeared to be exactly what his briefing said, a zoologist with no particular national security links.... probably drawn in because of what she knew as opposed to what her politics were. But he had to get her mind back on her own peril and not that of her loved ones. In Russia, worrying about her family would be a perfectly natural response in that situation. The SVR wasn't above taking their displeasure out on family members. "We don't know where it came from," she said in British English tinged with an unmistakable Russian accent. "I mean we know what happened to it, but not where it came from."

"Why don't you start at the very beginning."

"Do you think we have time? Will it be back?"

"Good point. Give me the condensed version. Right now, all I know is that my government is looking for biological weapons that they suspect are hidden somewhere down here, either in Antarctica or in Tierra del Fuego. Maybe southern Chile, but we don't think so. Pinochet let us go over the whole area with a fine-tooth comb back in the day, and we didn't find squat." He paused. "Also, please tell me that thing isn't the weapon."

"You're looking in the wrong place. You should have sent submarines, not some secret agent guy. The biological weapons are at the bottom of the Bellingshausen Sea."

"Then they existed? It was the Sverdlovsk anthrax?"

She hesitated, but then caved. "Yes."

"And the ship carrying it sank?"

"Yes."

"Holy shit. And what happened next?"

"The government sent ships out to try to find it. Well, not immediately, the eighties and the nineties were a bit of a mess for Russia."

"So I heard."

"Well, in 2005, the government got paranoid that the Chinese were setting up a presence in Argentina, and that they had somehow gotten wind of the accident. So they sent a small fleet out on maneuvers, with some treasure hunters on board."

"Treasure hunters?"

"You know the type. The ones who have reality shows about how they look for sunken ships carrying Nazi gold and that kind of thing. They already had the equipment we needed."

Breen laughed. The Russians were often strapped for cash, but they always found a creative way to get things done. He could only imagine what the Navy would say if they were forced to use reality show stars.

"So you found the wreck?"

"They did, yes. But they found some other things, too."

"Other things meaning… like the thing that attacked us?"

"No… I mean yes. Nothing that big, but they suspected there was something out there."

It all clicked. "So that was why they took you along. They needed someone to tell them what those things were…"

"They already knew what they were. The problem is that each time they went back, the things looked and acted different. The government began to worry that the anthrax strains were affecting them."

"Yeah, I'll say… I don't recall too many alligators that size from my high school biology classes."

"That isn't an alligator. It never was."

"It sure looked like one."

"No it didn't. You probably weren't paying much attention to it."

"I was kind of busy trying not to get killed."

"Whatever. The creatures are nothosaurs. Or at least they were before they came into contact with the bio waste."

"What the hell is a…" he felt his eyes widen, "a dinosaur?"

"Not exactly. It is an ancient reptile that coexisted with the dinosaurs, but modern scientists…"

"I don't really care about the taxonomy of the thing. Are you telling me we got attacked by a dinosaur as big as this ship?"

She looked unhappy but nodded. "Close enough."

"What the hell is it doing here? Where did it come from?"

"That's the beauty of it. They've always been here."

"The beauty?"

"You know what I mean. The thing is that this is cold water, and not a lot of people come here. At some point a subspecies of nothosaur adapted to the cold weather, and no one who saw them ever believed their eyes. There were reports about them in the early 1900s, even by British naval officers, but no one really paid them any attention. They were true, though."

"And Russia has known about this since…"

She shrugged. "2005. Or maybe one of the later expeditions. 2007 at the latest."

"Oh my God. Why didn't you tell anyone?"

"I have no idea. I was recruited for this mission… but I suppose it is because the effects of the bio agents on the creatures were interesting enough that it was worth keeping from other governments."

"Interesting? You seem to have a penchant for understatement."

"And you have no clue as to what the real problem we're facing is. You seem concerned about the big creature."

"If you'd seen that thing, you'd sure as hell be concerned, too."

"But that one can be tracked by radar, and its sheer weight would make it unwieldy on land."

"It can go on land?"

"Of course, nothosaurs are amphibious," Natasha said as if that was obvious to everyone who wasn't a zoologist or a paleontologist.

"Of course."

"No, the real problem are the small ones. The ones that can go through doors and get to the people in houses and bunkers. Those are the ones that hit our ship."

"And how many of those are we looking for?"

Again the shrug. "I don't know. It was dark and everyone was screaming, but I thought there might be twenty of them. I only got away because one of them grabbed Yuri."

"Yuri? They told me you were the only person on the ship."

"All I was left with was one hand. I think the doctor took it when he operated on me."

And she finally broke down and cried. Breen left her to regain her strength. She was going to need it.

CHAPTER 8

"We need to get under cover," Javier said.

"What about Martin?" Camila said.

Javier hoped his face didn't betray what he was thinking. As far as he was concerned, the student had become a meal for something. The best case scenario he could think of was that he'd survived long enough to die of hypothermia when the creatures pulled him into the sea. He was convinced that was where the attack had come from. The ocean could hide anything under that white wasteland covering. Drowning, of course, would have been worse. "He's probably back at the base. I didn't see him when we came down."

"And my copilot?"

"I think he might be dead. I think some large animal got him."

This elicited a snort of derision from Camila. "This is Antarctica. What sort of large animal would be hunting here?"

"I don't know. A polar bear, maybe?"

"Don't be idiotic. Polar bears live in the Arctic, not the Antarctic." This came from Ingrid, who managed to pip all the other scientists—each of which had started to speak—to the rebuke.

"Does it matter?" Javier asked.

That silenced them.

"I thought so. Now let's get back to the base."

"What for? The base doesn't seem to have been much of a barrier."

"I know, but I've been thinking about that. My conclusion is that they got caught by surprise, and weren't able to prepare." That was probably true, but the real reason was that cover, any sort of cover, had to be better than an exposed walk over the snow.

"How do you prepare for something that can rip a metal roof to shreds with its claws?"

"We don't know that that's what happened."

"It sure looked that way."

"I think the base was attacked by something smaller, probably more than one. I know you think polar bears are a stupid idea, but they fit the bill. They're big enough to attack a human and strong enough to carry them away. Also, it's probably much easier to hunt slow humans on land than wait for seals to pop up out of the ocean, which is a good enough reason for the attack. Hell, I'd be surprised if there were even seals here to eat."

"There are plenty of seals. Penguins too. But no polar bears, even if they fit the theory."

"Look, can we talk about this later? Right now, we need to lock ourselves in the base and try to stay safe."

They headed back towards the red buildings.

"Shouldn't we try to call the *Irizar*?" Clark said.

"The helicopter radio is destroyed," the pilot informed them. "It was the first thing I checked. Unless one of you has a satellite phone, we'll need to try calling from the base."

Javier sighed. The inability of Base Belgrano II to communicate with the outside world was what had started the whole thing in the first place. He said nothing, however; at least the party was moving in the right direction.

"We should look for a building strong enough to withstand," he almost said 'a bear', but checked himself in time, "an animal the size of a bear."

"And somewhere we can light a fire or connect a heater," Camila said. "Does the base still have power?"

"None of the lights were working. I tried. A fire's a good idea. And we need to get ourselves ready before nightfall."

He felt, more than saw, everyone rolling their eyes and remembered the past few nights on board the *Irizar*—nights in which the sun hadn't set at all. He laughed at himself.

"Camila, you seem to be the best-informed about goings-on at the base. Which building do you suggest?"

She stopped to think about it, looking at the base as they approached the slight rise upon which it was built. Javier admired her single-mindedness in looking forward. More than half of his attention was focused behind them. Everything indicated that the creatures, whatever they were, had come from behind, from the direction of the water, and regardless of whether they were or weren't bears, they certainly were strong enough to destroy a helicopter and break a wooden door to pieces. He kept his hand near his pistol.

"I know," Camila said suddenly. "The base of the observatory dish. It's a concrete cube. The only concrete structure anywhere in the complex. It's not ideal because it's not built on stilts, so we'll have a hell of a time heating it, but it's better than the rest of the buildings. Nothing is going to be able to get in once we reinforce the door."

"Good." They headed in that direction.

The building was precisely as described. Solid as hell, cold as hell, and about five meters to a side. A large satellite dish—some kind of radio observatory, he recalled—perched on the roof, and the mechanism for moving it occupied the top half of the cube. The door would need work, but they set about rolling some heavy drums that were stored inside to a place where they could quickly be placed as a makeshift barrier across the entrance.

Once the barrier was in place, Javier set out, pistol in hand, to see if he could locate the base's radio. He assumed it would be in the office space they'd only given a cursory glance to during their search for the base's inhabitants. That place had been hit, but not too badly.

It was a sign of how worried they were that no one tried to stop him and no one volunteered to go with him.

About thirty meters separated the two buildings, but it felt like leagues to Javier. The sound of the snow that crunched under his boots echoed on the walls and came back at him from unexpected directions. He pointed his gun first one way, then another, only to find he'd been jumping at shadows, and that there was nothing amiss.

He even wished the wind would pick up. He'd heard that the wind was what killed you in Antarctica, that it could blow right through countless layers of windproof clothes, that it howled like a train, that it would knock you off your feet.

None of that appeared to be true. The flag, forgotten and forlorn, hung limp from its frosted pole. Loose snow didn't swirl, and there certainly wasn't any howling. In the stillness, he felt as if he could have heard the slightest noise for miles.

But what he couldn't stop thinking was that anything out there could also hear him.

He rushed into the office building like the devil himself was after him, as if the sunny day outside was the coldest of dark Halloween nights.

Just as Camila had predicted, the base had a radio. It was an old UHF/VHF unit which, at present was serving as a tray for two coffee mugs and a dirty plate. It didn't appear to have been used this century but, of course, no one would ever throw it away. Eventually, it would just disappear under a mountain of bric-a-brac. The Argentine army never threw anything away. Equipment was repaired and duct-taped forever. Eventually, the government would need to start a war with someone just for the sake of getting all that old equipment blown up.

He sighed. The thing had a power cord and no backup batteries, which meant that, in order to check if it was running, he'd need to find and start the generator. The fact that it wasn't running was the least of his worries; those things were bulletproof, so it had probably just run out of gas.

Javier was about to go look for fuel when something moved in the corner of his eye. He desperately looked around the office, but there was nothing in there with him. Then he realized that the movement was outside the window. For a second, hope flared: had the *Irizar* tried to hail them and, upon receiving no response, realized that something was wrong? Had they sent the other helicopter, or a search party?

No. The movement was on the ground, something black against the snow in the distance. As he watched, whatever it was came into focus and he couldn't believe his eyes. A large, lizard-like creature was heading for the base.

It didn't look like any lizard he'd seen before, though. Those had reedy legs which stretched straight out to the sides. This one had muscular legs that went straight down from its body, and ended in enormous webbed feet… with what looked like daggers mounted on the ends. It also had a long neck with a disproportionately large head which it held up like… like the old pictures of the loch ness monster. A long tail balanced the neck and head. The walk reminded him more of a horse or a dog—a long, weird-looking horse or dog—than any lizard he'd ever seen.

He stared. That didn't look like a picture book dinosaur. Those appeared bloated and slow, plump and relaxed. This one appeared to be pure muscle. Even with its strange, ungainly proportions, it appeared to be moving quickly, even at rest. Dark greenish-grey color stood out against the snow. The creature would have looked more at home in a jungle swamp.

The distance made it difficult to judge scale but as he watched, mesmerized, it approached a small outbuilding. Javier gasped. Had it held its head up straight, it would have been taller than the little hut—at least four meters in the air. From tip to tail, it must have measured at least ten meters, probably more.

The creature didn't hesitate. As if tugged by an invisible string, it headed straight for the concrete cube that housed the scientists and the pilot.

Javier watched aghast. Would the door hold? Would the team realize that it had company of the worst sort? Were they ready?

The one thing he had no doubts about whatsoever was that the lizard had been responsible for the disappearance of both the members of his own team and the men and women from the base.

The monster reached the cube and roared, an awful, purely animal sound that somehow made the creature even more repugnant. A tremor ran down his spine, a desire to run that went past his intellectual faculties straight to the base of his spine, where some primal remnant of pre-mammalian instinct still survived.

As he fought the paralysis, the creature circled the concrete cube once, twice and then, with another roar, launched itself at the structure. He didn't have a good angle to see whether it was hitting the door, but if it was, the barrels wouldn't hold for long. This thing was four times the size of a polar bear. And once the door was down, he realized that the creature was—just—lithe enough to fit through the opening. It would be a massacre.

His sidearm was a Browning Hi-Power, a nine millimeter pistol, and the range, with such a large target was more than reasonable. He tried to control his breathing as he walked to the door, then, taking cover in the entrance, steadied his arm and inhaled. Javier fired once, then again and again.

Then he stopped to see whether his shots had had any effect on the creature.

To his satisfaction, it ran off towards the water. It ran much faster than something that ungainly should have been able to.

Emboldened by his success, he hurried back to the makeshift shelter.

At the door, he stopped in his tracks. The wood was splintered and cracked and, despite the drums behind it, the door had been pushed nearly twenty centimeters in. If he'd hesitated just a few more seconds, the creature would have been inside…

"Let me in!" he shouted. He'd seen the great lizard run off into the distance, but he still couldn't shake the sense that it was right behind him, just waiting for him to look away before hitting him in the back.

"Colonel?" the pilot shouted from within as the door opened a crack. "We thought you were dead for sure."

They all looked happy to see him, but Camila surprised him most by running up and hugging him. "Thank God. We were all so scared."

"Well, I have some good news and some bad news. The good news is that those things aren't impervious to bullets. The bad news is that they don't seem to be easy to kill, either. I hit it three times and it only ran away. It looked like it was perfectly all right."

"Where did you hit it?"

"I got it in the sides. I was trying to make it stop attacking you guys first, and worry about taking it down later."

They all studied the door. "I think we're going to need to beef this up a bit," the pilot observed.

"Yeah. When you close it, bring over more drums. All of them if possible."

"When *we* close it? Where do you think you're going to be?" Camila said.

"I'm going to hike over the ice to get to the *Irizar*."

Silence met this proclamation. Feet shuffled. Only Camila spoke up. "That's the most idiotic thing I've ever heard. Even if there wasn't some kind of overgrown monster out there eating people, you probably wouldn't make it anyway."

"Why not? The ice the ship was sailing through reaches the shore. I should be able to walk over in a while. An hour at most."

"We don't know if the ice is continuous. An insignificant crack, something four meters wide would cut you off completely."

Javier set his jaw. "I have to try. And I need someone to come with me."

The pilot immediately raised his hand, but Javier shook his head. "You've got your gun, so I need you to stay here and fight off those things if they come again. See if you can find a soft spot."

"I'll go." Javier was surprised to see Clark, the Australian, stepping forward. He'd had the guy pegged as a pretty boy who'd only act macho enough to get into someone's pants, and then conveniently forget all about it. But the guy didn't seem to be in the least afraid of heading out onto the ice.

Javier nodded.

"Then I'm coming, too," Anna said.

"No way," Clark replied. "Stay here."

"Why, because I'm a girl? I'm not staying here while you go out there. I just got you and now I'm going to take care of you."

Javier kept his mouth firmly shut. The Australian didn't seem like the kind of guy who would consider a few nights to mean anything more than a few nights, but Anna didn't look like a woman who would care what anyone else thought. Besides, though slim, she was taller than Javier was and well-muscled to go with it. He decided that letting her come might be better than getting decked.

"All right. But that's it. The whole point of me going out there is to keep as many of you safe as possible… and now there's just five of you here and three of us will be out there. Before we go, we'll help you roll some more drums."

Half an hour later, the three volunteers set off, pausing at the helicopter only long enough to retrieve its emergency flares, which Javier wanted to use to signal the icebreaker.

"We need to hit the ice over there," he pointed to their right, "where it makes landfall. But we should probably take an inland route. The creature I saw was moving towards the water."

"Did you follow it?" Anna asked.

Javier chuckled. "Are you kidding?"

"I'm only asking because of that big snow bank between us and the water. The creature might be hiding in there, although that would be strange."

"Stranger than other stuff that's happened already?"

"Reptiles are cold-blooded. They don't usually work all that well in freezing weather. It should have been nearly catatonic."

"The one I saw certainly wasn't."

"I know. That's why I'm doubtful about the accumulated snow. Normally, I'd have bet that the creature—assuming it actually is some kind of big reptile—would have headed straight back to the water because water is usually milder than the cold land around it. But this one seems to be fine on land… so maybe they nest here, too."

"Well, if you want to study them, I'm fine with that. But not now, and I'd recommend you come back with an armored division or two. It will make it more likely that you might return."

"I've worked with dangerous animals before, Colonel."

"I thought you worked with microbes."

That got him a cold smile. "There is nothing alive more dangerous than microbes. But while I'm a bacteriologist now, that is a relatively new development. I used to work at the Kruger Park tracking big cat and elephant populations. I only went into bacteriology because my sister needed help. She's going to win the Nobel one of these years… so I decided I might as well have my name on her papers."

He chuckled. "Sounds logical."

They reached the ice and had to jump from the shore—a place where the rocky grey beach could be seen poking through the snow in places—onto the sea ice. Clark and Anna managed to land softly, but Javier slipped and fell. He hoped the chagrin of taking a pratfall in front of civilians wasn't too visible in his face. To cover it up, he laughed and made a joke.

The ship was visible in the distance. It didn't appear to have made much headway since they'd landed at the base. They walked towards it.

It was impossible to make a beeline to the *Irizar* because the ice refused to collaborate. Every few dozen meters, curious pools of water, maybe ten meters across would appear. They weren't just holes but actually appeared to consist of oval basins filled with water disconnected from the ocean below. Where the water had made it through the ice, the sinkholes had drained into the sea, and all that was visible was a depression in the ice and a dark hole where the water below was visible.

One of the open holes held a family of seals, and Javier shuddered. An opening that could admit seals could also allow anything else to come up… and they'd left a bunch of these holes behind them. Javier's very first lesson in officer school, administered by a sadist who'd served in the Falklands War, was that you never left a live enemy behind you. Javier wondered how that man would have handled this particular terrain.

Time dragged on and the ship began to grow imperceptibly closer.

Clark held up a hand. "Do you guys see anything wrong with the ship?"

"Wrong? How?"

"The bridge looks weird." He passed around the binoculars, the only set they'd brought with them.

"You're right. As if something had exploded in there," Anna observed after she'd had a look.

Javier's turn came last. "That must be why they haven't moved. But we can worry about that later. First, we need to get there and convince them to send help to the people at the base. Other than that, the ship looks intact, and I don't see any smoke or anything."

"So we'll be better off there than here?"

"I have no doubt of that."

CHAPTER 9

Natasha had fallen into a fitful sleep, so Breen swallowed his questions and went out on deck to check his phone. All sorts of alerts were showing on the screen and he toggled to the encrypted messaging system used by Military Intelligence first. His orders were clear and succinct.

Your first priority is to stay in contact with the Miss Vodloyeva. Do not allow the Argentines to separate you from her—we will contact the Argentine government to organize a more thorough debriefing.

If possible, within the scope of your principal assignment, attempt to secure footage of the creatures in Antarctica.

They were never particularly emotional, these men of Military Intelligence. He knew all the officers who might have given these orders in person, knew all the dispatchers cleared to type them up and send them. He'd gone to dinner at their houses, attended their children's Bar Mitzvas and drunk with them at innumerable bars. And yet, every time he received orders in the field it could just as easily have been a bunch of strangers talking to him.

He supposed it was important to keep a certain level of detachment but it still seemed a bit harsh that, as soon as the shit hit the fan, communication became less warm and impersonal. Maybe the powers-at-be felt that a dead agent could only give away as much as the enemy could figure out from his equipment… and worked under the assumption that everyone on the planet could break encryption that would give Fort Meade fits.

In this particular case, Headquarters also appeared to be under the impression that monstrously mutated nothosaurs would be desperate to read his orders.

Well, it could have been much worse. All he had to do was to keep the Argentines from airlifting the girl out from under his nose, which, if they were smart, was one of the first things they'd try.

He headed out to find the colonel in charge of the contingent intended for the base. After the captain was killed, he and Javier were the ranking members of the expedition, even though neither was a naval officer. He would likely be in charge of evacuating the *Irizar* if it turned out the ship couldn't move under its own power.

The man appeared competent enough. He'd posted armed guards and was watching the water alongside his men.

Breen studied him for a few moments before speaking, trying to get the measure of the man. He was a bald, portly fellow, a bit shorter than Breen himself. He had a mustache that made him look like an Arab officer from the Six Days War. Apart from that, his face was smooth as a baby's bottom. He'd shaved within the last few hours… which probably made him a stickler for discipline.

"Good afternoon, Colonel."

The man looked at him askance. "They told me what you did during the attack. Would I be right in guessing that you're not actually a scientist, no matter what Colonel Balzano wants us to believe?"

"I've had some additional training which might be useful. I can handle certain weapons that a civilian might not be familiar with and also help advise on tactics if you want some help."

The Colonel nodded. There was no need to say anything more. Black ops were black ops everywhere in the world, and the regular army had learned how to extrapolate from incomplete answers.

"Fair enough. Keep the gun. We have plenty of them. Do you think the woman can shoot, too? Has she also received additional training?" He made quote marks with his fingers around the last two words.

"I don't think so. I think she's exactly what she says she is: a Russian zoologist pulled into a mission she had nothing to do with, on short notice." Then Breen smiled. "But, of course, she is Russian, so you never know. I'll ask her."

The Colonel nodded and began to turn back to his study of the dark sea below.

"That's not why I came, though. I wanted to know how we're organizing the evacuation."

"We're not. Right now I think we're safer staying on the ship than risking a four kilometer walk across the ice."

"Walk? We have two helicopters."

"One of them is at the base and isn't responding over the radio…"

"The other one is fine. It's in the hangar."

"True. But who's going to fly it?"

Breen felt sick. Had the Argentines actually mounted a polar expedition with two helicopters and only one set of pilots? Of course they had. In a place like Argentina, where the military was always cash-strapped because the only kind of fighting they ever did was against illegal fishermen and drug smugglers along the jungle borders, equipment would be at a premium, not manpower. Everything would be maintained as well as they could, but there would never be enough parts, and things would break down. So it made perfect sense to bring a spare helicopter along and not a spare flight crew, even though the country probably had ten more pilots than aircraft.

"Do we have any other plan?"

"Well, the Air Force has a Hercules that they sometimes rejigger to land on the ice, but that will take them a day, so we're basically waiting on that. Or for the other helicopter to respond."

"Any idea why it's not working?"

"None. But my guess is that they decided to get drunk with the base crew and haven't woken up just yet. Juan Manuel swears the radio was fine, and it was working when they went to check on the Korean boat, so I'd rule out a malfunction."

"So we're waiting for the Air Force?"

"Yeah."

At least the radio link between the icebreaker and the mainland seemed okay… a relief, considering that every other Argentine communication line appeared to have broken down completely.

Breen wandered to the front of the ship, itching to keep debriefing Natasha, but knowing she would be asleep much longer than the half-hour he'd given her so far. The woman was exhausted.

A familiar sound caught his attention. Normally, the sound of a plane flying overhead wouldn't have interested him in the least… but here, in the empty skies above Antarctica, it called like a siren, in much the same way that it would have caught his attention over a battlefield where he'd been told the friendlies wouldn't be flying, but instead of terror, he was filled with hope.

His cabin was a few steps away, so he popped in and brought out his binoculars. The plane was visible to the naked eye, but the glasses would help with type identification.

The first view wasn't encouraging: the plane might have been a number of small cargo aircraft, but one thing it wasn't was one of the Hercules planes the Argentines operated. He kept looking for markings, straining his eyes to see if anything was visible.

It appeared to be descending to land at the Belgrano II landing strip, a patch of ice kept in shape by the station's crew, albeit seldom used. Most refurbishment was done by airdrop or, in the summer, by the *Irizar* when she was available, or via icebreakers rented from other countries when the Argentine icebreaker was in dry dock.

The aircraft flew right above them, close enough to see that it was painted grey, but not close enough to make out the lettering. It shouldn't matter—most planes tended to reveal their operators, especially medium sized cargo haulers like this one. A lot of countries built them, and then couldn't export them anywhere. He snapped a picture of it and sent it to Fort Belvoir.

Ten minutes later, he received his answer.

You're slipping. That's a Curl.

A list of commercial and military operators of the type followed. Specs, which he couldn't have cared less about were also attached.

He cursed. Not because of the implied failure of his abilities, but because the Antonov An-26 was one of the world's most ubiquitous military planes. Petty African dictators had them, and so did major players like the Russians and the Chinese—although the Chinese flew a pirated version under a different name. The presence of this plane, here and now, meant that it had probably been chosen precisely because it would lend the operator some degree of anonymity unless you got close enough to read the markings.

Despite dozens of operators, Breen knew who was running that plane: the Russians. In fact, he would have bet his next paycheck that he knew exactly which Russians were landing at the remote Antarctic base: the SVR, Russia's post-Soviet answer to the KGB… optimized for a more modern world. These guys had military strike capability globally; and they were about to show off that when they said "global" they weren't fooling around. This was about as global as you could get.

The plane disappeared from view behind a slight rise in the snow just as his phone vibrated.

We believe the plane is Russian. Investigate but stay out of sight. Get a decent picture of the plane's markings. If possible, take Vodloyeva with you.

Now that was more like it. He was beginning to wonder when the mutually incompatible orders would begin to come down the line.

Well, at least this time they'd equipped him correctly. It was time to open some crates.

Then he would choose between ignoring the plane or kidnapping the girl.

***

A chink in a corner where the concrete that formed two walls hadn't quite blended together allowed a little light to come into their fortress. It also allowed their warmth to escape. They'd debated whether to block the slit off, but eventually decided not to. No one wanted to sit in the dark and wait for monsters to eat them.

But now the slit served another purpose.

"It's a grey plane with skis," Ernesto said. "There's Russian writing on the side."

"How do you know it's Russian?"

"Because of the funny letters."

"That's just Cyrillic," Camila said. "The plane might be from anywhere in Eastern Europe."

"Yeah, but I doubt Montenegro would send a plane to rescue us. We should tell them where we are."

"Let me look," the pilot said. He glued his eye to the small opening for some minutes. "We might not all want to go out there."

"Why not? Do you think we're better off waiting for the lizards to knock our door down?"

"Because four guys just stepped off the cargo ramp. They've got enough weaponry to start a war and they're dressed in black jumpsuits complete with balaclavas." He chuckled. "They really, really don't look like the Red Cross."

"Who cares? They'll help us, won't they? Any civilized human would," Camila said. She began to try to budge one of the barrels beside the door. All they needed to do was to explain their plight. The fact that the men were armed, under the circumstances, was a huge plus.

"Wait. They don't look like they want witnesses."

"Don't be ridiculous. They have to help us. Come on!"

The pilot sighed. "Then let's just send one person."

"Fine," Camila replied. "I'll go."

"No, you won't. I get paid to risk my life for my countrymen. That means I get to go get myself shot by the Russians."

"Don't be so dramatic. Just don't leave without us."

They struggled with the barrels until the door opened just far enough for the pilot to extricate himself. "Keep this," he said, handing Ernesto his pistol. "And close the door behind me. I'll wait here until you finish."

"That's silly."

"Stop arguing."

Camila watched the pilot cross the open snow and wondered why men were always so dramatic. They saw conspiracies and enemies at every turn. If there was a single place in the world in which ski masks were appropriate attire against the weather, this was it.

About two hundred meters away, the men in black saw him. They watched him approach until he was about fifty meters away, and then one of the men opened fire. The pilot fell immediately.

Camila screamed. "They shot him!" she told the rest of her team as the sound of shots echoed and died away in the distance. "He didn't do anything, just walked up with his hands in front of him and the animals shot him."

Silence reigned in the makeshift bunker before Ingrid spoke up. "What are they doing now? Are they coming this way?"

"No. They're heading towards the sea. They didn't even bother to check if he was dead. They just left him there. He might be suffering, bleeding out." Camila tore her eyes from the wall.

"Would it be better if they finished him off?" Ernesto asked.

"No… I mean it would be better if they started acting human. I'm sure they have a doctor on that plane."

"Like the pilot said, I don't think they're particularly interested in witnesses."

Again they went quiet. Camila seethed at the brutality. She wanted to go out there and scream at the murderers. But all that would achieve was to add her own body to the mounting count. The helplessness infuriated her.

Eventually, Ingrid broke the silence. "So what do we do now?"

Camila sat, head in her hands. "I don't know. This isn't what I signed up for. I… I've never been in a situation like this one."

To her surprise, Anderson, the normally quiet Venezuelan spoke up. "I have. Five years ago, before I came to Argentina, I was at a rally against Maduro. It was a peaceful demonstration, but the police attacked us for no reason. Dictatorships hate it when you protest."

Camila was about to argue. She wanted to tell him that he must have been wrong, that Venezuelan socialism was for the people, and that provocateurs from the right must have been responsible for any violence. But the look in Anderson's eyes made her suspect that her opinion wouldn't have been welcome.

"They came after us with hydrant tanks and nightsticks and a few of us, two boys and about six girls, took cover in a small shop. We closed the door and hid behind the counter. The owner let us stay and didn't give us away even though he looked like he was about to shit his pants. Outside, the cops were attacking the protesters with tear gas. A horse ran past as we watched.

"And you know what? Just by staying inside, we managed to avoid the worst of it. Once he realized we weren't going to rob him and murder him, the shopkeeper acted like our father, lecturing us about the folly of youth and the fact that street protests never achieve anything."

"So you're saying we should stay here?" Ernesto asked.

"Yes. I still remember going back out after everything had blown over. The street looked like it had been bombed. There was even a dead girl, she must have been seventeen, dumped off to one side with a bloody t-shirt covering half her face. But I was fine… except for some irritation from the tear gas. My clothing wasn't even wrinkled."

"This is different. If we stay here too long, we'll either freeze or starve."

"I know that. But it feels the same. I think we'll come out of this unscathed, wondering how the whole thing could have passed us by."

Camila thought it was the first sensible thing she'd heard all day. Everyone else appeared to have bought into the fact that it was a military expedition, and they all seemed hell-bent on going down in a blaze of stupid, useless glory. "I agree with Anderson, but it's not my call. Does anyone have a better idea?"

"I'd rather wait until they get out of sight and go try to get our pilot back."

"He's dead, Ernesto."

"I won't believe that until I see it with my own eyes."

Camila leaned on her years in academia to move the discussion along. "All right. Noted. Ingrid, what do you think?"

"I… I don't know. I don't care. This is all so awful."

"All right. Then we stay here."

***

Javier's delight turned to shocked disbelief as the men in balaclavas opened fire. Instead of the expected rescue and evacuation, now there was another group on the ice that wanted to see them dead. He hoped the lizards got them, although with that kind of firepower, it would take a lot of reptiles to do much damage.

"What do we do now?" Clark asked.

Every bone in Javier's body wanted to sneak up on the bastards who'd shot the pilot and put one bullet into each skull from behind. But tactically speaking, it made no sense. There were four of them and only one of him, and he had to close a gap of three hundred meters which actually meant walking nearly six hundred, because he had to get back to the mainland along the ice. By the time he reached them, he would have been spotted by someone in the plane or by the men themselves. Even if they were blind enough to miss a guy walking in sunlight over a snowfield, there was no way he'd get them all.

Even if it had been possible, it actually made more sense to keep going and let the other group make as much noise as possible… maybe the lizards and the guys in masks would take each other out.

Also, the *Irizar* had men and weapons on board. These guys certainly looked the part, but there were four of them… and they had no air support, no cover and no particular advantages other than, most likely, superior training. But that only counted for so much when you were caught in a crossfire against a numerically superior opponent.

Of course, they might also have twenty more men in the plane. But there was nothing he could do about that if it happened to be true.

"We keep heading towards the ship."

"But…"

"Yes, I know. And trust me, I want nothing in the world more than to shoot those bastards. But now isn't the time. We need to tell the *Irizar* what's happening out here."

Clark and Anna nodded, obviously relieved not to be in command, and they turned to keep walking in the direction they'd been moving. The ice that had appeared as smooth as a billiard table from the ship now showed its true colors. Ridges as tall as they were crisscrossed in their path and the easiest road often led to deep pools.

Every once in a while, they had to climb to the top of a ridge to be certain they were on the correct course.

The closer they got to the *Irizar*, however, the stronger Javier's sense that something was very wrong grew. The lumpiness on the upper level of the main structure resolved into obvious damage. It appeared as if the ship had been struck by a missile. The bridge area was a mass of torn and pulled out metal. He said nothing to the others, but he suspected that, perhaps, the airplane had made a pass at the ship before landing. Strangely there had been no exterior launch tubes on the fuselage. The aircraft looked like a cargo plane.

For the first time, it occurred to Javier that the *Irizar* might need more help than they did. He made them increase their pace. The three slipped down ridges and moved as fast as they could in the conditions.

A roar echoed across the frozen plain. They were still a kilometer away from the icebreaker, but that made no difference. Even at that distance, the enormous creature that shot out of the water and landed on the ship's aft deck, behind the helipad, could be seen clearly. It could be heard even more clearly, like a dog barking in the yard next door.

Metal screeched as the monster applied its claws to unprotected metal doors and bulkheads. Javier saw a gigantic Sea King dragged out of its hangar, inspected briefly and then torn in half and discarded on the ice.

"Holy crap," Anna exclaimed. "It's like the one that attacked us, but bigger."

The sound of automatic weapons fire carried across the ice and the thing screamed, but didn't desist. It began to tear chunks out of the decking. It was too far away for Javier to see… but he imagined screaming sailors being scattered like so much confetti, and contemptuously tossed into the terrible maw.

They stood there in utter shock.

"What now?" Anna asked.

Javier didn't have an immediate answer.

CHAPTER 10

Breen lurched under the onslaught.

He'd convinced the sailors—who believed he'd lost it completely—to lower his specially modified snowmobile over the side using one of the ship's cranes. It had barely made contact with the ice when the ship suddenly shuddered in a way that was terrifyingly familiar.

Everyone ran to get their guns. Everyone but Breen, that is. He had other orders.

But he also saw an opportunity.

Clutching his FAL—since the first attack, he'd taken it everywhere he went—Breen sprinted forward along the aft deck. He was lucky: a set of claws that, at close range, looked bigger than a car, landed where he'd been, striking a furrow in the steel. Breen redoubled his pace. The cream-colored cube that held the ship's cabins might not represent safety, but it was certainly better than standing out in the open. Besides, he was on autopilot, higher functions suspended. All he wanted was to hide behind something, anything.

A couple of sailors opened fire on the monster with small arms, and Breen wondered if there was someone manning the slightly bigger guns the ship supposedly carried. His briefing had indicated that the *Irizar* was equipped with a couple of 40mm cannons suitable for threatening illegal civilian craft. He hadn't seen them, but they had to be on board somewhere, probably in storage since this wasn't a patrol run but an Antarctic expedition. The crew would be well-served to get them out of storage: those might actually do measurable damage.

He reached the cube and sprinted into the infirmary. To his relief, the doctor was nowhere in sight. Breen would have hated to have to hurt the man. He found the doctor to be the most familiar archetype on board. Apparently, all military doctors were exactly the same, no matter where one went.

"Come on, we're leaving," he told Natasha.

The Russian woman looked at him with wide eyes. "What are you saying?"

"We're getting off this ship before that thing tears it apart."

"The nothosaurs? But they're not that big…"

"Have you looked out your window lately?"

She did. Her eyes got even wider. "I guess I thought you were exaggerating before. But… how can that be? Nothosaurs can't get that big. They'd weigh too much for their bone structure. Also, where would they get food to feed a body like that?"

"You can tell me all about why it can't be done once we're off the ship. For the time being, I'm more concerned with not getting eaten by your impossible monster."

"It's not my monster."

"Well, you'll be its lunch if you don't move. Get dressed."

"Turn around."

"Don't be an idiot. You can't dress yourself with one arm."

"Turn around."

He did so, fuming, with one eye looking out the window and his mind racing furiously in an attempt to figure out which would be the best way to climb off the ship without being seen by the monster… or, if possible, the crew.

The crew was probably the least of his worries. It seemed that every man on board was sniping at the creature from whatever cover they could find but judging by the screams, they were losing. If they even noticed him leaving, they'd probably think he was the smartest fellow on board and his problem would become how to keep the deserters from trying to tag along.

The monster tired of being shot at in the back of the ship and pulled itself all the way out of the water. Then it advanced and, using the helipad as a stepladder, tore into the ship's central structure. Breen heard glass shattering all around him.

"All right, turn around. Help me," Natasha said.

She'd barely gotten started. Her snow pants were about halfway up her legs, and her bra was hanging by one strap as she held it in place with her free hand.

"These aren't my clothes," she said apologetically.

He didn't waste time on words. He pulled up the pants, adjusted her bra and grabbed a t-shirt and a sweater from the foot of the bed. Those took precious seconds to put on around the plastic cast the doctors had put on her arm. At least they hadn't used plaster… even though that would have been much better for her in the long run.

Finally, he added a red jacket. He would have preferred something less visible on the ice, but the clock was ticking, and if she froze out there, she wouldn't be much use to anyone.

The sound of tortured metal right beside them made him jump. He half-expected to see a claw rushing towards him, and then a mouth, and then nothing, but what he saw was that the wall that led to the exit was crushed.

"It's kicking in the wall," Natasha yelled.

"Yeah. We won't be able to get out that way."

Which really sucked. He didn't think breaking the window would be a good idea. The view through the glass was now completely greenish-grey: the monster's belly blocked everything.

"This way."

He dragged her through a dark passage which echoed with the sound of the ship being demolished. It led to a stairwell with only one option: up.

They climbed, and he felt like a character in a bad teenage slasher flick. One of the ones that, instead of running like hell out the open front door ran up the stairs instead, presumably on the assumption that being trapped and massacred was preferable to having to run all the way to the police station.

Another passage greeted them on the next floor. This one opened into a small lounge with three sofas and a TV set. It had also once held a window.

That was gone, a jagged tear in its place. Cold air washed into the room.

Suddenly, the belly disappeared and an eye looked in on them.

"Shit, it's seen us. Get back!"

Even as he said it, he knew there was no chance they'd make it. A huge claw flew at them. He tried to shield Natasha from the brunt of the impact and took a deep breath. He'd imagined his death many, many times… but never thought it would come at the claws of a mutated dinosaur.

Something exploded all around them, a deafening, concussive crash that repeated a thousand, a million times. Breen's overloaded senses took a moment to realize the sound was perfectly familiar, and that the metal walls had caused it to become overwhelming: automatic gunfire.

The claw drew back like a human pulling away from a wasp sting.

Breen ignored the ringing in his ears and risked a look. One of the sailors stood in the doorway they'd just entered, a FAL braced against his hip like Rambo. It was a terrible idea because the recoil on that gun was more than enough to cause some serious injuries if it happened to slip… especially if it got him in the nuts.

"Thank you," Breen said, but he could barely hear his own voice.

The sailor just smiled and pointed at his ears. The man—not much more than a boy, really, an impression made stronger by his baby blue eyes—appeared to be happy as a bedbug, with a smile that spread from ear to ear. Breen had seen this happen—not often, but he'd seen it—to men who entered real combat for the first time: that sudden sense that this was what they'd been born to do, and that they would never again be happy unless they were fighting for their lives.

Their savior strode towards where the windows had been to inspect his handiwork. After a few seconds, he turned back to them, satisfied with a job well done.

That was his last mistake. A sharp nail the size of a rhinoceros' horn suddenly burst through his stomach. He looked down on it, the blue eyes confused, his smile gone. Of course, he couldn't turn his head to see that the nail was attached to a claw which had just thundered back into the room.

The boy opened his mouth to scream, but a gush of blood preceded the sound. Then, when he saw that, he began to shriek in earnest, loud enough that it made it past the ringing in Breen's ears.

He was pulled back, as if by a string. He struggled to avoid it, but his feet could get no purchase on the blood-slick ground.

The monster removed the sailor from the room, gashing him against the jagged edges where the window once stood.

The boy writhed in pain, still screaming, and the monster appeared to realize he was there. The rest of the clawed paw closed around him and… squeezed.

Blood sprayed in every direction as something inside the kid's body exploded with an audible pop. Breen felt the droplets hit, felt the warm liquid begin to run down his face.

Suddenly, the other side of combat came back to him with a thud: how quickly a human could go from a smiling laughing person, a person you could sit down and play cards with, to a pile of mangled flesh and gross goo.

Natasha screamed.

That brought him back to life. "Don't go catatonic on me," he said. "I need you alert."

They ran out of the room and tried to make it towards the stairs on the other side of the cube at the center of the ship, but that way was blocked by pipes and wiring that had been pushed into the hall in front of them.

"Dammit," Breen growled. "This is stupid, but what choice do we have? Up it is, then."

They went up a flight of stairs, but the corridor they reached was full of smoke. They went up another. Breen knew the ruined bridge had to be on either the next level or the one after that, so, even though this floor had a certain amount of smoke as well, he decided to risk it. Natasha came after him zombie-like, but at least he didn't have to drag her.

They were in luck. The way was clear and they made it to the stairwell on the far side without getting shredded or crushed by any of the tremendous blows that landed on the ship while they were in the corridor. The stairwell, despite being right on the outer skin of the ship's superstructure, was still, miraculously, intact.

It wasn't quiet, though. Every sound—the beast's roars, the machine guns and the yells of frightened defenders—echoed. It sounded like there was a large war in there with them.

Finally, they reached the ground floor and were back out on deck.

There was no way they were going to make it aft past the creature on deck. Breen looked for one of the stairwells that led beneath, and saw that they had to cross nearly ten meters of open deck to get there. He turned to Natasha.

"Do you see that door over there?"

She nodded, tears making tracks down the spatters of the sailor's blood.

"Good. We need to run there. Can you do that?"

Another nod. Less certain this time.

"All right. On my signal."

He knew he had to time it right. At the moment, they stood in a small oasis of peace in the middle of hell itself, but nothing guaranteed that the monster wouldn't spot them and pounce as soon as they left their dubious cover. On the other hand, he suspected that it was only a matter of time before this little patch of ship was torn apart, too. So the question became one of choosing exactly the right moment to run: when the creature's attention was elsewhere, but without waiting too long.

A burst of machine-gun fire opened up on the opposite side of the ship.

"Now! Come on." He half-dragged Natasha across the open space.

Breen had always had a sixth sense about when someone was watching him, whether it be a person standing behind him in an office setting or a sniper on a hillside a thousand yards away in the mountains of Pakistan.

Perhaps it was a change in the quality of the air or perhaps he saw a flicker of shadow out of the corner of his eye, but something made him stop, turn back and throw himself on top of Natasha just as the enormous set of claws flew over them. Apparently, his uncanny ability also worked with reptiles. It was something to think about later.

The creature had overbalanced when it tried to decapitate the two and that gave them the opening they needed to scramble to their feet and reach the relative safety of the lower deck.

Suddenly, peace reigned. If Breen hadn't known what was going on above decks, he would have thought the ship was sailing in reasonably calm water—or, more likely, he would have guessed that it was in port and that workers were carrying out repairs. The cacophony had been reduced in scale to a series of intermittent clangs and thumps.

Natasha relaxed visibly. Her shoulders straightened and she began breathing normally.

"You okay?" he asked. It wasn't the right time to talk about it, but he was impressed. Natasha had followed without missing a beat. Injured and untrained, she'd still held up much better than some soldiers he'd known.

"I think so."

"Good. Let's see how far we can get."

The first thing he did was to find a corridor which took them another level down. The paint on the upper level was a welcoming white shade, while the one below had been painted green, with exposed piping and wiring replacing the more human amenities of the floor above. The message was clear: this was a place for machinery and the men who worshipped it.

The corridor extended all the way to the back of the ship and emerged in the far rear below the heliport. It was nearly perfect, except for one detail.

"Let me check where the monster is."

He climbed a ladder far enough to stick his head above the heliport deck. The nothosaur was still ahead, ravaging the bridge. Other than a few swatting movements, it appeared to be ignoring the men around it… in fact, it reminded Breen of horses swatting at flies with their tails as the rest of the animal did something else.

"All clear, come on." He headed for the port-side rail and looked down. There were no ladders, but the stern was low enough at that point that they could jump onto the ice below.

Natasha stopped dead. "We're leaving the ship?"

"Of course. I don't think there's going to be a ship much longer."

"Wait. Are you sure about this? I prefer to stay on board. The crew will drive it back."

"With what?"

"I don't know. Doesn't this ship have guns? Now that they know what they're up against, they shouldn't have trouble. It's just an animal."

"It's a big animal."

She said nothing.

"Even you said it shouldn't exist. Come on. The crew can't get this under control. You'd need an armored battalion, not just a barely armed ship's crew." He decided not to tell her about the 40 mm guns. Those could probably deal with the creature… but his orders were to take her with him, they said nothing about having to tell her the truth. "Besides, I have a snowmobile with spiked treads down there." He pointed to the crate that he'd finished unloading a few minutes before the monster hit them again. "We won't have to walk."

"All right. You go first, though."

There was a narrow fringe of water between the *Irizar* and the ice, and the fall was a little over a meter and a half. He wanted to be certain that Natasha didn't feel threatened and decide not to try it after all—the height and the jump over the open water would make climbing back on board to get her a risky proposition.

He jumped, and the ship lurched, launching him out onto the ice in a much higher trajectory than he'd intended. He landed on his feet, but they slid out under him and that meant that, an instant later, he was on his ass. It hurt like hell.

Damn. Now he'd have to convince Natasha that she would be safe. He turned back to the ship, half-expecting to see her heading back belowdecks as fast as her feet would carry her.

Instead, he found her laughing. His face must have shown his surprise because she stifled it immediately.

"I'm sorry. It's just that I was expecting you to land like Tom Cruise in *Mission Impossible*."

He chuckled. "Man, I hate those movies. They never get anything right. What I just showed you is how real secret agents land."

"So you admit it now?"

"You were going to realize it as soon as you saw the equipment I have over there anyway. Do you think you can land better than I did, or would you prefer for me to catch you?"

Natasha jumped and landed on her feet, though it was a close thing. She swayed a couple of times and waved her uninjured arm in circles, but stayed upright. Then, after walking about twenty meters away, slowly, deliberately, she turned back to the ship and watched the monster.

"Come on, what are you waiting for? When it finishes them, it's going to come for us."

"I… I'm not so sure."

"What do you mean?"

"It looks like it's attacking the ship, not the people."

"Could have fooled me, it's killed a lot of guys."

"That's just incidental damage. I think the ship is what it's after. I think it sees the ship as a threat. Something big swimming around in its territory and making a lot of noise. It's defending its turf."

"You've got to be kidding me."

"No. I mean it. As long as the ship stays here, it's going to keep attacking until one or the other is dead."

He shook his head. The woman was right. It was obvious once she pointed it out. Of course, it also helped that they were no longer in the line of fire: it was one thing to be cool and collected when you were watching the conflict from a reasonable distance, quite another to try to analyze what was going on from within.

"Well, with the bridge gone, I'm not sure the *Irizar* can leave," Breen said. "But we can, and we should get the hell out of here. My stuff is over there."

The snowmobile was black, which made him suspect that it had come out of one of Langley's skunkworks. The boys from the CIA loved black things. Black helicopters, black cars, black glasses. Apparently, no one gave a thought to the fact that a black snowmobile on a continent-sized patch of ice would stick out... well, like something black on a white background. They went ahead and painted it black anyway.

He'd also piled up some more stuff they'd sent with him. Most of his equipment was still on the ship, including his weapons, which were mostly small arms. The one thing he'd brought with him was a Matador portable missile launcher, on the off chance that he would run into the big creature again. He stifled a small pang of guilt at not having offered its use to the men defending the ship, but for one thing, he didn't know the monster would attack the *Irizar* again... and for another, they weren't his responsibility. If they couldn't take care of their own toys, they didn't deserve to keep them.

The rest of the weapons had been left behind because, in all honesty, nothing in the arsenal he'd brought along felt as satisfying as the FAL rifle, so he decided to keep that one and had brought a number of ammo clips. He hoped the Russians wouldn't be prepared to be attacked with a big infantryman's rifle.

Of course, he didn't know what to expect from them, either. Probably well-trained special forces types, and those guys didn't fool around. Unless he received a direct order to the contrary, he would watch them from a safe distance.

"Is that a missile launcher?" Natasha asked as he discarded the bulky packing case for the Matador unit.

"Yes."

She nodded. “Good idea. But I don’t think it will be much help.”

“We’ll see. That thing might be big, but it’s covered in flesh, not armor.”

“Oh. If we run into the big one again, you’ll be all right, I suppose. But that’s not the one you need to worry about.”

“What? Did you see what it did to that boat back there?”

“Yes. But did you see that it wasn’t eating any of the men? It has no interest in humans, I tell you. The little ones, on the other hand... Well, I think they eat people, as many people as they can.”

“And the missile won’t work on them?”

“Of course it will. But they’re pretty fast, and there’s a whole bunch of them,” she said as she mounted the heavily-laden snowmobile behind him. “How quickly can you reload?”

CHAPTER 11

Javier stood, slack-jawed, watching the carnage. The thing on the *Irizar*, the thing *demolishing* the *Irizar*, was not something his mind could wrap itself around. It was just too big. For a split second, his mind told him that the creature wasn't trying to destroy the ship but involved in some bizarre and disgusting mating sequence. But then it slashed again and he saw a largish chunk of metal fly off.

"All right. Change of plans. We're going back to the base. Maybe we can get the generator started and use the radio."

His companions just nodded. They looked as dazed as he felt. Anna asked: "But what about the lizard? The small one, I mean."

"We'll have to deal with it. I scared it away last time. Maybe I can do it again. It's the only hope I see right now."

Carl and the Swedish scientist nodded glumly, and they began to trudge back.

Javier shook his head and wondered if time passed differently there. How long had it been since he slept last? Had it been a couple of hours? A couple of days? The sun appeared to be circling around above them, not moving across the sky the way it should have. His watch said four o'clock... but four o'clock in the afternoon or four o'clock in the morning? His cell phone might have told him, but he hadn't bothered to charge it after its battery ran down on the last night on the *Irizar*. There were no cell towers in Antarctica, and the whole reason they'd come was that base had no internet connection.

He might have asked one of the others, but he preferred to remain silent. The scientists tended to be smug, all-knowing. Better not to have them believe that he was losing his mind.

His body seemed as tired as his brain. He was amazed at just how hard it was to put one foot in front of the other. His stomach growled with hunger, and he was glad to have been trained by the Argentine army, where cadets never really had enough to eat. He knew hunger was just a distraction and could ignore it.

A few minutes passed. A thin mechanical noise which he realized had been going on for a few minutes forced itself onto his notice. He automatically looked up, expecting to find that the guys in black had sent a drone up, but there was nothing in the air.

Within moments the buzz was loud enough to be a distraction. It reminded him of a motorcycle for some reason. Hope surged: maybe someone from the base had survived and was now coming to rescue them in a vehicle?

He quickly realized that would have been ridiculous. No one would be riding a motorcycle over the ice.

He was right. Moments later, a black snowmobile whisked into view and stopped beside them. It was towing a kind of trailer on skis, also black, carrying what appeared to be a missile launcher.

Remembering what had happened to the pilot, Javier reached for his pistol, but the driver said. "No need for that." And pulled down his hood. It was Breen.

The passenger, likewise, uncovered her head. She had some difficulty because one of her arms was still in a sling. Natasha smiled at him. "Hello, again," she said. "I don't think I ever thanked you for saving my life. In the long run, it looks like we're all going to die anyway, but at least you gave me a few more days."

"Don't mention it," Javier said, thinking that the people who called Russians morose might be on to something. "If it hadn't been me, it would have been someone else."

"But it was you."

He realized that, when she smiled, and now that she'd gotten a bit more color in her face, the Russian girl was much prettier than he remembered. Those blue eyes and bright, perfect smile contrasted with her black hair and pale skin for a stunning impact.

He smiled at her. "Let's make a deal. You can accompany me to dinner when we're back in Buenos Aires and there are no giant lizards or guys in black around to kill us."

Breen broke in. "Why do you think the guys in black are here to kill us?"

"They shot our pilot."

"Are you sure?" His face went very hard.

"Of course I'm sure. You don't get to be an army colonel if that kind of thing confuses you."

"Right. Sorry." Breen thought for a minute. "That does put a different slant on things. We'll have to be careful. What were you planning to do?"

"We saw what happened to the *Irizar*, so we were trying to get back to the base. There's a concrete structure there that should be strong enough to hold out against the lizard we saw, if we can reinforce the door. Well, against the small one, at least."

"Hop on. I'll take you as close as I'm going."

There was a spot on the back of the snowmobile seat so, seeing that Clark and Anna were trying to accommodate themselves on the trailer,

Javier took that one. He soon grew very conscious of Natasha sitting in front of him. He tried to avoid any contact with her by keeping his legs spread wide, but he had nowhere to hold on to; when the snowmobile jerked into motion, he almost fell off the back.

Instinctively, he grabbed onto the nearest available object, which happened to be Natasha's waist, just above her hips.

"I'm sorry," he said, thankful that she couldn't turn around to see that his face, by the heat he felt, must have turned scarlet.

"Don't worry about it," she replied. "I'm just glad you didn't grab my arm… I'm pretty sure that would have hurt like hell."

And then, she actually moved back and snuggled against him. She was likely just trying to get into a more comfortable position, but it was extremely distracting.

Luckily, the American chose that moment to accelerate again and Javier forgot all about Natasha as he held on for dear life.

The distance that had taken what seemed like hours to cross disappeared in a couple of minutes, and they were soon back at the point where the sea ice met land. The snowmobile's speed allowed it to follow the ridges and valleys in the ice instead of cutting across like they had when they were on foot. Breen appeared to have some kind of sixth sense for the uneven Antarctic terrain. Every time Javier was certain that the American had misjudged a curve and that they would be plunged into a sinkhole, the man would make a tiny adjustment which kept them from dying.

Breen drove right up to the spot where the ice ended and the water began. Then he pulled out a pair of binoculars and studied the terrain.

"I think the way back to the base is clear," he said, handing the glasses to Javier.

Breen was right. There were no monsters and, perhaps more importantly, no men in balaclavas between their position and the station. He returned the binoculars.

The snowmobile moved again, along the coast, slowly. After a couple of hundred meters, Javier was going to ask whether they were going to turn towards the base.

He never got a chance.

A colossal roar tore across the frozen landscape. Javier, who'd only heard it from afar, couldn't believe the volume. He looked around in confusion, not knowing what to expect.

What he saw was the monster, the big one that had been mauling the *Irizar* only moments before, towering above them as it dragged itself out of the water. Two steps later, it was between them and the base.

Breen didn't hesitate. He gunned the motor and drove along the coast away from the abomination. He wove around snowbanks he could avoid… and over others he couldn't. This run made the earlier mad rush seem like a walk in a meadow. Javier hung on for dear life.

Clark and Anna screamed behind him, but he didn't dare turn his head to look. They'd just have to hold on as best they could. To his own shame, he realized that he was much more concerned about the missile launcher than he was about the scientists.

Then he realized where they were going. "That's the way the guys in black went," he shouted.

"I know," Breen replied. "But we don't have a hell of a lot of choices here. The thing's coming this way."

Javier half-turned. It was true.

He looked forward again. "Watch out!"

His warning was too late. Breen, still glancing behind them, didn't see the crevice, a white hole against the white background of snow. The front right ski went over the side of the snowmobile and, before the American could correct, they had gone over the side.

As the nose of the snowmobile hit the bottom, it stuck firm. The impact threw Javier and Natasha off. He hit the ground with bone-jarring force.

The snowmobile didn't stop there, however. It cartwheeled down the narrow opening, throwing snow, equipment and pieces of black bodywork everywhere. Out of the corner of his eye, he saw it slam into a wall and disappear around a bend.

Javier lay stunned for a few moments, taking stock of how he felt. His left shoulder was numb, and he had to gasp for breath. A hand shook his arm, someone behind him.

"Are you all right?"

It was a woman's voice, English with a slight accent. Natasha.

"I… I think so. I took a big hit." He turned to look at her.

"I think I owe you another thank you. It's starting to get to be a habit. I landed on something soft. Now I think I know what it was… you."

He couldn't imagine how that was possible. She'd been ahead of him on the snowmobile. By rights, she should have hit the snow before him. But he couldn't argue because his memory of the event coincided with hers: he'd hit the ground first, and then something had landed on his chest and shoulder.

He laughed. "I'm glad I was there. There's no way I could have set your arm for you if you'd re-broken it."

"The doctor says there isn't much chance of that. He told me he screwed a plate in there. His exact words were 'if you get hit by a nuclear blast, there won't be anything left of you except for that bone. Nothing will ever break that bone again'."

"Yeah, that does sound like him." Javier smiled. The doctor was a prick, but he was a competent prick and Javier was glad of it for Natasha's sake. If the man said that the arm would be fine… the arm would be fine.

He sat on the snow, too dazed to move or even to make the effort of remembering how they'd gotten there.

And then the monster roared again.

Javier jumped to his feet, or at least he tried to. He slipped on the solid ice below him and ended up stumbling to his feet. They walked to the kink in the crevice where the snowmobile and their companions had disappeared.

Natasha gasped. "Oh my God."

Anna lay in front of them, and there was no doubt that she was dead. Her head was bent at an unnatural angle, and her bright eyes were open wide, staring into infinity. A jagged piece of the snowmobile had lodged itself between her ribs, and blood had soaked her jacket around it. Whether she had died of the wound or of a broken neck was impossible to tell. All he knew was that Anna was dead.

Javier checked her pulse anyway, and then he shook his head and took Natasha's arm. "Let's go."

Pieces of snowmobile were strewn everywhere and they found Breen and Carl lying in a field of debris. Carl was just beginning to stir, groaning in pain. Breen was alive but unconscious. Ahead of them, the crevice opened up onto a wide rocky beach below an accumulation of snow, the bottom of which had been eroded by the water to form a wide ice cavern tall enough for a man to walk through without bumping his head. From where they stood, they could only see part of the cave—the rest was blocked by the crevice walls.

Javier went down on one knee and began to slap Breen's face. He knew it wasn't the best way to revive an unconscious man, but he couldn't think of anything else. Breen needed to come to now… and they could only hope that his injuries weren't bad enough that they would stop him from walking. If they were, they might have to hole up where they were or drag the man to the cave. Either option would offer a bit of defense against the wind, which was beginning to pick up.

"Where's Anna?" Carl's voice was weak.

Natasha hugged him, even though she'd only known him briefly. "I'm sorry," she said.

The Australian was stunned. "Are you sure?"

"Yes. Trust us on this."

"What am I going to tell Ingrid?"

"It wasn't your fault."

Javier stayed silent. He'd always been bad at that kind of thing. From where he was standing, it appeared that Natasha was a natural. He also would have preferred that the girl not hug the good-looking geologist quite as warmly as she was… but he stomped on the feeling. What kind of guy thinks that way in light of a tragedy like this one?

He was relieved when she let go of the Australian and returned to his side, pausing only to grab a handful of snow in her good hand. She pressed the cold wet mess against the unconscious man's neck.

Breen made a noise and shuddered. "Can you hear me?" Javier asked.

Before the man could respond, the sound of shooting, echoing against the walls appeared to reach them from everywhere at once.

Breen opened his eyes.

"Can you walk?" Javier shouted.

"How the hell should I know?"

Though he probably had a concussion, there was no time to let him recover. Javier pulled him to his feet, and left him standing, swaying slightly, while he went for Carl.

The Australian made it to his feet without much help, but stood looking dumb. He was obviously in shock.

"Listen. Someone's shooting, and I think it's probably the guys in the black suits firing at the creature we were running from. We need to get somewhere we're safe from both."

"What about the small ones?" Natasha said.

"Small ones? I only saw one of those."

"There are several, possibly even twenty. I tried to get a count on the ship—the ship I was on originally, not the *Irizar*—but it was too dark to get an accurate number."

"How fun. Well, we can't worry about those now. Unless someone has a better idea, I suggest laying low in that cave over there and letting our friends in black deal with any monsters that might pop up. What do you think?"

No one answered, so he took Clark's arm, and led him to where Breen was slowly pulling himself together. "You with us?"

Breen nodded, then shook his head as if to clear it. "Got my bell pretty thoroughly rung. Good thing I'm not an NFL player… they wouldn't let me back in the game."

"Can you move?"

"Sure, but we'd better get the gun. I had a rifle with me at some point. A rocket launcher, too."

Javier raised an eyebrow, deciding against speaking. There wasn't really much to say. He found the FAL almost immediately. It looked essentially intact and, when he dismounted the clip, it slid back easily. He'd trained for countless hours on this rifle—it was, after all, the basic weapon of Argentine infantrymen. He'd strip it down and clean it later.

The missile launcher was a complete loss. It had been bent nearly in half by the impact. Javier knew it was the only weapon they had that might have proved effective against the big bastard and mourned it.

He half-led, half dragged them towards the mouth of the crevice and the safety of the cave. About three-quarters of the way across the beach that fronted it, he realized his mistake. The men in black were standing on one side of the cave entrance. They'd been hidden by the walls of the passage. Luckily for their little group, the Russians—Javier was convinced that they were Russians now; what else could they be?—had their hands full. They'd been spotted and were firing upward at the large reptile.

Smaller creatures flocked around the big one, but they appeared reticent to engage the men with guns, prompting Javier to suspect they might be smarter than they looked. One of the monsters was on the ground.

It was too late to stop now. Hoping the men wouldn't spot them, Javier led his companions into the overhang and as deep within the cave as he could. The big one couldn't see them there… but the small ones would have no trouble rooting them out. Hopefully, the FAL would be as effective as whatever ordnance the commandos outside were using.

Though the big creature's head was out of sight, the men fighting it were all in view. They'd spread out in a rough diamond with about ten meters between them. Only three were firing, Javier now realized. The fourth, standing behind the other three was carrying something big in his arms. A large sack of some sort… black, of course.

The soldiers were retreating in what Javier, unless he'd gotten turned around by the mad dash and subsequent accident, believed was the general direction of the plane, gradually moving away from the cave and backing up a slope. The foremost shouted a command, and all three fired a long burst before running upwards out of Javier's sight.

All except the man on the right. He was farthest from the slope, and he never made it. Before he was halfway to where the others had disappeared, the monster's foot caught him midstride.

He saw it coming and dodged, almost managing to avoid the blow completely, and causing the impact to be a glancing strike. But even that was enough to tear a jagged hole in his side and rip off one of his arms. The man pirouetted and fell in a spray of crimson. Javier never saw where the missing arm ended up, but the man himself was most likely dead before his body hit the ground.

Then, the big creature walked past. It was clearly in pursuit, but didn't appear able to move too quickly on land. That seemed to Javier to be the only good news he'd received since the helicopter had landed.

Once the long tail disappeared from view, Javier motioned to his companions to remain where they were and advanced to the mouth of the cave. He didn't dare leave the cover of the overhanging ice, but in the distance, he could hear the sound of occasional gunfire punctuated by the roars of the monster. They seemed to be getting more and more distant.

Emboldened by this, he climbed up the hill, carefully concealing himself from view until, finally, he saw the monster far away. It was facing the other way, so Javier took another step.

The firefight was now nearly three hundred meters from the cave. Whoever those soldiers were, they were admirably disciplined. They kept moving slowly, using the same patterns as they'd done initially and giving ground towards the plane with the monsters following behind. Javier knew that the last few meters would necessarily need to be a mad dash, since the plane would get shredded by the largest of the creatures if it came to that, but the men appeared to be in no hurry. He supposed it was only natural: for men such as these, fighting something that couldn't shoot back had to be much easier than what they were used to.

At one point, the soldiers concentrated their fire on the group of smaller reptiles who'd been creeping towards them. The creatures scattered and ran towards the red buildings of the base. Javier's heart sank.

The battle wouldn't last forever. He needed to get back to his companions and discuss what their next move would be. The clock in his head had started ticking, for some reason, he supposed that the monsters would return to the cave once the interlopers were gone.

He was also frightened that night would fall at any moment and he didn't want to face the creatures in the dark. Not even the small ones. *Especially* not the small ones.

He knew it was ridiculous, knew that night might not fall for another week or two, but the human animal is not a purely intellectual one. The urgency drove him on.

Just as he was about to enter the cave, Natasha ran out, crying hysterically.

She fell to her knees on the snow and vomited. It didn't stop until she'd been dry heaving for nearly a minute with nothing more left in her stomach.

CHAPTER 12

The air inside their refuge was thick with the smell of fear. Though there were only four of them inside and the temperature had been low to start with, it still felt stuffy. Sweat from under her arms ran down Camila's sides.

She gasped. It was her turn to man the lookout post, the chink in the concrete wall. "They're coming!" she yelled back at her three companions.

What she saw was a huge colossus advancing towards them, flanked by smaller versions of itself. It took Camila a few moments to realize that the miniatures were actually large reptiles of the same kind that had already terrorized them once. The big one… the big one was like something from a monster movie.

"What do you mean, they?"

"Lizard things. Lots of them and also… something huge."

"What?"

"I think you'd better see for yourself. You wouldn't believe me if I told you," Camila said, moving aside.

One by one, the others took turns staring through the hole. None of them said anything; the most demonstrative was Anderson, who, when his turn was over sat heavily in the corner furthest from the spyhole.

Camila turned to Ingrid. "What are they?"

"They're not anything. At least not anything alive today. Some kind of dinosaur, I'd say, if that wasn't ridiculous."

"And the big one?"

"Nothing like that has ever existed. Not even the biggest dinosaurs were that size." Her face hardened. "I think this is probably some kind of genetic experiment. If you ask me, that's why the American was with us. He probably came to oversee this operation."

"That guy? He wouldn't know a cell wall from a cell phone."

Ingrid looked grim, but said nothing more.

Camila wondered if she might actually be on to something. This was, after all, the kind of thing the American government loved to do. That didn't account for the plane with Cyrillic lettering, though. Could the Russians be working alongside the United States on this one? She wouldn't be surprised. Oligarchic, paternalistic and imperialist regimes tended to stick together.

"What do we do?" Ernesto said.

"I think we should stay as quiet as possible. I'll keep watch," Camila replied.

At first she couldn't understand why the reptiles were milling about as though they were confused. Then the soldiers came into view over a slight rise and the sounds of distant cracks began to make sense. She took some satisfaction from the fact that only three of the black-clad soldiers were visible... and hoped that the missing man had died painfully.

Then, to her disbelief, the smaller creatures broke and ran under the hail of bullets and headed straight towards the base.

"They're coming," Camila whispered.

"Of course they are," Ernesto moaned. "We're all going to die."

"Not so loud. Just keep still. The door is blocked."

She took her face away from the tiny chink, allowing the eternal sunlight to seep into the room. The outlines of the door and the drums staked in front of it became visible and she wondered whether the door could possibly hold. Their defenses were awfully thin.

A shadow flitted past their bunker only a few meters away. Camila attempted to warn the others... but the words stuck in her mouth. She was too frightened to speak.

Bang!

One of the creatures crashed against the door. Inside the confined space, the sound was like an explosion. Camila whimpered. She couldn't move.

Crash followed crash and the door began to deform. Light could now be seen around its edges, and the bulging impact marks showed where something had struck with superhuman force.

One of the drums fell away and rolled to one side. Ernesto ran forward and manhandled it back into place, desperation lending him strength.

Now Camila could see the fatal flaw in their defenses. The drums only reached halfway up the door. The upper half was unblocked. A human, of course, would have found himself stymied by this arrangement: he wouldn't have had the strength to bend the top half of the door out of the way.

The creatures outside had no such limitations. Though the blows against the doorway appeared to be equally distributed along its height, the ones on the upper reaches were inexorably knocking pieces out of the door. Splinters showered the pile of debris beneath. Even if the creatures weren't smart enough to take advantage of the weakness, they would still kill her in the end.

A sudden blow against the top half of the door knocked out a board and allowed light in. The interior of their bunker became bright enough to see clearly.

Now the creatures realized where the weakness was. She remembered having read that dinosaurs, even the biggest of them, had brains the size of a walnut. Whether that was true or not, she had no idea, but even if it was, it appeared that a walnut-sized brain was all an animal needed to realize that where a hole had appeared, a hole could be made bigger. Subsequent strikes all landed on the upper portion of the door.

The view out allowed Camila to see how the dinosaurs—from this distance, she had no doubt that that was that they were—attacked. They weren't using their armored claws as she'd imagined, but bashing the door with their heads, swinging the heavy skulls on long, muscular necks. It looked painful, but she assumed that the skull had some kind of armor plating… and that the creatures' brains really were as small as advertised.

Two more strikes were enough. The entire top half of the wooden door toppled inward with a crack that resonated in the enclosed space like the Trump of Doom. Four heads attempted to crowd into the resulting opening at the same time. Then they disappeared from view, and growls and grunts—a scuffle for primacy?—filled the room. Finally, a head squeezed through the opening and a single pair of eyes studied them.

The look reminded Camila of a fat woman at a buffet. The head turned from Ernesto to Ingrid and back again, as if unsure which to nibble on first.

The Swedish woman panicked. She threw herself to one side, trying to take cover in the safety of the room's depths, but the effect was exactly the opposite. Attracted by the movement, the creature struck.

Ingrid vanished. One moment she was trying to dive behind a pile of boxes, and the next, she was simply gone. Camila supposed that the neck must have stretched forward and that the creature must have grasped her in its jaws… but it happened too fast for Camila to be certain. A bump against the door—probably Ingrid being dragged through an opening too small for a fully extended human—and then the head in the opening was gone.

Camila pressed her eye against the chink to watch the creature disappear towards the sea, Ingrid's blond hair trailing in the wind. It seemed that Ingrid was actually striking it with her free arm. Could she possibly still be alive? Camila didn't think it was possible, the movement of the creature must have been shaking the arm.

Then she realized just how lucky Ingrid actually was: her ordeal was over, while the rest of them would also die, but still had to suffer first. Another head appeared in the opening, and wasted no time in poking deep into the room. It came straight towards Camila. She screamed, and felt her bladder letting go, warmly soaking her pants. She didn't care. She was going to die.

Ernesto attacked the thing's neck with a section of wooden plank he'd pulled from the pile at the door. He landed a colossal blow just below the back of the creature's head.

The monster felt the blow but didn't appear to suffer any damage from it. It just turned its head towards the tiny human attempting to attack. Ernesto shouted with rage and struck it again. This blow never landed because the creature dodged with unexpected speed and closed its huge jaws over the plank… and over much of Ernesto's arm.

A sickening crunch echoed over the concrete and the creature swallowed: plank and arm disappeared.

Ernesto stood for a moment, staring uncomprehendingly at the stump that was pouring blood onto the floor. He swayed and looked like he was about to fall, but the creature moved too fast. This time Camila saw it close its jaws around his torso and grasp. There was no chance that Ernesto would survive the wounds the teeth made as they opened the skin of his gut and tore into his intestines.

Then, like Ingrid before him, Ernesto was dragged out. Droplets of his blood landed in front of her and he disappeared into the distance, screaming and unsuccessfully trying to keep his intestines on the inside.

Another head appeared. She'd known it would. There would be no quarter until they were all dead. There had been four monsters outside, she remembered. There were four of them inside—or at least there had been at the beginning. This obviously wasn't just coincidence. A plan, something sinister orchestrated by the forces of the universe itself, some kind of karmic action she couldn't fathom, was at work.

Camila decided to get it over with. She took two steps towards the colossal head. It was important to be killed quickly; she didn't want to die like Ernesto, with her guts hanging out and her limbs bitten off. It was bad enough that she would die covered in her own pee.

Anderson yelled. "Don't just stand there looking at it, shoot the thing. Shoot it!"

She turned to look, uncomprehending. He'd grabbed on to a pipe, a metal water pipe that obviously served the astronomical instruments above them. The pipe was embedded in the concrete.

Unfortunately for Anderson, the creature also turned to look. It struck with lightning speed, gripping his leg and attempting to pull him away. But Anderson's panicked grip was much stronger than the bite-weakened flesh of his thigh. The leg tore away in an arc of blood that splashed over Camila's face.

The man, however, kept screaming at her. "Shoot, oh, God, please, shoot it. Please."

The reptile bit him again. Camila watched, fascinated as the jaws opened wide—wide enough to encircle his waist, just above the hips. With a crunching of bone, the teeth, long as knives, took hold. Then, like a puppy worrying a chew toy, the reptile shook its head.

Anderson shrieked, and then fell silent. Gobbets of meat flew everywhere, but nothing broke his death-grip on the pole. The top third of the Venezuelan student still held on. It took the creature another couple of minutes to gnaw away the man's arm and carry its prize out of the room, leaving the rest of the fragmented body scattered all over the place.

As soon as it was gone, another head appeared. "Of course. I am going to die." Camila was blubbering, talking to keep herself from fainting. "And look at me," she said to the huge, malevolent head in front of her. "I've pissed myself. What will people say at my funeral?"

She gestured towards her wet crotch, to show her humiliation to the monster that would end her life, and realized she was holding something. Her eyes fixed on a black shape, all business.

The pilot's pistol.

Confusion lasted only a few seconds. Camila raised the gun and began firing just as the creature's mouth flashed towards her. Her world was filled with teeth and tongue. She, in turn, filled the gaping maw with round after round. She expected the magazine to run out after the sixth bullet. But then it didn't. Seven. Eight. Nine. She lost count somewhere around twelve, but the gun kept firing. After the bullets ran out, she kept pressing the trigger, again and again and again.

When she stopped, the first thing she noticed was the pain in her arm and shoulder. The second was the ringing in her ears. Only after that did she recognize the fact that she was still alive.

The creature was not. It might have a brain the size of a walnut, but the odds had been stacked in Camila's favor. One of the rounds had to hit something vital… and one, evidently, had.

She waited, Zenlike, for the next monstrous head to appear, for the following monster in the queue to pull back the corpse of its fellow and avenge it. She could already feel the blades of teeth tearing into her.

But a minute passed, and then another. Nothing happened. A flicker of hope began to burn in her breast, but she quashed it. Why make the suffering worse? She would die there. That was all.

And yet, she didn't. The minutes turned to a half hour, and time stopped having meaning. She started feeling things other than fear and desperation. Cold. Her legs were cold, the urine against her skin was clammy and uncomfortable. The creature's neck didn't take up the entire opening. There was a gap wide enough to see out of, and wide enough to squeeze through if the coast was clear.

She would leave. Evidently, the universe had decided that Camila didn't deserve to die. She must have passed some cosmic test and been reserved for a different task... so she would live, but only if she managed to understand what that task might be.

Camila went. There were no more creatures in sight as she left the charnel house. The snow was white all around her except where long red streaks headed towards the sea. Camila turned her back to those. She'd seen enough blood already.

The buildings. They were red, too. She couldn't go there. But it was that or the sea and the blood of her friends. She decided to dart between two of the structures, closing her eyes against the crimson of their walls.

Success. Now there was nothing in front of her but pure white snow. She walked into the open plain, away from the sea and the buildings. Away from the red. One foot in front of the other until, when she turned, the buildings were just children's toys in the distance. Then she kept walking until they were hidden by a ridge.

There, she stopped and realized that she was thirsty. Kneeling on a soft white patch, she removed a glove and melted some snow in her hand, rejoicing in the bitter cold that told her she was alive. Then she drank the drops.

Finally the pain of the cold made her stop. She put her glove back on.

There was a gun in her other hand. She threw it away and walked some more. She stopped again when she could no longer see the black pistol in the snow behind her.

The sky was wrong. That was why these things had happened to her. It was the sky; the sky was to blame. How could anything work correctly under a sun that never moved other than to change its position capriciously with the hours? It should be night by now. Darkness should make her safe from the monsters that roamed, protected by the velvet cloak of the heavens.

But there was no night.

There would never be another night.

The wind picked up as she waited. Within minutes, snow particles that lay like dust upon everything around her, had been kicked up into the air. They hung suspended everywhere and made the blue expanse above her head even more alien and unbecoming. The sun, the ever-present monster in the sky, refracted off the crystals to create a halo around itself. She stared up at the ghostly circles of light and cried for night.

The faces of her companions, men and women she'd selected herself, and who'd trusted her to bring them along, flashed before her. They were all dead now, and she'd seen most of them die with her own eyes. It was her fault.

Even worse, Ernesto and Ingrid and Anderson had died awful deaths for no reason. She could have saved them all if only she'd remembered to use the gun.

But she hadn't. She'd failed them and let them die. They would never return to their families and friends, their lines of research—Nobel-worthy in the case of the Götthelm sisters—would be dropped forever, or passed on to researchers who would only give a passing note to the fact that the queries had been begun by someone else… if that.

She cried. Her tears fell into the snow, and she watched them, expecting to see them turn into tiny frozen diamonds. Summer in Antarctica was determined to be disappointing, however. The temperature was nowhere near freezing and the tiny drops simply disappeared into the snow.

Finally, her tears dried up, not because she wanted to stop but because she no longer had the physical capacity to cry.

The sky mocked her and the ice crystals danced.

"It wasn't my fault," she said, realizing, as the words came out, that they were true.

"Javier. Javier is a military man. He had to know what was going on, he certainly knew what he was leading us into. *He's* the murderer, not me."

And the man had abandoned them on the flimsy pretext of going to find help. Ha! If he'd wanted to help them, he would never have brought them here.

But that wasn't the way that men—it was always men—in the military thought. They put civilian lives in danger because they were convinced that they were invincible, that they'd be able to deal with anything that came up, and that the civilians, if any were present, would be perfectly safe. In fact, it was better if civilians were there so someone could ooh and ahh at their macho antics.

Of course, like everyone who took unnecessary risks, the lives of the people they were endangering meant much less to them than the possibility of showing off or going about on some great adventure.

Adventurers never admitted they were wrong, and if someone dared to point it out, they banded together to defend themselves and mock the accuser as a worrier, a small-minded conservative. A brotherhood dedicated to taking risks with other's lives, unassailable in their superior numbers.

But she would show them. She'd get back to the *Irizar* and then to Buenos Aires. She'd report them to the police. She'd go on TV and write to the newspapers. She'd make people aware of what these cowboys were really like. It might not be enough to stop them in the future, but it would put this set of clowns, particularly Javier fucking Balzano, out of business.

Camila remembered Ingrid—poor dead Ingrid—and her suspicions about Breen. Javier would have known about that, too. He was obvious about it, in fact. No one had ever pretended that the American was really part of the science crew. They hadn't even bothered to try to make it look good.

If she couldn't make it back to the ship… well, then, if he was still alive, she would take matters into her own hands.

She looked out over the empty white plains and grinned into the teeth of the wind. In this emptiness, the bastard wouldn't have anywhere to hide.

Perhaps it was time to see deserving blood spilled. God knew that enough innocent blood had fallen on the virgin wastes of the white continent.

She faced the sea and began to retrace her steps. There was no need to keep running into the endless interior of the landmass. Panic was gone now that she had a purpose. She knew why she'd been spared.

"Javie-er…" she called into the wind. "I'm coming for you Javier."

CHAPTER 13

The cave was a place of nightmares brought to life.

They stared at the tableau in front of them, rooted to the ice. Now Javier understood why Natasha had needed to run out and empty her stomach. Even Breen, hardened as he likely was by his military and paramilitary background, looked a bit green around the gills. The Australian, on the other hand, just took the new horror dully. He appeared to still be in shock from the death of his lover, unable to take anything in, and even something as appalling as the scene before them held no power to move him.

The mystery of what had become of the crew of the empty fishing boat and of the people stationed at the Argentine base was now solved.

The deepest corner of the ice cave, the place where the top and bottom of the hole came together in an acute angle, was packed with frozen human bodies, piled in a roughly semicircular wall. Some still wore the red parkas of Argentina's Antarctic missions, others had had those outer garments torn away. Some were completely naked, or wore only socks. A few of the bodies were mangled and missing limbs. A disembodied head had bled onto the ice and frozen there. Fortunately, it wasn't anyone he knew, just some blond man with a scraggly beard who was most likely one of Natasha's erstwhile shipmates.

"Look at this," Breen said after they'd all been standing with their mouths open for several heartbeats. Javier approached.

At first, he couldn't see what the American was going on about, but then he realized that the ice of the floor was streaked with parallel red lines. Javier's stomach turned. He knew exactly what that was. "Fingers," he said. It wasn't a question.

"Yeah."

"What does it mean?" Natasha asked. "There's blood everywhere, why focus on this?"

"These marks show that someone was still alive, they were trying to stop themselves from being dragged onto… whatever that is over there." Breen gestured to the piled bodies with his head. "I'm not going to follow the marks to see where he ended up. Alive. Can you imagine what that must have been like?"

Natasha looked confused. "Of course he was."

"What?"

"That structure over there is meant to keep something warm. I'd guess eggs. So it makes sense to grab something warm-blooded and pile it up around whatever you want to warm up. That is likely an instinctive behavior. The problem, of course, is how, if you're a dinosaur with the intelligence of a brick wall, you keep the warm bodies alive long enough to do you any good. And I think we already have our answer to that."

Javier was confused, or at least he hoped he was. The only explanation for her words that he could think of was bad... really bad. "I'm sorry. I don't follow."

"Their warmers—the humans they took—kept dying on them. Most of them were probably dead by the time they arrived, which meant they were no use for incubating anything. If this was the middle of the Triassic era, that wouldn't be such a problem for a number of reasons. In the first place, the higher temperatures that reigned then would have meant that there was little problem with organisms freezing to death, but even if they did die, the bacteria that would decompose them also generated heat. So, dragging them underwater, like they did to my Russian shipmates wouldn't be as self-defeating as it seems at first glance." She pointed to a grouping of pale, bloated bodies, and Javier reflected that she certainly didn't seem all that horrified to learn their fates. He supposed he wouldn't be too happy with a bunch of spies who press-ganged him into an unexpected expedition, either. "Also, the amount of heat needed would be much less."

"That still doesn't explain how you know the answer."

"Oh, that part's easy. If you don't have the warmth you need… you go look for more warm bodies. That's what's been happening. In fact, the repeated attacks by the smaller nothosaurs are the only thing that has made sense since we got here. Well, that and the guys in black."

Breen looked at her sharply. "Do you know anything about that?"

"Not really… except that, judging by the fact that they got here without anyone's help, it's obvious they knew where to look for the bodies…"

Breen slapped his head. "They chipped everyone on that ship."

"Yep." She held up the forearm of her uninjured hand and pulled back her jacket and sweater. A small, puckered white dot could be seen on her pale skin. "Everyone. It wasn't optional."

Breen took a step towards Natasha. "We need to pull that out."

Javier stopped him. "Are you crazy? We're not pulling anything out. Not here, anyway. The doctor should look at her."

"They'll come after her."

"Why? Unless they put in some really advanced diagnostics, all they have is a little thing that tells them she's here. They've been here, they know what people in here look like." He gestured at the corpses all around her. "Do you really think they'll come back for that?"

"They've got to have some pretty powerful transceivers to track them globally without amplification. So the implant is probably sizable. Why not add in biometrics? She might lead them straight back to us."

"Who cares?"

"They don't want witnesses, Javier. You know what that means as well as I do."

An image of men in black balaclavas gunning down the survivors of the *Irizar* flashed before his eyes.

"Maybe. But I'm willing to risk it if that means we can avoid cutting into Natasha's arm without her permission."

"Damn it," Breen said. But he backed off.

Natasha pressed closer to Javier and whispered the words: "Thank you," softly enough that only he could hear them.

"Now that that's settled," Breen said, "how about explaining a little more about what's going on here?"

"You've heard most of it."

"Go over it again in case I missed something."

Javier listened as Natasha went through a wild tale of cold war biological weapons made out of weaponized anthrax, surviving dinosaurs that no one had ever noticed and a Russian program to study what happened when you combined both of them.

"Jesus. And these things are the result?" Javier said.

"I… I don't think so. I think most of them, the small ones, were probably just created by evolution itself. All but that big one… That certainly isn't natural. It would take some really unusual evolutionary conditions for an amphibian creature to grow to that size and still keep its legs. The bones need to be reinforced to take weight that grows proportionally to the cube of the length and width. My conclusion is that the sea floor is littered with the bones of creatures that also got dosed with anthrax, but whose mutations didn't flourish. It was only our bad luck that one of them survived. As for the rest… I think the small ones would have been here anyway."

"You're seriously trying to tell us that we're being attacked by lizards bigger than a car, and that's fine and natural?"

"Of course. From what I can tell, from everything the intelligence people back home managed to piece together, they're just nothosaurs."

"Nothosaurs?"

"Triassic reptiles."

"Dinosaurs?"

"Not quite. But close enough that it doesn't matter all that much. The thing is that they appear to be perfectly natural. The only unusual things I was able to discover from the material I was allowed to see is that in the first place, they survived until the present day, which, I'll admit, is pretty unusual in itself. They're also a bit larger than anything we've seen from this species before, which might be a question of evolving to have more fat and consequently more bone and muscle mass to adapt to colder climates… or it might just be due to gaps in the fossil record."

"This isn't getting us anywhere," Breen growled. "Can you tell us why no one saw them before if they've been here all along? It would have been kind of hard to miss these things when humans first explored Antarctica. We've been here for a hundred years and more, after all. Dark grey things the size of whales walking around aren't exactly difficult to spot over ice cover, are they?"

"Nothosaurs were amphibious. They live and hunt in the water, like sea turtles, and they come up to land only occasionally. I think this place is a nest, and if I'm right there are probably eggs behind those bodies."

She strode over to the ghastly wall and walked around the arms and legs and dead, gaping eyes until she came to a gap. No sign remained of the frightened woman who'd been throwing her guts up out on the ice just moments before. Javier had seen it happen to specialists in high-stress situations before. They focused on the problem at hand to the exclusion of everything else, no matter how appalling the circumstances.

Javier himself had to look away from the faces frozen not in the peaceful expressions of someone dead in their sleep, but in horrified—and horrifying—expressions of pain and bewilderment. Faces of people who'd been torn, kicking and screaming, from the horrible nightmare that had been the final moments of their lives.

"Bingo!" Natasha exclaimed. Javier couldn't believe her eyes when she actually clapped her hands. "I told you it was a nest. This makes sense at least."

Javier walked up behind her. He'd expected to see something leathery and slimy, like the eggs in the movie *Alien.* Instead, these almost looked like bird's eggs—slightly larger than that of an ostrich and pale brown in the light that filtered in from the entrance.

"Well, I'm glad something makes sense to somebody," Breen said.

Natasha peered at him. "Actually, most of it does. If you accept the fact that nothosaurs somehow survived for hundreds of millions of years without anyone noticing, and that they adapted to live in cold-water environments, most of this is perfectly rational. But not the eggs in the ice. That's weird."

"*That's* weird? What about the huge thing that tore up an entire icebreaker?"

Natasha shrugged. "I suppose that's what you get when you cross an ancient reptile with a specifically selected and purified strain of anthrax. It's a special case, like the two-headed snakes one sees in museums. Mutations can happen, but they're normally something physical. Weird behaviors like this? That is something to take note of."

"How is this strange? Don't penguins lay eggs in cold weather?"

"Penguins are birds."

"Birds are dinosaurs," Javier said. He was proud of being able to say that, but it came with the territory: he had a four-year-old nephew who knew more about dinosaurs than anyone on the planet.

Instead of praising him, Natasha gave him a put-upon look. "Birds are dinosaurs, but nothosaurs *aren't*. Dinosaurs were high-metabolism animals, like birds or mammals. Nothosaurus are just reptiles." She held up a hand. "Yes. I know what the name says, but trust me on this one. They're reptiles, and that means that their eggs shouldn't really be laid in ice. Not even knowing they've been collecting bodies to try to keep them warm. Nature is never stupid, and it always makes sense once you understand it. It's possible that the anthrax might have messed with the brains of all of them. This may be a complete brood that got exposed. One mutated into that huge abomination, and the rest became addled enough to lay eggs in a snow mound." She suddenly blanched. "What in the world are you doing?"

Breen looked up. He'd emptied most of the contents of his backpack—miraculously still with him and whole—onto the ice, and was gingerly taking an egg from the ground and laying it inside. "What does it look like? I'm getting a sample." He pointed at empty spots in the clutch of eggs. "The Russians who just left took a bunch of them, and that tells me they're important."

"We need to leave them here. Do you have any idea how valuable this nest is to the scientific community?"

"Nope. All I know is what I saw. I work for a government which will want to know what the hell we have here without waiting for the whole question to go through the United Nations."

Natasha's eyes burned, but she simply stamped her foot and turned away. She knew perfectly well that the world worked exactly the way Breen had said.

As Javier turned to follow, something caught his eye. "We might just have a way out of here," he said. "Look."

A deep fissure ran into the back wall of the cave, not an inviting hole, but apparently big enough for a man to crawl into. Javier strode over and bent to look. It was about ten, maybe fifteen meters long. Sunlight, the pale light of the Antarctic summer could be seen at the far end. As far as Javier was concerned, no yellow glow on a tropical beach had ever looked more inviting.

"Ugh," Natasha said. "I don't want to go in there."

"The only other way to get back is the way the creatures left. I'm assuming you don't want to run into them, either," Breen said. He'd finished packing the egg, using cloth cut from the clothes of the frozen bodies around them as damping material. Javier had looked away.

Natasha looked glum. "I hate small spaces. I can't even get an MRI without panicking."

"I'll be right behind you."

Her wan smile told him she wasn't convinced.

Something roared.

"Oh, God," Natasha said. "They're here." She dove into the hole before Javier could react, leaving him behind. He grinned—clearly some phobias were stronger than others.

"Go now," Breen told Javier. "I'll hold them here. Unless the big one comes, I should be all right. But hurry." He held out his hand and Javier placed the FAL in it with a nod of respect.

Javier jumped into the hole behind Natasha, only to find her collapsed a couple of meters in. "Move it," he whispered. "They're coming."

From behind them, voices could be heard. "You're next, Smith."

Clark finally spoke. "Wait. Look. That's Anna!"

"No, it's not. Anna's dead."

"She's right there. That thing has her in its mouth. She's alive. We have to do something." Even from deep inside a hole in the ice, Javier could hear the desperation in his voice.

"There's nothing we can do now. Come on."

Gunfire erupted behind them, echoing in the closed confines of their escape route. Javier redoubled his efforts, pushing against Natasha's behind. He abandoned modesty for a moment and pressed her forward, pushing her along the ice. The shooting had reactivated her somewhat, and it appeared that she'd left her claustrophobia aside, but she was still having problems: it was difficult to crawl with only one arm. "I'm sorry, but we need to move," he shouted.

"Keep pushing," she screamed.

Behind them, the argument raged. "She's alive, you bastard, we need to get her back!"

"Shut up and get in there, or I'll shoot you myself."

Javier turned back to see Clark, his face a mask of fury, enter the tunnel. Behind them, three more shots exploded in the cavern before Breen himself darkened the entrance.

By then, Natasha had made it to the exit and, not waiting for Javier to push her, she scrambled out, balancing herself on her good hand. Javier exited as well and helped Clark to his feet when he arrived. Breen was last and, as soon as he was on his feet, the big Australian took a swing at him.

It should have been a massacre. Clark was nearly a head taller than the American and thirty kilos heavier. Javier, an ex-rugby player himself, saw the telltale bulk along the chest, legs and shoulders of someone who'd once been part of a pack of forwards.

But Breen stepped nimbly out of reach and grabbed Clark's hand. He moved quickly, and twisted the hand backwards, while, at the same time, getting behind the bigger man's back. "Now, just calm down. Breathe."

"You utter shit," Clark gasped between clenched teeth. "That was Anna back there. How can you just leave her like that?"

Natasha put a hand on his arm and Javier felt a pang of jealousy. "Anna's dead. I'm sorry, but I saw her myself."

Javier nodded. "She's right. She was definitely dead."

"Then who's that back there? She saw us. She even talked to us. She needs our help. Breen, you saw her."

"I didn't hear her talking."

"But you saw her. You saw her moving."

"She was moving around, but that was probably just the way the creature was holding her. Besides, I couldn't see her face through all that hair."

Javier suddenly understood, and his heart broke. "It must have been Ingrid," he said. "The creatures must have gotten into the bunker."

Natasha nodded. "That makes sense. Now that all the humans they had are dead and cold, they must be hunting for more to heat their eggs. I wonder if the eggs might develop in spurts when they're warm and then go dormant while they're cold. It would be an amazing adaptation, don't you think?"

They stared at her like she was crazy. Breen let go of Clark's arm and grunted. "Well, at least they're not eating them."

"Of course not. It's much easier to eat fish around here. Hunting prey on land would consume a lot more energy just to keep the creatures warm. It's totally inefficient. The air out here is colder than the sea for most of the year."

Clark wasn't listening. He half-turned to face Breen and then appeared to think better of it. He walked off, ten paces from the others and, ignoring the bitter cold, sat down on the ice. "That was Anna. I don't care what you say. And she was alive."

***

Breen wanted them to get moving. His vote was to attempt to make their way back to the *Irizar*. He'd done what he needed to do, and now he wanted some kind of metal plating between himself and the dinosaurs or reptiles or whatever the hell they were. He knew the ship wouldn't be much defense against the big one—that had been proven over and over again, but it was better than nothing, and would make a nice landmark to send the rescue choppers. If it didn't sink first, of course.

He was sure that somewhere in The Pentagon, someone had hit some alarm bells, and that somewhere in the ocean, a Navy ship with helicopters would conveniently appear just in the right place to offer the Argentine government assistance on the inevitable rescue operation that they would have to mount. It was probably already close enough to rescue them… but no one would move unless the Argentines allowed them to. Breen, for all anyone knew, was just a scientist, another civilian sadly stranded in a fluid situation. Overreacting would blow his cover miles high. He wondered if that mattered anymore.

Breen's satellite phone was still up and running, and he had three fully charged batteries in the pack for when that stopped being the case, so he took advantage of the lull and checked his orders.

Hold on to the woman. We've already told the Argentines she's an American citizen and that we want her back because we believe she was involved in illegal activities in Russia.

Breen chuckled. He wondered how the US would handle the fact that it would be their word against that of an Argentine colonel with a spotless record? If he knew the State Department, it would be smoothed over. A couple of Coast Guard cutters, obsolete in the U.S. but better than anything in the Argentine Prefectua, would change hands and the incident would simply never have happened.

Have secured a sample of nothosaurus egg, he sent back. *Confirmed that landing force was Russian. I'm trying to confirm whether they have taken off again. They're not currently in my line of sight. I'm pretty sure that the Russians also have egg samples, probably more than one. I could really, really use a pickup team right about now, and I suggest they come loaded for elephant. Or nothosaur.*

Fort Belvoir was going to be furious about the openness of the communication, but he was too tired and too angry to care. As far as Breen was concerned, if someone cracked the encryption, they'd earned the right to read it. He suspected that, by the time anyone could manage that, the news of what had happened in Antarctica would have traveled across the globe.

Now, if only his companions would see reason. They needed to get out of there.

But even Javier had agreed that the proximity of a bolt hole too small for the nothosaurs to enter was more important than putting distance between themselves and the nest.

CHAPTER 14

"All right. We've dithered long enough. Let's get back to the base," Breen said. The clock in his head, honed by years spent in unfriendly territory, was telling him that time was nearly up. Something or someone would find them soon... and none of the people or things roaming the ice were friendly.

His companions stood. Grudgingly, but they stood. "Why the base?" Smith asked.

Javier replied. "Because the base has a radio and a generator."

Breen nodded. "That, and the fact that the base is pretty much the best place to organize a helicopter pickup. We don't really need the radio," he held up his phone. "I'm in contact with the US government, and they're trying to help." Breen had been thinking hard about it. There were only two realistic potential pickup spots: the base and the icebreaker. While there were more people on the *Irizar*, it also appeared to be the large creature's primary target and therefore nowhere near ideal for a rescue. That opinion could change, though; he hadn't yet had a chance to evaluate the situation at the base.

"Have they contacted Buenos Aires?"

"I suppose so. They don't tell me those things." Breen knew they were probably putting everything in place before speaking to the Argentines, and that the only rescue they could legitimately be expecting was in the form of the US Navy... but there was no need to tell his companions this. It was unlikely to make them happy. "Even if we don't use the radio, the base is the right place to go."

Javier said: "Good thinking. We can hold off the small ones, and the big one appears to be much more interested in the *Irizar* than in us for some reason. It's weird."

Natasha's head snapped up and she gave a startled look. "It's not weird," she said.

"What?" Javier asked.

"What Breen said... it's not weird. It's just another thing that makes perfect sense."

"To you, maybe," Javier grumbled under his breath, just loud enough to be heard.

Natasha went on. "Think of it this way. Pretend for a minute that you're a monster big enough to eat whales and dominate the ocean for miles around. You'd pretty much feel that the ice is your domain." She looked around like a teacher in a class of dull students gauging whether she had everyone's attention. Her file said that she'd done some teaching, so perhaps it was just her usual way of pontificating. Breen found it very irritating. "What would you do if a great honking ship comes, engine noise blaring, into your ice patch. Animals defend their territory." Another look around. "In fact, we were already thinking this way when we tried to study them from the fishing ship. We had equipment to create sound waves we thought they could hear."

Breen had heard her territoriality theory already, but this was new to him.

"So that was the stuff at the prow?" Javier asked.

"Yes. It's like a big speaker that used the ship's hull to cast sound deep into the ocean." Now Natasha's demeanor changed and she cast her eyes down. "We were expecting them to come up to the ship and swim around, not to climb aboard in the middle of the night and grab the crew. And we didn't see any sign of the big one." She shuddered. "That was a good thing. I think it's probably because we were using sound pitched a bit too high. A good engine grunt like the *Irizar's* sounds a lot more like the monster's roar."

"So if we keep the *Irizar's* engines off, it won't attack?"

Natasha looked doubtful. "I'm not sure. It already knows where the icebreaker is. I don't think it will just leave it alone. But it might be worth a shot."

"This is all very interesting, but it's not getting us anywhere," Breen said. "I'm going to the base. Anyone who's coming can come. Anyone who isn't, can stay." Of course, if the woman decided to remain behind, he would be screwed… but he didn't think so. Unless he was reading her completely wrong, she'd go wherever Javier went, and Javier was with him on this one.

So he began the trek in the direction of the red buildings. The first thing he did was to climb the small rise hiding them from sight. It was decent cover, but had the disadvantage of hiding everything else from them at the same time.

The base was visible across a few hundred meters of flat, unthreatening-looking ice. If nothing untoward befell them, they should be there in a few minutes. But you really couldn't count on that. Nothing but untoward things had been befalling them since they crossed the Antarctic Circle.

He set out across the plain, only glancing back once to verify that the rest of the team was coming. Javier and Natasha were nearly beside him while the Australian, Smith, was a few feet further back, walking with a dazed expression… but coming.

As they crossed the open field, he gripped the FAL hard. It was the only real defense they had against the small nothosaurs unless one counted Javier's handgun.

About halfway to their objective, Breen nearly threw himself to the ground, startled by movement to his right.

He looked in that direction and was relieved to realize that the movement was just the Russian plane taxiing for takeoff.

While the ideal solution would have been to overpower the Russian commandos and force the pilots to get them out of there, there was no way to do that. Even if darkness had fallen, the Russians would have posted sentries with night vision goggles or, even better on the ice, infrared. It was academic; night wouldn't fall for weeks.

So, while not the perfect solution, removing one enemy from an already confusing battlefield represented a welcome simplification. At least now, no one should be shooting at them. The creatures would have to physically reach them before any harm could be done.

They reached the wrecked base and Javier led them in a beeline to a small cubical building set beneath some kind of enormous red sphere. The building had once had a metal door, but the top half had been torn away. Everything was covered in blood and one of the creatures filled the opening.

"Look! It's attacking them," Javier said, pulling his Browning from its holster. "We can still save them."

Breen put a hand on his arm. "Wait. Look. That thing isn't moving. Nothing is. I think it's dead."

Javier peered at it. "You may be right. Let's go see if anyone's alive in there."

They approached cautiously. The creature was completely immobile, but what if it was just resting? He held the assault rifle at the ready, just in case.

They got within ten meters when the Russian plane flew overhead. The sight of the monster combined with the roar of the engines touched something primal within him and it was all Breen could do to avoid running away in a panic. The feeling only passed when the drone of the aircraft dwindled into the distance.

Javier appeared unaffected. The colonel was the first to reach the opening. He squeezed his head into the space between the creature and the doorframe. A second later, he pulled it back out. He cursed in Spanish and turned back to them. "It's dead all right. Someone shot the hell out of it… but there's no one left in there. I don't think any of them survived. Blood all over the place… and pieces."

"If none of them survived, then who did the shooting?"

"I don't know. My guess would be on your friends in black."

Breen put his head in the opening. Javier was right. Even in the dim light that entered around the creature's neck and from a chink in one upper corner, he could tell that the ground was painted red, and it didn't take too much imagination to predict the color of the spatter stains on the wall a couple of gobbets on the floor... he didn't look at those too closely. The air smelled of blood and, just slightly of urine. He pulled out again.

"I suppose this is the strongest building on the base?" Breen asked.

"Yes. But I won't go in there even if the alternative is getting eaten."

Natasha broke in. "They're not eating anyone. Didn't you see the bodies. They're harvesting warmth for the nest." Natasha, after her initial reaction back in the cavern, appeared to have become engrossed in the mystery of the creatures, to the point where the human suffering around her no longer held any importance. That was actually a good thing. Better to avoid having anyone go into hysterics at the wrong moment.

"Let's go somewhere else, then. I'd rather be inside."

"Which building?" Javier asked. "None of them are safe from the creatures."

"Let's use one with a north-facing window. That way, we can see if anything is coming. As long as they don't catch us napping, we should be able to stay safe."

Breen thought of how the Russians, a mere four men, had held back not only the myriad small ones but also the big bastard using nothing but assault rifles and suffering minimal casualties. He fumed. He was sure someone had known something, or at least suspected something... but no one had told him what he might run into. They just sent him off with good wishes and orders that basically amounted to "keep your eyes open."

The result was that the US's only asset on the ground had essentially been rendered useless except as an observer because he was too busy running from a bunch of lizards. Big lizards, granted, but lizards. Humans had shown, in the course of their history that the size and strength of the creature in front of you made little difference if you were ready for it. He assumed the Navy didn't send its SEALs into shark-infested waters without at least telling them that there was a possibility of running into big fish with teeth, but that was exactly what Military Intelligence had done to Breen.

He'd give them that particular piece of his mind when he got back, in writing, in triplicate and with everyone who needed to be copied in, copied. But that would come later. Now, he needed to get out alive, and try to get as many of the people with him, as well as whatever was left of the crew of the *Irizar* out, too.

They selected the cafeteria, not only because it had the necessary window, but also because it still had an intact door and there was no blood or interior damage. The room was about ten meters by five with three tables and a counter, all made of white plastic. The floor and walls were wood and the roof sloped to either side from the centerline. Chairs were stacked against a wall, and the cafeteria also held a couple of microwave ovens. A door in one end opened onto a small kitchen area.

"All right. We should probably try to find the generator. In the middle of summer, we probably aren't in much danger of freezing to death, but we'll be much more comfortable if we can use the lights."

"I still want to try the radio," Javier said. "Maybe I can raise one of the other bases."

Breen would have preferred to avoid that, but he didn't want conflict, not yet. Things might come to that later. They might not. "That's fine by me."

"All right. Then let's see where the generator is located." To Breen's surprise, the Colonel walked to a map on the wall and stared at it for a few seconds. He stabbed his finger on one of the squares depicted. "Here we go. This is the machine room. I assume the generator is there, but we should probably find the fuel first. The generator wouldn't have broken, but it could very easily have run out of fuel."

"Who's going to search?"

"I'll go," Javier said. He turned to the Australian. "Clark, do you want to help?"

The big man shrugged. "I guess," he said.

"Good. Breen, I'll leave Natasha in your hands."

Breen nodded and watched them leave. He wondered if he should try to take off with the girl now, and save himself trouble later… but he hadn't heard back yet about when the rescue would be ready, and where it would be centered. It was probably better to stick together for now.

***

Javier suspected that the fuel would be stored in one of the big hangar-like semi-cylindrical buildings. The one that had been torn to pieces had contained food, so that left the second.

He didn't relish the idea of rolling a big drum of diesel over the slippery terrain to the machine shed, which, in an unfortunate twist, was located on a small hill. But that wouldn't matter unless they could locate the fuel—of course, it would matter even less if the generator had been trashed by the nothosaurs. He led Smith towards the machine room first.

Firm pressure opened the door. Everything inside appeared to be in working condition. Unscrewing the generator's gas tank with his gloves proved a little trickier than expected—he imagined the base's crew complaining about this year after year, and being ignored year after year. The generator itself was a Mercedes-Benz unit that looked like something from the fifties... and probably was. Not a large motor, but more than enough to power a base that size.

They searched for fuel, but there was none in the machine room, so they headed to the big hangar.

"Javier," Clark Smith said as they walked. "Can I ask you something?"

"Of course."

"Is Anna really dead?"

"I took her pulse myself. She was dead."

"Do you swear?"

For a second, Javier was angry. He was an officer and a gentleman, in a way that few people outside the armed forces of a select number of nations would ever understand. He would never lie about a thing like that. But he was also a human being, and recognized the suffering behind the question just in time to cut short the curt reply. "I do. On my honor as a soldier."

Clark nodded. "Then I must be going insane. I know she moved. I saw it myself. And it wasn't just because she was getting bounced around by the dinosaur thing. She was alive. She was trying to get away."

"I don't know what to say. All I can tell you is what I saw... I was in the tunnel already when the monster came in behind you. I didn't get to see it."

They reached the storeroom. The door was dented and damaged, with a small part of it pushed all the way in, but it didn't appear as if the monsters had entered. It certainly hadn't been clawed to pieces by the big one like the other hangar, probably because they'd smelled neither food nor humans within. They crawled inside and waited for their eyes to get used to the light.

The first thing Javier saw was a box with the unmistakable markings of the red cross on its side. He slit the cardboard open and pulled out a small metal case. He handed it to Smith. "Hold onto this, it's a first aid kit, military grade... with stitches and some decent anesthetics. I hope we don't need it, but if we find anyone who got out of that room, I'm pretty sure we will." *And much more than this... and probably a priest*, he thought, but didn't say. He went deeper into the storeroom. "Can you get that door open? I need more light."

He heard Clark trying to push it out and, after much grunting and cursing, a shaft of clear grey light pierced the gloom. "There."

At first, all the new light achieved was to remind Javier of how tired he was, of the fact that there was no night, that he might never see the moon and the stars again… or even a sunrise for that matter. One of the few perks of a soldier's life was that getting up really early afforded some excellent views of the sky.

He shook his head to clear it and to snap out of his reverie.

The fuel was in drums, but at least there were a couple of hand trucks leaning against a wall, which meant they wouldn't have to roll the things halfway across the continent. They were able to wrestle one of them up the hill to the machine room. Then they had to return to the storeroom to look for a hose or a pipe with which they could siphon the pungent diesel oil into the tank which, fortunately, was located under the floor, which made pouting possible without having to lift a heavy drum.

Once done, they took turns cranking the freezing generator until, with a sputter, multiple coughs and a cloud of black smoke, it came to life.

"What do we do now? Do we have to connect this to something?"

"I don't think so. Let's get back and see if the lights are on in the cafeteria."

Clark laughed ruefully. "Or maybe just try this." He flicked the switch on the wall beside the door and the fluorescents above them flickered on. "Always try the easier experiment first."

Javier was in a much better mood as they made their way back to the cafeteria. For some reason, getting power back up made him feel that the prehistoric nightmares were being pushed back into the realm of imagination where they belonged.

But the joy lasted only a few moments. By the time they were halfway back, the wind picked up and was blowing snow into the air. The world turned grey and dark.

When they got back, the ice crystals were stinging their exposed faces, and Javier was sure the temperature must have fallen by ten degrees. They shut the cafeteria door behind them gratefully.

Breen wasn't as happy. "We won't be able to see anything coming through this soup," he said.

"At least we have lights," Javier replied. "Besides, they're animals, but they're not stupid. Why would they come after us in this weather?"

"I can answer that," Natasha said. "The temperature drop will mean that the nothosaurs need more warm bodies for their eggs. The only good places around to get them are here and at the *Irizar*."

"There are more people on the *Irizar*," Breen said.

"That's true. But we are much closer."

"I suppose you're right. And worse, I don't think anything can land until this clears and the wind dies down."

Javier had intended to get some rest on one of the tables, but now he was filled with a need to do something, anything. To get things moving again.

"I'll go see if I can fix that radio."

Before anyone could object, he walked back out into the eternal gloomy light. Even the snow would be bearable, he thought, if only it would get dark.

CHAPTER 15

Camila watched the group approach. She clenched and unclenched her hands as she saw the light tan uniforms and the guns. More soldiers. Sailors from the *Irizar*, probably sent out to help Javier.

They hadn't spotted her yet. In fact, they were looking in the wrong direction because Camila had stopped to study the body of the pilot, and therefore she was in the landing field, well off the direct path between the icebreaker and the base which the men had followed. She'd spotted a dark blotch in the snow as she walked towards the ship—which was where she thought Javier had gone and had decided to detour and see what the mound was, and the trip had paid off. The pilot was long dead, but she'd been happy to discover that the man carried a serviceable knife, wickedly serrated on the side opposite the razor-sharp blade. It was a strange thing for a pilot to have, but she was grateful to find it—the man's pistol, after all, had been abandoned in the snow far away.

Then the wind had picked up, and she'd hunkered down, using the slight mound of the pilot's body to keep at least some of the snow off her. It allowed her to avoid having to close her eyes.

"You're keeping me safe even now," she told the dead face. "First, your gun saved me, and now this. You're the only man who ever gave me so much."

The pilot had nothing to say to that, so Camila continued.

"You know another thing I like about you is that you're a man of few words and a lot of action. Of course, if we were together, you'd have to leave the service and get a less ridiculous job. Everyone in the military is a fascist, you know."

Silence met her, and she snuggled closer. If it hadn't been so cold, it would have been perfect.

"You're not like Javier. That guy is a bastard. He stole my dream and took it over, and he didn't bother to tell us that we were walking into a nest of monsters. Look where he got us. You're dead. So are all my students and the scientists. Those Swedish girls might have looked like models… but they were on track for a Nobel. Now they're just food for some lizard thing. That shouldn't happen in the twenty-first century, and it's all the fascists' fault.

"So you'll need to find a different job. Well, if you were alive, you would. Yes. I'm not crazy, I know you're dead, and that you can't change jobs no matter how much I want it."

The wind died down slightly. "Look. There are people coming. People! Are they here to take us back to civilization?"

She stared at them. Disappointment filled her.

"No. They're sailors from the *Irizar*. Just another branch of the oppressors marching us towards their own goals." Then she brightened. "But I suppose they might be able to tell us where Javier is. Did I tell you what I plan to do to Javier when I find him?" She laughed to herself. "He won't expect it in the least. It will be funny to see the look on his face, won't it?"

She stood, and vacillated. On one hand, she didn't want to leave the poor pilot alone in the snow, but on the other, he wouldn't even notice because he was dead. She wondered whether the sailors would be a real part of the problem or whether they were just following orders. Enlisted men often taken from the working classes—forced to serve the very powers that had ground their ancestors and still ground their families under iron thumbs because the alternative was to starve. The true tragedy was that the brainwashing and resignation ran so deep that protest, rebellion against the system, never occurred to them.

There was so much she could have taught them, had the situation been otherwise.

But, of course, it wasn't. On board a ship like the *Irizar*, there would always be a captain, or a lieutenant or someone looking over her shoulder ensuring that the men couldn't be influenced. The officers, of course, were from a different class: they had Spanish last names, often street names. The patrician families, of course, had named the streets of every city in the country after their major figures.

The sailors still hadn't seen her, so she began to walk towards them. The group soon resolved into three figures hunched against the driving wind. Only when she was almost on top of them did they react. As soon as they realized that she wasn't some prehistoric monstrosity hell-bent on tearing their flesh from their bones, they ran towards her, waving, shouting, and smiling.

"You're Camila, aren't you? The leader of the scientists?" the young lieutenant who appeared to be in charge asked. They'd told her his name at some point, but she hadn't been paying attention… after all, officers were interchangeable to her. What difference did the name make when his rank was the only thing that mattered?

"Yes, Lieutenant," she replied. "Though the Colonel will likely take exception at your description."

If he heard her response, the young man—he couldn't have been more than twenty-five, could he?—gave no indication. "I'm so glad you're alive. How are the rest of them? Did you reach the base? Did you see any creatures?"

"We're scattered all over. I'm afraid that some of us are dead. I think the Colonel is still alive, but I'm not sure where he is… he told me he was going back to the *Irizar*."

That did get an expression from the man: he looked grave. "He never made it."

Could it really have been that simple? Was her nemesis dead of nothing more interesting than the big teeth of an animal? Could the universe really hate her that much? All she wanted, her deepest desire, was to be able to take her own revenge on the man who'd casually appropriated and then destroyed her life-long dream and left her wandering forever in that nightless purgatory.

It couldn't be. She refused to believe it. It wasn't *right*. "He must have turned back to the base," she said.

"We hope so. That's where we're going to look for them. How is the previous base complement?"

"I don't know."

"Weren't you at the base?"

"Yes, but there was no sign of anyone. Either they ran off when the creatures appeared, or…" she left that in the air. There was no need to belabor the obvious.

"We'll look for them, then. I'm glad you're all right, though. In these conditions, anyone being alive is a blessing." He gave her a genuine smile.

She smiled back, and hoped he couldn't tell it was faked.

They started walking towards the base. Visibility had gotten so bad that the lieutenant was trying to get his bearings with a compass.

"This thing is useless," he shouted in frustration.

Camila laughed. Soldiers were all the same. None of them had any brains. "That's because we're too close to the pole. The needle will always point directly away from the magnetic south pole, no matter where we go in Antarctica."

"So… how does that help us?"

"Do you know the exact location of the pole?"

"No."

"Then it doesn't."

He looked so dejected Camila almost felt sorry for him. Almost.

She went on. "I can tell you how to get there, though." She was reasonably certain she could give them the right bearing. She was normally very good at not getting turned around. "That way."

He smiled again and they set off, obviously assuming that she would walk with them. After only the briefest hesitation, Camila did so, lining up behind the two enlisted sailors. Her original plan had been to return to the *Irizar* and seek Javier out there, but that had been scuttled.

As she walked, she wondered about the man in front of her. He was a short, wiry fellow—at least as far as she could tell through the voluminous uniform jacket, also tan—who struggled through the snow. By his facial features and slightly darker skin, he was obviously not descended from Europeans, or at least not of pure European stock. Unlike most countries in South America, Argentina's native population had essentially been wiped out in the wars of colonization. Criminal colonists had killed without second thoughts, hiding behind the excuse that the natives had been hostile and murderous from the first.

It might even have been true… but anyone, upon seeing themselves displaced from their ancestral homes by strange invaders, would have reacted violently. Argentina's shame was that the desert campaign in response was not a war of pacification, but a war of extermination.

Most of the native survivors had been in the north of the country… a population that had been continually supplemented by immigration from neighboring Bolivia and Paraguay. She guessed that the man ahead of her had probably come from those, not from among the few survivors left in Patagonia.

Northern Argentina was a warm place, a place of deserts and near-tropical jungles. Like many such areas around the world, its inhabitants were poor… and, for them, like for so many poor people in other places, the armed forces were a quick path to respectability.

But even if that man—he looked to be about forty—had seen every expectation that he'd had upon enlisting fulfilled, it was still cruel to send him to a place where the summer wind could cut through heavy jackets and fling snow into the air.

Camila wished she could explain the error of his ways to him. After all, the political implications of his situation were probably lost on the sailor. But this wasn't the right moment. Camila reflected, as she followed him, that there truly was such a thing as being in the wrong place at the wrong time. At any other period in her life, Camila would have tried to awaken the righteous political anger that should have been his. Any other time, she would have saved him from himself.

But not that day.

She closed the distance between them and drove the point of the knife deep into the exposed side of the man's neck. His gasp was swallowed up by the wind and the other two men never realized their companion was gurgling to his death, already a dozen paces behind.

The warmth on her hands only lasted for a few seconds. Soon, in the wind, the blood turned cold… cold and slick. The temperature wasn't quite low enough to freeze it, but it was most certainly sufficient to turn the warm essence of a comrade, the essence of human companionship, into an uncomfortable reminder that she'd just snuffed his light like a covered candle.

The next man ahead had to die as well, another common sailor. She didn't want his blood on her hands, neither figuratively or literally but, like so many others before her, sacrifices needed to be made in the name of a greater cause.

So she hesitated and wondered about this man's life story. He, unlike the other, sported the pale skin of the invader. Of course, an enlisted man was still one of the oppressed, even if he acted as a cat's paw and looked similar to the people who ran the country.

He walked with a slight limp, so she concentrated on that. The walk to find Javier was one of those missions that screamed "volunteers only". She imagined that he'd signed up for it despite that pain. The agony was likely made even worse by the cold and humidity. She cried as she thought of him, a wounded warrior, volunteering out of concern for his fellow man.

Camila stabbed him in the right kidney, the razor-sharp point making short work of several layers of fabric. She pulled the knife away quickly to avoid getting more blood on him.

That was lucky. The man grunted, but didn't fall. He turned towards her with a confused look and she was able to slash at his neck. Now, he fell, but the cost was that Camila ended up spattered with gore.

She cursed under her breath. It was almost as if the karma of having murdered the man couldn't be expressed without the physical manifestation of the crime.

They walked on and, without warning, the wind died down. The ice crystals suspended in the air settled slowly and the base came into view, fifty meters to their left.

The lieutenant turned back, a smile on his face. "You were right. We're almost on top of the base." Then he stammered to a stop. "What happened to you?"

There was little need to fake the fear. She knew the lieutenant would shoot her if he found out what she'd done. "It happened so fast," she said. "Two of those… creatures came out of the snow. They attacked us before we could react. They took your men."

The lieutenant looked down at her hand and she followed his gaze. She put the bloody knife in front of her as if she were seeing it for the first time. "I must have managed to hit one of them. I… never even realized what I was doing."

The lieutenant's eyes went wide. "That's amazing. I've seen men run away at the mere sight of one of them… even the small ones. And you attacked one with a knife? You're incredible." He nodded in respect. "But come on. We should be able to see them escaping." He did something to the big automatic rifle he was carrying. "This time they won't catch us by surprise. And maybe the boys are still alive." He peered into the snowy landscape and pointed in the direction the second man had fallen: "There. I think I see something. Come on!"

He ran off in the direction of the murdered man, and Camila rushed behind him. "I think it's José!" the lieutenant said.

He was too far to stab in the back, and would certainly reach the dead man before she could catch up. Her only hope was to be right there, right beside him when he reached the corpse, so he wouldn't be able to react before she did. This one, she had no qualms about killing. This onc deserved it.

He reached the body and fell to his knees beside it. "Dammit," he said. "They killed him. Tore out his throat. Poor man."

The lieutenant reached out and closed José's eyes. He bent his head and said a prayer over his lost sailor.

Sometimes the oppressors can fool us, Camila thought, perhaps remembering some long-past political science class, perhaps just reminding herself of what she knew to be true. *Sometimes they almost seem human. It's important to stay strong, to know that the fight is more important than anything else.*

And yet, she couldn't bring herself to stab this man in the back.

This man will defend Javier from you.

That thought, apparently out of the blue, galvanized her. She struck without thinking any further, and this time without mistakes: the neck was the right place to attack, and a sweeping, untidy blow from behind hit the lieutenant just below the right ear.

Though it was a messier strike than the others, and spilled much more blood, the man didn't die immediately. He desperately tried to hold his blood in as it began to spray, and then he collapsed onto his side. But he still wasn't dead. His hands opened and closed around his neck.

She sat beside him and pulled off his hat. He had thin black hair, which was a pleasure to run her fingers through, even though the blood from her hands matted it.

He'd stopped trying to put his neck back together and now was just letting her stroke his head and sobbing into her clothes.

The crying got softer and softer until it finally stopped and he died.

Camila stood up and looked around. The sun, now that she could see it, was still up, even though her body told her that it must be about three in the morning. She didn't know. Her cell phone had died long ago, so she had no clue what time it was.

She sat there, unsure of what to do next. Was Javier even alive? Had he turned back to the base for some reason?

In the distance, a man walked, zombie-like towards the coast. It was a strange direction in which to be walking: neither towards the *Irizar* or towards the base. Then she remembered that the men in black had been going in exactly the same direction. There must be something there.

She smiled as she recognized the man. It was Clark Smith, the Australian geologist. And if Smith was still alive near the base, that meant that Javier's team had come back.

"Javieeeer," she called softly into the cold air. "I'm coming for you..."

CHAPTER 16

"Where's Clark?" Javier had returned to the cafeteria after a long, frustrating struggle with the radio. All he wanted was to lie down on a table and sleep for a week. If he was killed by some prehistoric monster while he was asleep... well, c'est la vie.

Breen looked around sharply. "He was here a few minutes ago. I thought he'd bunked down in back, but he must have slipped out when I went to the bathroom. Natasha?"

"I must have dozed off. I didn't see him leave."

They searched the cafeteria, but that only confirmed what they already knew: he wasn't under a table or sitting in one of the microwaves.

"Damn. Where's he gotten himself off to?" Breen said.

"You think he left on his own?" Natasha asked.

"Unless those things have learned to open doors without tearing them down, he left on his own."

"I didn't see any sign of nothosaurs outside, either," Javier added.

They opened the door and looked out into the snow. The wind was dying down.

Natasha pointed with her good hand. "Look. Over there!"

A tiny figure headed away from them, in the same direction they'd arrived from.

"Oh, God," Javier said. "He's going after her."

"Too bad."

"What do you mean? We have to bring him back."

"Really? Are you suggesting we should take Natasha back into that nest with us? A woman with only one good arm? Or would you rather leave her here alone? We already saw how that works out for unarmed people."

Javier barely thought about it. "You stay here with her, and I'll go get him. No, don't try to talk me out of it, you should know it's useless by now."

"Yeah, I'd gathered that. You'll want this." They swapped weapons, Javier took the FAL and Breen, reluctantly, accepted the Colonel's Browning.

Two minutes later, Javier was slipping and sliding on the snow as he followed the wayward Australian. Though convinced that Clark was heading towards the nest, he didn't want to lose sight of the speck in the distance.

He jogged as fast as he dared, with his head on a swivel searching for the nothosaur that would appear out of nowhere to tear him to pieces, but none presented themselves.

As he ran, his mind wandered, and he found himself thinking of having traversed that particular patch of snow an endless number of times. It was as if he was caught in an infinite loop, destined never to be able to break out, never to be able to go on with the rest of his life. The loop continued… and night seemed as far away as it always was.

A dead nothosaur, riddled by bullets from the Russian assault team, lay in his path, and he hardly gave it a second thought, other than to think that Natasha was right: they *were* just animals, and they could be killed easily—if you were prepared for them. Even the big one would likely not last too long if someone got a few planes in the air armed with missiles. Even just helicopters with anti-tank ordnance could cut it into mincemeat.

The rifle he was carrying, though, wasn't going to do it. The best he could hope for was not to run into the big bastard.

Javier kept going. He'd halved the distance to Clark, but he wasn't going to be in time to head him off. Clark would enter the cave before Javier reached him; the Australian was already descending the big incline that the Russians had used for their retreat. His head soon dropped out of sight.

"Damn," Javier said, and redoubled his pace.

But extra speed didn't mean that he was catching the other man any quicker. All he achieved was to hit the ground a number of times before deciding that he'd make better progress by slowing down. He'd reached the top of the descent and was in sight of the cave mouth, so he reduced his pace to a walk and unslung the FAL.

Clark was nowhere to be seen. Javier shrugged and began his descent, rifle at the ready. There really weren't too many options: he was either in the cave or he'd jumped into the sea.

The back of the opening was invisible to Javier from that angle, but he thought that swinging out to see the cavern would only put him in sight of whatever happened to be inside, so he maintained his angle of approach.

The clock in his head ticked and tried to tell him that time was running out for Clark, but Javier forced himself to go slowly. Haste was his enemy.

A scream pierced the wastes. It sounded like it would carry all the way back to Buenos Aires, and it spurred him into action. Throwing caution to the wind, Javier rushed headlong towards whatever might await him in the cave.

At first, he couldn't find the source of the yelling. He was five meters into the cavern before he realized it was coming from his left, near the wall of bodies.

Javier ran towards the sound and, clearing a pile of fallen ice, he was confronted with a grisly scene.

Clark Smith lay on the ground in a pool of his own blood. He was missing a leg, which had been violently torn from its socket and lay halfway across the cave. Despite the horrendous injuries which must have led to enormous blood loss, the Australian was still alive. He was using his hands to crawl across the ice towards the pile of human bodies around the eggs.

His objective was a shock of blond hair that fell from the pile onto the floor. Its owner was sprawled atop the rest of the bodies, clearly a recent addition. She lay where she'd been dropped: legs on the pile, head dropping over the edge, one arm beside it, the fingers dragging in the snow.

Clark reached her hand and took it in his. To Javier's astonishment, the girl's hand first jerked away slightly, and then closed around his.

The nothosaur struck. One moment it was standing to one side watching Clark crawl with its head tilted to one side in a strangely human-like way, and the next it moved, lightning-fast.

Javier flinched as the enormous jaws closed around the Australian's midriff. He expected them to snap shut and cut the man in half but, instead, the creature lifted him off the ground almost gently and laid him on top of the pile. At some point Smith lost consciousness, but he managed to keep hold of the girl's hand. The two were now strewn haphazardly across the pile, the ultimate layer of a macabre sculpture.

It was too much for the colonel. Without checking to see if there were any other creatures waiting within, he opened fire on the nothosaur, using the FAL on full automatic. He knew it was less precise, knew that all he was really achieving was to spend his ammo wastefully, but he didn't care. He wanted to see the creature and its smiling, jagged teeth blown into tiny fragments of flesh and bone and enamel.

The nothosaur screamed. It wasn't the roar he'd come to associate with these creatures, but something more akin to the sound that he remembered that pigs being slaughtered made when he was a child: high-pitched, plaintive, almost like a woman's yell of terror in an old horror movie. The sound was both an expression of pain and, somehow, a sound of warning. Nothing that heard the sound could fail to understand the message: "Danger! Danger!"

Was it also a cry for help?

Javier didn't care. The creature staggered towards him, obviously badly hurt. He'd concentrated his fore on the neck and forward portion of the torso on the assumption that those areas were full of delicate organs… organs hopefully not shielded by a thick skull.

It was evidently working. The nothosaur's walk became more and more erratic before it finally collapsed in front of Javier.

He finished emptying the clip, and stood above it, shaking and, he realized, shouting and cursing. When the magazine was exhausted, he kicked the nothosaur in the head again and again. There was no need for that, nothing to be gained, but the terror in his body demanded a release.

Gradually, sanity returned and Javier remembered the creature's screams, and the certainty that they were desperate calls for help. In military terms, he thought, the lizard expected backup. He stopped kicking it and turned his attention to Clark.

The man's hand was moving. He was alive.

Javier rushed over and put his hand on the Australian's neck. He would be weak from blood loss, of course, but the Colonel wanted to see just how weak and try to figure out what he could do. The missing leg had been torn off at the hip, there was no way to apply a tourniquet.

And… Clark wasn't bleeding as much as he should be. That wound should have been gushing blood like a river during snowmelt season, but the fall was barely a trickle, mostly dripping downward along the bodies below him.

As he observed this, Javier searched for a pulse, but no matter how hard he pressed, he was unable to feel anything. The man had to be dead.

Except… The hand had moved again.

It wasn't his hand.

The girl!

Two steps brought him over to where she lay face down on the pile. He gently disentwined the woman's living fingers from Clark's dead ones and turned her over to face him. Long blond hair fell across her face, and though her exposed skin felt cold in his hand, her body wasn't stiff, didn't feel dead. In fact, it almost felt like she was moving along with him.

Could Clark have been right? Could he have been wrong about Anna? Had she survived the crash of the snowmobile after all? It seemed impossible: both he and Natasha had been convinced that she was dead.

She coughed and the movement blew her hair away from her face.

Ingrid.

Her eyes were barely open, but when he came close the lids slammed apart and she tried to lift her hands to push him away.

"It's all right," he said. "You're going to be all right."

He was pretty sure he was lying to her. Ingrid's jacket, once electric blue like her sister's, was stained with blood, some dry and flaking, more of it dark and cold. She looked to be on death's door.

Nevertheless, she was trying to speak.

"Water…" Ingrid whispered.

He cursed himself for a fool, pulled his canteen out of his pocket and poured a few drops onto her lips. She swallowed and he waited.

"More." Stronger this time.

He poured a little. She drank greedily and tried to sit.

"Wait. You're hurt."

"I... know."

"I'm afraid to move you."

"I think I can sit up."

To Javier's amazement, she did, with his help. She grimaced and yelped in pain, but she sat.

"Are you all right?" He felt like a fool asking such a moronic question. She obviously wasn't all right… but her determination was nothing short of amazing.

"Hurts," she replied.

"I know."

And then she tried to stand.

"Don't do that. You…" He stopped. How could he tell her that she wasn't in any condition to walk? That her only real option was to stay in a cave and either bleed or freeze? He couldn't, so he put her arm around his neck and helped her stand. She swayed a little, but managed to stay on her feet. He was amazed.

And then their time ran out. A roar, too large to be contained by the cavern, shook the world.

"Oh, shit! It's the big one."

But they had more immediate problems. Smaller grey streaks, at least three of them, tore into the cave.

One of them jumped towards them.

Javier reacted instinctively, forgetting that Ingrid was badly hurt. He rolled to one side, out of the way of the hurtling animal, and pulled her with him. They tumbled off the pile of dead bodies and slammed into the cold ground—fortunately, Ingrid landed on top of him, so Javier took the brunt of the impact.

He pulled her back to her feet as he stood, but she wasn't up to it and began to collapse again. He let her fall and fell on top of her, just as knife-sized teeth snapped shut above him.

Then, for the second time in… two hours? Three? A century? He'd lost all sense of time... he found himself shoving a woman into the crack at the back of the cave and diving in behind her.

But this time, he was just a fraction of a second too slow. Fire coursed down his back as something sliced through his jacket and skin.

"Damn," Javier said.

"Are you all right?"

"I don't know. I think so. But it hurts like hell." Then he laughed.

"What?"

"I'm pretty sure I should be more worried about you than about me. You should see yourself."

"The blood, you mean? I think most of it belongs to other people. Some of it's mine, but I think I mostly got bruised. Those things aren't gentle." She cocked her head, listening. "What's that sound?"

"Digging. They're coming after us."

***

Breen looked at his phone in disbelief, unable to believe what he was being ordered to do. Kidnapping the girl? Abandoning the other survivors if they couldn't make it to the rendezvous point in time? The Pentagon must be getting seriously worried about something to risk a PR nightmare of that magnitude.

At least he still had some time to try to keep things from becoming a total disaster… maybe even lower the fallout of the inevitable diplomatic incident.

The last line of the message, however, burned in his mind:

Navy Seahawk will be there to pick you up. ETA: 1500 hours.

That was just ten hours away. The coordinates given coincided almost exactly with the position of the *Irizar* as far as Breen could tell.

"He's been gone a long time," Natasha said.

"Yes. If he doesn't come back soon, we might have to return to the ship. We can't hold these buildings without that rifle. We just can't."

"They'll get us if we try to cross."

"Not necessarily. We've already done it once. We should be fine."

She gave him a look. "And what will you do with me if we make it? You're not going to let me go back to England, are you?"

Breen sighed. "I would personally let you go back wherever you wanted. All I want is to go to a beach somewhere peaceful where there are no lizards and stay there until they have to lock me up in a nursing home."

"You didn't answer my question."

"All right. No. You're not going back to England. The U.S. government is going to debrief you, and then give you a choice. You can go back to Europe and continue to live the life you had before, or you can get asylum in America. If you're smart, you'll choose the asylum."

"What?"

"Exactly what I said. If you go back to England, how long do you think it will take the SVR to have you in a basement somewhere in Vladivostok talking about your experiences here?"

"This isn't the Cold War, Breen."

"I know. The communists would have hesitated at snatching someone off a London street and getting them back across the Iron Curtain. You don't have that particular protection."

She growled under her breath, but said nothing.

"I wouldn't worry about that now, though. It's all moot unless we can find a way to make it out of here alive."

He stood to get some water. All they had was snow from outside that they were melting in a pan on an electric stove, but it tasted incredible. He was parched and ravenous… but there was no food.

He wondered why anyone would choose to spend half a year marooned here. It was bad enough in the supposedly warm summer with its eternal day, but he couldn't even imagine what it must be like in winter, with inhuman cold and howling winds and endless night.

He'd been sent to some hellholes over the course of his career. Mountains in Pakistan and deserts in Somalia came to mind immediately, but this… there was no question of living here without infrastructure. The people who came here were eternally one equipment malfunction away from an unpleasant death, and for what?

Most of the other hellholes he'd been to represented some kind of political flashpoint. Africa was the wild border of Islam, where its extremists could hide from the entire world. Pakistan, likewise was at a crossroad.

But Antarctica? It was nothing. Even the science done in the stations was mostly of interest to environmental groups. Politically, the place was irrelevant. The major powers, or at least some of them, had bases there, but it was only to show off a little. No one really cared.

He wondered how this incident would play out on the worldwide news. There was no way it wouldn't get out. Someone on the *Irizar* would have had a phone and filmed the whole thing… and there was no way to get a cleanup crew—complete with icebreaker—here in time to erase the evidence. The Argentines would definitely reach the scene first in sufficient numbers to make any difference… and they were terrible at keeping secrets.

Besides, they had no incentive to keep this secret in particular. This was essentially a case in which the U.S. and Russia had clashed and innocents had taken the brunt of the casualties… It had happened before, and it always raised a hue and cry.

This time, the incident would be worse. Argentina was not a world power, but it was an established democracy and a nation that had been at peace with everyone on the planet for more than thirty years. Their voice would be listened to.

"We should probably get back to the ship," he told Natasha.

She shook her head. "I'm not going anywhere until he gets back."

Breen just nodded curtly. He still had time.

CHAPTER 17

The FAL clicked uselessly and Javier cursed. "I'm out of ammo." He knew, every soldier knew, he shouldn't have emptied the clip at the other creature… but that was easy to say now. In the moment, with the giant teeth facing him, there was no way he could stop.

Pushing the blond woman ahead of him, he pressed deeper into the crevice.

Ingrid said nothing. She just hyperventilated where he'd dropped her. A cut on her face was bleeding.

"We've got to get out of here. This crack leads to a small depression in the ice. We can walk back to the base from there. It's maybe five hundred meters. Do you think you can make it?"

"I… I'll try."

Javier had grave doubts. She looked dizzy and her voice sounded weak, which didn't surprise him in the least. Even if she was right about not having been hurt too badly, the stress of what had happened to her, combined with having been out in the snow for a couple of hours would be enough to leave her reeling. And Javier wasn't too convinced about her assessment of her injuries.

They crawled out of the tunnel, loud scratching behind them a constant reminder that they were not alone, and that slowing would mean an agonizing, inevitable death.

Ingrid grunted in pain, interspersing the sounds with even more eloquent yelps. She was clearly in a huge amount of pain, but Javier knew that she would have to hold up. There was no way they could stop. It just wasn't an option.

They reached the tunnel exit and he led them out. The first hundred meters or so on the open ice were the least dangerous because they were completely hidden from the view of anything on the beach or in the cave.

But after that, the terrain flattened out and speed would be of the essence.

He took Ingrid's forearm. The woman felt solid, muscular… maybe she'd be fine after all. They set out on the gentle rise which led towards the base. Ingrid matched him stride for stride, so he let go of her arm and concentrated on choosing the most direct route through the snowy crenellations.

They reached the top of a small ridge. The base was in sight across a flat plain and the going—though tense—should be easier. Javier took two steps.

Ingrid dropped to her knees and then collapsed on the snow. "You go ahead," she groaned. "I need to rest."

"Don't say that. You'll be fine." He tugged on her arm, tried to put his hands around her waist and pull her to her feet, but it was no use. Ingrid's legs appeared to have turned to jelly.

It soon became very apparent that no amount of tugging or whispered cajoling would get her walking again.

Javier took a deep breath and bent down to pass both arms under her. He groaned, grunted and, after nearly slipping multiple times, lifted Ingrid in a fireman's carry.

He wondered if the Swedes fed their children ball bearings. Though she looked lithe and certainly wasn't fat, this woman was probably heavier than Javier himself—and he was basically all muscle.

There was no other choice, however. Either he could carry her back to the base, praying that the nothosaurs would insist on digging their way through the tunnel after them and lose all that time… or he could leave her there to die.

In Javier's world the answer was a foregone conclusion.

He tried to keep his breathing steady as he walked. He kept his eyes on the ground at his feet, thinking only of the next step, not of the hundreds still to come.

Javier's stomach groaned. When was the last time he'd had anything to eat? Could he stay on his feet long enough to reach the base, or would they both be devoured where they fell? He'd heard Natasha's theories about the creatures and the fact that they wanted the bodies to heat eggs, but that wasn't how it felt to him. His gut knew that big lizards only wanted him for one thing: food. What science might say was irrelevant.

The hair on the back of his neck stood up every time he thought about the creatures behind him in the same way they would if he were being chased by wolves hell-bent on eating them both. He was sure that, if they fell, they'd become dinosaur food.

"Just leave me…"

"No."

They had the same conversation over and over again, and Javier was actually grateful to Ingrid for insisting. The annoyance he felt at the suggestion that he might be capable of leaving an injured woman out on the ice to die kept him going. Each exchange bought him two steps.

Unfortunately, Ingrid was only semi-conscious part of the time. When she was out of it, his progress had to come from deep inside with no help from his companion.

Each step was a conscious effort.

Javier looked up. The sun was still in the same place it always was, circling overhead like a buzzard over carrion.

Perhaps in this place, at this moment in time, it *had* replaced all the other scavengers. Penguins couldn't circle overhead. They couldn't fly at all, in fact. He wondered whether penguins would eat dead mammals. He couldn't remember.

In fact, the only thing that came to mind when he thought about penguins was how hungry he was. He'd eaten penguin before—not by choice. It had, simultaneously been the most disgusting thing he'd ever tasted and the most wonderful.

Part of traditional Argentine Army training for officer cadets was to set them out in an uninhabited wilderness and pick them up a week later. Patagonia, especially the desert-like Patagonian coast, was ideally suited to an exercise of that sort. Empty of food and water, with howling winds and summer temperatures that could drop to near-freezing at night, it was a true test of mettle and ingenuity.

Thc cadets were dropped off in small groups—after being thoroughly searched for hidden food—and picked up at the same spot a week later. The dregs of what had once been soldier candidates were usually emaciated wrecks at the end of it.

Javier's crew, unusually, had been lucky. Just three days into what promised to be an unpleasant sojourn, one of the men had stumbled upon a nesting Magellan's penguin. It had immediately become dinner, and had, in the end, seen them through.

The fishy taste of its flesh was still fresh in Javier's memory… even if he told anyone interested, in all honesty, that penguin tasted like crap but that crap was a glorious alternative to starvation.

He could almost taste it as he walked.

Javier shook his head. He needed to clear his thoughts; he was losing focus, and that wasn't something he could afford. He was on his last legs in a hostile terrain surrounded by creatures that wanted to kill him. The one thing he didn't need was for his own mind to betray him.

In fact, he should probably begin to worry. Just moments ago, he'd been sure that something was approaching from ahead of him and to his right. Maybe one o'clock.

But when the image got through his addled brain and he looked in the right direction, there was nothing to be seen, just a snowy waste like any other.

He kept walking. Nothing from that direction was likely to kill him. The real problem would come if something approached from behind. But if that was the case, he'd never know—he was much too exhausted to look back.

It made no difference. Had he seen a nothosaur coming, all he really could have done was to fall forward onto his face and make it easier for the creature to strike. There was nothing left in his legs.

There. A flicker of darkness against the white background. Closer now, but when he turned, it was gone. He tried to focus, but all he could really see was that the ground where he was looking consisted of broken, uneven patches. And that was only visible because of the shadows in the snow that separated patches of white from other patches of white.

Damn this stupid white-on-white world, anyway. His nightmares had always been dark, not brightly illuminated with the light reflecting from every available surface. It was maddening, confusing, insane.

He saw it again. It lasted longer this time. The figure was getting closer.

Whatever was coming was still distant, but his mind created the image of the grim reaper, black robes billowing in the wind, scythe glinting in the light. Death, coming for him as inexorably as any other natural force, indifferent to the ways of flesh and mortals. He tried to redouble his step, but only managed to stumble on the uncertain footing. It took superhuman effort to keep him from tumbling headlong.

Javier looked away. He was half-convinced that the oncoming figure lived only in his imagination. He tried to face the base, ignore it. Incredibly, the enormous distance actually appeared to have shrunk to something manageable. Just a few more hours… maybe a year… and he'd be there.

He put another foot ahead. And another.

Now there was no more doubt. There was no longer any room to doubt. The figure was fifty meters away, and he could see it clearly enough to realize that it held a blade that glinted in the sunlight. He hadn't been imagining it. The eternal nightless land had finally sent its angel of perdition after him.

"Javier!"

Strong arms suddenly supported him and he focused on the face in front of him.

"Breen?"

"Yeah. I thought you were a goner for sure. Is that Ingrid? What happened to the Australian?"

"Dead."

"Oh."

But Javier wasn't thinking about Smith's sacrifice. He just wanted to get Ingrid off his back. Sharing the weight would feel like heaven. Even as he lowered her to the ground so they could carry her between them, something nagged at him. In his addled state, he took a few moments to know what it was. It was important.

"Over there," Javier said, suddenly remembering.

Breen looked in the direction the Colonel was pointing. "There's nothing there."

Javier looked. The American was right. The empty white wastes stretched out forever.

But even though it wasn't visible, Javier knew that the angel of death wouldn't be gone. It was out there somewhere, just waiting for its opportunity. None of them, he knew, would be leaving this place of pale light alive.

***

Had it only been thirty minutes since he returned? It felt like he'd followed Clark Smith onto the snow a lifetime ago. He could barely remember what he'd been like then. The walk, burdened with responsibility for the life of another human being had represented his rebirth.

It was a touch of the sublime.

And then, the quotidian. A cup of stale coffee. Some crackers that Natasha had found stashed somewhere, and… he'd felt normal again, for the first time in ages.

Javier shook his head. He'd always considered himself a rock, the kind of guy who could go through the fire without losing his head. And there he was, seeing figures in the distance and having all sorts of prophetic visions.

Breen was looking over the FAL. He grimaced when he realized the clip was empty. "Did you hit anything?"

"Yeah. Killed one of the small ones."

The American grunted his approval. "Good. You should take extra ammo next time you decide to go after the nest, though."

"Good idea." There was a long, uncomfortable pause. "How is she?"

"Remarkably well, actually. I thought she was a goner, but once we got her stripped down, we realized that most of the blood belonged to someone else. Her own injuries are mostly minor, although she does have a couple of deep gashes I had to stitch. It's a good thing you found that first aid kit… It's not the kind of thing I would have attempted without decent anesthetic."

"I knew that would come in handy. So you're saying she's fine?"

"Unless there's internal injury… yeah, I suppose she is. She was pretty well dehydrated, but I put her on an IV."

Javier smiled. He'd been uncertain of Breen's decision to move out of the cafeteria and into the infirmary, but most of his objections had evaporated when they'd placed him on a soft bed and given him coffee. The rest had disappeared as soon as he realized that Breen intended to examine the Swedish scientist.

"I need to get back there."

"Go ahead. I'll be fine," Javier replied.

Breen left.

Natasha, who'd been sitting unseen on the couch, stood and closed the door.

"I… I want to apologize," she stammered.

"For what?" Javier asked.

"For… before."

Javier knew exactly what she was talking about. When he'd entered, half-carrying Ingrid, half-supported by Breen, she'd rushed forward and thrown her hands around his neck. She'd kissed him full on the mouth.

Now that he was feeling better, he was tempted to say something like 'I don't know what you're talking about, please be specific', but a single look at her anxious face deterred him. "There's no need to apologize. I'll forgive you if you promise me something."

She was suddenly wary. "What?"

"Never tell anyone."

Now she looked hurt. "Why not?"

"Because Argentine men aren't allowed to be kissed by beautiful women and not kiss them back. I'd get thrown out of the country."

She laughed with relief. "Then it didn't bother you?"

"Of course not. I just wish I'd reacted properly. A gentleman has standards."

"Would you like me to kiss you again?"

"If you like."

"Well you're going to have to wait." But she was smiling as she said it.

"What? Why?"

"Because you teased me. Now you will wait. And besides, I want to ask you about the American, and I don't want to forget."

"What about him? He's a spy. He'll probably stab us in the back as soon as we turn around."

"Do you really think so?"

Javier thought back at the man, appearing like the good Samaritan out of the haze and saving him from the snow, the dinosaurs and himself. "Maybe not."

"He wanted to go back to the *Irizar* after you left."

"How long was I gone?"

"When he wanted to leave? An hour. No more. Ten minutes later, he ran out and brought you back inside. I thought I'd lost you."

"Did he tell you to come?"

"I don't think he'll leave without me. He wants to take me back to America with him. He says it's the only place where I'll be safe."

Javier considered it. The men in balaclavas, the Russian government's decision to recover... something... at huge cost, all pointed to the fact that the American agent was right about that. She would definitely be safer in the US than in Argentina. "I think he might be right."

"There's another thing. He wants to take the chip out of my arm."

Javier sat silently for a minute. "He's serious about that?"

"I think so. He... he did an amazing job with Ingrid. I went in there because I didn't trust him. I thought he might..." She blushed. "But he was absolutely professional. He's not a surgeon, but he's definitely had some kind of training as a doctor."

"Then you should get the chip removed."

She nodded and, as if she'd been waiting for his permission, she tripped out of the room towards the operating room.

He sat there in a daze, wondering how he'd managed to miss his second chance at the kiss, and whether he'd ever have a third attempt.

With that thought, he dozed off.

***

A touch woke him. He didn't know whether minutes or hours had passed but unlike most times he'd had that sensation, Javier didn't care. What difference did it make in this land of eternal days?

He turned away from the contact, too tired to care if it was a nothosaur, but the contact was insistent. He opened his eyes to find Natasha's face inches from his own, a half-smile on her lips.

"I hope you haven't changed your mind," she said, pushing him further to his left.

Someone, he noticed, had put a thick comforter over him and Natasha had climbed under it. He could feel her chest against his. It felt warm and very female, even through the cloth of her sweater.

In response, he leaned forward and, opening his mouth, brushed his lips against hers, an exploratory gesture to see what she would do.

Her response surprised him. She pressed forward hungrily, greedily taking his mouth with her own.

Javier didn't have to be told twice. He joined the passion and was soon pressing himself at her, one hand behind her head, the other moving down her back.

He stopped himself. "Are you sure about this? I mean… you aren't going to regret it? It's not just because you're scared, is it?"

She laughed. "How should I know? All I know is that yes, I'm sure about this. I just wish I could take off my sweater. Stupid broken arm."

He let the hand continue down her back, pressing into the cloth of her clothing until he came to her ass… which was bare.

She pulled away, grinning wickedly. "Nothing wrong with my legs, though."

Javier lost himself in her.

CHAPTER 18

Snick.

The blade made a pleasant noise as it swiped along the stone she'd found. Camila didn't know if the flat grey rock, rounded by eons in the sea, was honing the edge or ruining the knife, and she didn't care. A blunted knife would hurt all the more.

The slut was riding Javier like there was no tomorrow, the kind of desperate lovemaking that you saw in the movies. She clearly didn't imagine that someone could be watching. Although, from the looks of it, she wouldn't have cared if she did.

Snick.

A reckoning was coming, and this woman, no matter how badly she'd been mistreated by the world, had chosen to align herself with the side of the oppressors, of the patriarchy and of the rich.

Even a woman from Russia should have been able to take a single look at the high-class Javier and understand that he was the enemy, a much greater enemy than even the strange creatures that roamed the open ice.

Snick.

So she would die, too. It was the right thing to do.

Giving herself to the enemy made her an enemy.

Snick.

The cold was beginning to get to her. She'd been out in the open for what seemed like hours, waiting and watching. She thought Javier was hers when he was carrying the woman back from wherever it was he'd found her, but that interfering American had spotted him just in time.

A second earlier, and he would have seen Camila ducking down behind a ridge.

Snick.

She should probably kill the American, too. After all, the American domination of the world, and its interference in Latin American politics for the past sixty years was what had made Javier and his kind possible in the first place.

But this man was not really one of the oppressors. He was a tool of the oppressors and, unlike the sailors, wasn't in a position to stop her yet.

Therefore, he would only die if he had to.

Snick.

She watched the figures in the window finish having sex. The initial mad rush had subsided first into a more rhythmic dance and then, finally, the woman had collapsed on top of Javier, and they'd become lost in a lingering embrace.

Almost as if they loved each other, she thought. The bitterness she felt wasn't for herself but for the Russian girl. Did she really think a man meant what she thought when he embraced her? Could she truly be that silly?

Camila didn't think so. They'd told her that the woman was a scientist herself, educated in Great Britain. She would have experience with men, know a little bit about their ways. Of course she'd know that they were more fickle than cats, loyal only to other men.

She thought of the men in her own life. Particularly about Juan Carlos. Juanca, as his friends and soccer buddies called him. He could have been the one... No. He *should* have been the one. He was the one.

It had all been going so well. They'd had their ups and downs, of course, but that was normal for any couple. She'd told him not to worry about it. He'd asked her for a little more space, but she'd held firm on that ground. She knew he'd be happier once they were married and could finish unifying their plans. There was no need to waste time with space, with projects that didn't run along the same track. Life was too short to become distracted.

At first, she didn't know what madness possessed him, or why he walked away from a perfect future... but then, with the help of her friends, she came to understand that many men were intimidated by women who were their intellectual and professional superiors. His masculine pride couldn't deal with being just a normal mid-level office worker while his girlfriend had received more and more attention from the scientific community, eventually earning leadership roles at the Museo de La Plata.

He'd pretended to be happy for her, of course. In fact, back then, she'd believed him. He truly did appear to be delighted. But now she knew the truth, knew how threatened he must have felt.

It was better that way. Juanca had been a good man in some regards; kind, funny, loving, but in the long run, being with her would have made him unhappy. His constant requests for space were just a false front behind which he hid other insecurities.

Javier, in a roundabout way, reminded her of him. Same kind of family, same kind of upbringing and same soft-spoken personality.

Yes.

She would enjoy killing him.

Snick.

And she would enjoy killing his little Russian whore even more.

***

Breen said nothing as they entered, just nodded to his right and said: "The coffee machine is working, take all you want." He'd settled down beside a window in the tiny nook that served as a kitchen for the infirmary.

Javier and Natasha descended on it and he stifled a laugh. They weren't even trying to disguise what they'd been doing.

He had no issues with it, other than the fact that he would have preferred for them to save their strength for more urgent pursuits. On the other hand, anything that helped them to relax was a positive… even if he knew that a relationship between them would create complications later.

The clock was ticking, but they still had plenty of time. Of the ten hours he'd been given, only four had passed. It wouldn't take them more than thirty minutes to return to the *Irizar* in normal conditions, although he preferred not to risk cutting it that close. But even allowing two hours, they had some time to kill.

"How's Ingrid?" Natasha asked.

"She's doing well. I'm letting her rest a bit."

Natasha nodded and drank. The coffee appeared to be much more important to her than the stricken woman at that particular moment.

"Can I ask you something?" Breen said.

Natasha blushed before saying: "Certainly."

"How did the sound machine on the fishing boat work?"

"That?" She seemed bemused by the question. "That was just a simple speaker, boosted by the shape of the hull to carry the sound long distances through water. There wasn't much science to it at all."

"I imagine it must have occurred to someone, though. Did you design it?"

"Oh, no. It was already there when I arrived. There's a man called Oleksandr Pripyenko, a paleontologist in St. Petersburg, who has a theory about dinosaur hearing, and the frequencies that they would hear. It's all based on the shape of fossil skulls and no one ever took him very seriously. The machine was built on his theories, just a speaker that broadcast on a specific tone, in rhythmic pulses." She chuckled. "Turns out he was right all along—too bad no one survived to tell him about it."

"You've survived."

"I thought you were going to kidnap me and have the CIA hide my voice from the world."

Breen felt uncomfortable at the direct way she said it, but not guilty. When he'd said that the Russians were very likely to kill her for what she'd seen, he meant every word of it. Russia was no longer the enemy of the West that it had once been—in many ways it had become an enlightened, modern society—but there were still things that, for strategic reasons, had to be kept secret. This certainly fell into that category.

And one of the most admirable things about Russians had always been their pragmatic approach to life's little problems. There was a legend about the space race that held that, while the U.S. was pouring millions into developing a pen that could write effectively in zero-g, the Soviets simply sent pencils.

Whether that old story was true or not, Breen didn't know. But it sounded true. It sounded consistent with the Russian approach.

So, faced with something like an embarrassing violation of international treaties, some countries might simply accept the consequences. Others would protest their innocence and attempt to discredit their accusers.

All of that would seem hugely unnecessary to a true pragmatist when you could solve it all with a single bullet.

He changed the subject. "So we can build one?"

"Sure. All we need is a couple of speakers and something to amplify with."

"What about the sound source?"

"Just download a rock song through that phone of yours.... But why would we want to build one? I thought the point was to stay away from the things, not call them to us."

"I was thinking that if we could get them to come here while we run for the *Irizar*, it would definitely go a long way towards making it much safer to run across the open ice."

"That isn't a bad idea."

"What isn't?"

They all turned towards the source of the new voice. Ingrid stood just inside the door, a blanket wrapped tightly around her body. She gave them a wan smile. "I'm not a ghost, you know."

Then her face fell. Breen had filled her in about what had happened while she wasn't present. He believed she was still processing the loss of her sister. It clearly hadn't hit her yet. Or at least not completely.

Javier rushed over to her. "How do you feel?"

"Much better now. I..." It was clear she was fighting back tears. "Thank you for what you did. I'm sorry I couldn't be more help out there. I still can't believe you went back for me. I can't imagine anyone being so brave. And Clark…" Now she was crying, unable to keep up the strong front.

Javier didn't even hesitate. He walked up and hugged the Swedish geologist. She hugged him back, tightly enough to look painful, and bawled into his shoulder. Breen watched Natasha out of the corner of his eye, but if the Russian was jealous, she didn't let on.

Ingrid composed herself and looked around the room. Breen expected another round of apologies, but the woman surprised him. "You were about to tell me what isn't a bad idea."

"We're thinking of setting up a sound lure to bring the creatures here while we try to get back to the *Irizar*."

"But why go back to the *Irizar*?"

"Because, it's better protection than this base, even if it isn't perfect."

Ingrid gave him a strange look. "Then why did you come here in the first place?"

Breen knew it was time for honesty. "I wanted to get a better look at the guys in black. Part of my job is to report on what they were doing."

"Did you know they would be here?"

"No. Not until they appeared, but once they were here, it was my duty to watch them."

"Fair enough, I guess. How does one build this snare?"

Breen released the breath he didn't realize he'd been holding. The one thing he didn't want to have to talk about is why he'd brought Natasha with him. An injured woman without recon experience wasn't exactly the standard choice for that kind of mission.

"The first thing we need are speakers."

They cautiously exited the infirmary and walked over to one of the barracks. The empty bunks and discarded possessions reminded Breen of the pile of frozen bodies in the nest. In that sense, the emptiness was even more chilling than the damage done to the room by the nothosaurs.

"No one thought to bring a stereo," Javier remarked.

"But we have one of these," Breen said. He pulled two round objects a little bigger than his fist from one of the bedside tables.

"What's that?"

"Cell phone speakers. Here's the headphone jack."

"Well, at least we won't have to leave our one working phone behind," Javier said. "This one is full of music, and still halfway charged." He showed the Russian women the screen of a phone he'd found in an open drawer.

Breen handed the speakers to Natasha, who plugged in the phone. They listened to the sound for a few moments at full volume before she turned the rig off. "I don't know if those will be strong enough. They're loud, but we need a certain amount of bass."

"That's a relief. I would have felt naked without it."

Javier gave him a hard look. "Any news about a rescue?"

"Only that we need to get back to the *Irizar*."

"All right. I think there might be some bigger speakers in the office. Let's go look."

Javier and the two women filed out of the barracks, Natasha stuffing the speakers into her jacket pocket with her good hand. Breen had taken the phone and was crouched under one of the beds in hopes of finding a bigger set of speakers, or maybe one of those bass boosters. If he knew one thing about soldiers out on boring duty, it was that they'd have their tunes with them, and be willing to share with anyone who couldn't shoot them to make them stop. The louder the better.

He was halfway under a bed when the wooden wall of the barracks exploded inward. That probably saved his life.

The nothosaur, one of the small ones, shook itself like a wet dog, but what actually flew off were chips of wood and plaster.

It was only distracted for a second, however. Almost too fast for Breen to react, it pounced onto him, or rather onto the bed he was under. The monster lifted the bed, mattress and all, and shook it like a cat shaking a mouse.

That was all the opening Breen needed. He pulled the FAL into position and opened fire on it.

The roar filled the room, dwarfing even the crash the creature made when it came through the wall. The nothosaur reared back, breaking a window in the process. Then it studied him.

The lay of the land was complicated. The reptile, injured, presumably enraged, stood between Breen and the door. He could hear the others yelling to him.

"Get back to the *Irizar*!" he shouted. "I'll deal with this one."

Then, not caring whether they paid any attention to him or not, Breen shot a short burst into the window nearest his position and dove out onto the rocks outside. Blood immediately began seeping into his eye, and he brushed it away as he got to his feet and sprinted towards the building he thought was the offices.

He was relieved to see that he'd guessed correctly. A pile of recently disturbed components marked what must have been Javier's attempts to revive the radio.

The colonel's recollection had been correct: a set of dusty speakers and an amplifier stood beneath a shelf across the room. Breen looked around and located a metal filing cabinet. He propped it against the door as best he could and headed for the speakers.

Breen pressed the power button, but nothing happened. He swore in frustration just as the door reverberated with the sound of something slamming into the frame. He was overjoyed that dinosaurs were as stupid as he'd always been told… even after going through a window in the barracks, the nothosaur appeared unable to realize that glass was much easier to penetrate than wooden doors.

He desperately followed the power cord, wiping blood from his forehead every moment. Finally, he found the plug and jammed it into the nearest outlet.

The building shook again.

"Dammit," he hissed. Time was running out. The last impact had actually caught part of the door and moved it inwards, displacing the cabinet a little. He could see the white of sunlight reflected off snow through the small opening.

It would take a really, really dumb animal to miss that.

He stabbed the power button and was relieved to see a small amber light blink on. Then he slammed the phone into place, inserted the cable into the aux plug and pressed play.

The soft sound of guitars emanated from the speakers.

"Nah," Breen said out loud, "that's not the way to listen to Metallica."

He turned the volume knob all the way to the right and smiled.

"That's more like it."

A single burst from the FAL took out the window, and he exited the office just as the door came down. He got around the building quickly enough that he was sure the monster hadn't seen him and then stopped to catch his breath.

He paused to catch his breath and to curse himself for being an idiot. Why had he bothered to do that? They couldn't really be certain that the sound would shield them from pursuit anyway. He could already be hundreds of meters away.

But if it did work… having the big sucker out of the way would be truly useful in attempting to prepare for its eventual attack on the *Irizar*. He tended to agree with Natasha's assessment that the largest of the creatures wouldn't just leave the icebreaker alone. It would be back.

But the longer it took, the better.

He slalomed between the tightly-packed buildings of the base in an attempt to throw off any pursuit and then headed out onto the ice. Javier,

Natasha and Ingrid had gotten clear of the base and could be seen, starkly outlined against the white background, a few hundred meters ahead.

He began to run after them when, from behind a large drift, the mottled skin of one of the small nothosaurs materialized in front of him. He froze. The thing was close enough that he could have reached out and stroked its chest, close enough to smell the stench of death it emanated.

Yellow eyes flickered briefly over him and then the head looked away, towards the base, from which the unmistakable chords of *Enter Sandman* could be heard clearly, even at this distance. It lunged off, running with a strange, uneven gait that made him think of a cross between a skink and a camel.

Desert creatures both. It certainly wasn't the kind of movement one expected on the icy plains near the poles.

But then, if it hadn't been unnatural and unnerving it would have been out of place somehow.

CHAPTER 19

The crew of the *Irizar* lowered a rope. The sailor who peered over the railing appeared shocked to see them, but wasted no time in getting men to assist the injured women on board.

"Did you see some sailors down there?" This was addressed to Javier. The fact that he was the only uniformed Argentine military man in the group apparently held a little weight.

"No," Javier replied.

"The lieutenant took some men to look for you. Everything was fine, he even reported that he found a survivor, but then we lost radio contact."

"We didn't see anyone." Javier didn't want to say what that meant: the men from the ship, probably friends of most of the crew, were most likely cold meat now added to the pile surrounding the eggs.

But everyone who met them knew what losing contact meant. Heads turned to look down at the deck, a quiet moment in memory of shipmates they never expected to see again.

Javier broke the somber mood. "What news? What is Buenos Aires saying? When are they coming to get us?"

"There's a ship on the way from Ushuaia with troops on board. They're going to get us out of here and then try to secure the airfield to fly in the Hercules. They don't want to land if there's any danger of the big monster destroying the plane."

"There was a team of Russians out there. They had no trouble. But the Argentine government refuses to risk it to rescue us?" Javier said. "No. Don't answer that. I already know what you're going to say. Just tell me when the ship will be here."

"A day from now. Well, twenty hours."

Javier saw Breen checking his watch. He wondered what the American knew and wasn't sharing with the rest of the team. Unfortunately, he had a feeling that he'd find out soon enough, and he suspected he wouldn't like what he learned.

"All right. Do you know if my cabin survived?"

"What floor were you on?"

"The second."

"I don't think so. But we moved her stuff," he pointed to Natasha, "out of the infirmary and into a belowdecks room."

Javier turned to her. "Mind if I join you? I really need to sleep."

Natasha smiled.

***

Breen watched the Colonel take the Russian woman aside. He checked his watch again. In five hours, a large helicopter would arrive to fly him—and as many others as he deemed suitable to his country's interests—to safety.

His orders were quite clear: he was expected to have Natasha with him when he boarded that chopper. As simple as that.

But, as always, his orders were emphatically not clear about how he should go about it. Was he expected, or indeed authorized, to shoot Colonel Balzano if the man attempted to stop him?

He supposed that if he did shoot Balzano, he would probably be fired. And if he failed to get the woman secured, he would be yelled at by the experts at Fort Belvoir.

All right. So the lesser evil would come from failure. International incidents and shooting high-ranking officers from the militaries of friendly nations was worse. Nevertheless, he could probably convince Javier of the advantages of putting the two injured scientists, and the only two female civilians, on the first vehicle out of the theater of operations.

That vehicle would be an American helicopter.

Failing that, Breen could try to sucker punch him. But he had to do it some time when no one was watching, and even then, the odds of success were limited. Javier wasn't some guy just off the turnip truck. He knew how these things went, knew that even though Breen had a healthy respect for the colonel, he knew the American wasn't above a certain amount of duplicity. Balzano might see him coming a mile away.

It was definitely something he had to think about.

Though he was utterly exhausted, Breen decided not to go back into his room—assuming it was even still standing—to rest. There would be plenty of time for that on the flight out.

He was much more concerned about what might happen to him in the interim. Five hours was still a long time, and judging by what he'd heard, no one had any inkling of where the big creature had gone off to. From what the sailors reported, after the second attack on the *Irizar*, the monster had sunk back into the depths. Some of the sailors speculated that with the amount of ordnance it had absorbed, it was probably dying, but Breen had his doubts. FAL bullets would be nothing more than pinpricks to a creature that size: annoying, possibly even painful, but unlikely to do much permanent damage.

A lot could happen in five hours… and though his body ached, he knew it could be suicide to spend the time resting.

Instead, he headed aft towards the storage room where his equipment had been held. To his relief, subsequent attacks from the big monster hadn't damaged the area, and his crates were still exactly where he'd left them.

His snowmobile, the item that had inhabited the largest crate might be dashed to pieces on the ice, but there were still a number of goodies in storage.

Although his superiors had told him that all the mission entailed would be a bit of driving around the Antarctic plain to points they'd tell him about later and doing a whole lot of watching, perhaps some infiltration work if he saw something suspicious, he was coming to believe that he should have questioned the briefing a little more closely. The Pentagon had plenty of resources, but it didn't often send recon people into the field with enough equipment to fight a small war.

And, like it or not, that was what he had. In certain parts of sub-Saharan Africa, the six RPGs he'd shipped with would have made him quite the warlord.

He packed a couple of them into a duffel bag. He could have armed them right there in the hold, but he really wasn't comfortable doing so in full view of witnesses. Part of it was his natural tendency to be secretive, but another part wondered what he'd say when the crew of the icebreaker asked him why he hadn't shared them once the nature of the threat to the ship became evident. A couple of well-placed missiles would have made a world of difference and probably saved a bunch of lives.

The answer was complicated, and the Argentines wouldn't have wanted to hear it: he was there to carry out a mission and, as long as the stuff going on around them didn't jeopardize that mission, he would not divert a single piece of equipment away from it.

Yes, the *Irizar* and its crew were in danger, but it wasn't his job to save them. He had to shut down and do what was needed in service of a much bigger picture.

Perhaps losing a ship today might mean saving an entire city from a biological attack tomorrow.

Unfortunately, most people didn't see things that strategically. How, they asked, could a soldier with a packful of MREs pass a starving village and not hand them out? How could anyone accept a single life as collateral damage? The truth was that, when taken in the greater context, those villagers, those men and women and children who would only appear in partisan newspapers or tabloid websites as victims of some atrocity, actually were a down payment in blood on lives that could, if the side of the angels emerged victorious, be saved later.

The true power players knew the score, both in the West and in the countries that opposed the Western way of life. Josef Stalin had once said that a single death was a tragedy but a million deaths were a statistic. He'd known exactly how to leverage both for his own ends. He understood strategy.

But most people didn't. That single death, that tragedy, colored and annulled their capacity to consider the bigger picture. They couldn't think beyond the death of that single innocent… no matter how it was explained to them that preventing that tragedy could have terrible consequences for the lives of many more. They just weren't built to see beyond it.

For some reason, Javier was the man he thought of as he headed back to the cabin area. The Colonel should have been ready to make the necessary sacrifices to reach his objectives. Even Argentines must teach their officers the realities of life…

And yet, the man struck Breen as a bit of a starry-eyed idealist. Competent, certainly. Brave… of that there was no doubt. But perhaps not the kind of man who'd do what had to be done without thought for the price. He didn't look like a guy who could see past the tragedy.

That made Breen nervous. He had a feeling in the pit of his stomach that the end of sacrifices was not yet at hand.

***

Javier wasn't thinking of Breen. He'd fallen asleep nearly immediately when his head hit the pillow in Natasha's room. He'd actually been relieved when she laid down with all her clothes on, hugged him tightly and closed her eyes. She was a stunning woman, but all he wanted was to get some rest.

Again, Javier slept without a sense of time. The next thing he knew, someone knocked on their door, and he spluttered to wakefulness, trying to remember where he was. Were they under attack?

The soft electric light reassured him. It felt safe somehow, civilized.

He looked down at Natasha. Her fine hair framed delicate features. The contrast between the peace he saw now and the mindless terror he remembered from the first time he'd seen her was striking. She hadn't heard the knock, but started slightly, muttering in her sleep when the sound repeated.

Javier disengaged gently and padded to the door. He cracked it open.

The ship's surgeon, haggard and sporting a couple of days of beard, stood in the hallway.

Javier pulled the door open all the way and gave the surprised man a bear hug. "I'm so glad you made it."

"Yeah, so am I. It was a close thing, though. I made the silly mistake of trying to pull an injured man across the deck. One of the creatures grabbed my pants and tried to pull me off the ship. If a sailor hadn't fired on it, I'd be dead now."

"And the guy you saved?"

"He was already dead when I got there. I wasn't able to do much with the other guys who'd been hurt. The injuries were either scratches or complete dismemberment with not much in between. We set up an infirmary belowdecks, but I've only got one patient that I couldn't discharge after applying a few bandages. Well, two now that you've brought that Swedish girl on board. How come every woman you encounter gets brought back to me in terrible shape?"

"It's a knack I have."

"Well, stop it."

Javier was about to continue the banter when he remembered that a couple of other women he'd set out with—and a good number of young men—were never going to return, not even in less-than-mint condition. "What brings you here?" he said instead, lamely.

"I'm here to check on my other patient. And to ask what you were doing in her bed. She needs to be resting."

"She was. We fell asleep immediately."

"I know. I listened at the door before knocking. But… it would still be better if you left her alone. She was in surgery just a couple of days ago. She shouldn't be doing… any kind of strenuous activity."

"You should talk to Breen about that. He's the one who took her off the ship in the first place."

"I already talked to him. He says she was safer with him than on a ship being attacked by Godzilla." The doctor shook his head. "He's insufferable, but I can't really say I can fault his logic."

"Tell him he can come in," Natasha said. "I'm awake now."

The doctor entered and gave the arm a quick but thoroughly professional once-over. "Have you felt any pain?"

"No."

"Have you had to do anything strenuous?" He raised an eyebrow at both of them as he said this.

"We fell off a snowmobile. I suppose we were going… maybe twenty-five or thirty kilometers an hour…"

"Please tell me she's kidding."

"I was there. It's true. But we also fell into a hole. The impact killed the Swedish woman's sister."

The doctor nodded gravely. "Did you hit anything?"

"No. I think I kind of slid along and landed on Javier. Everyone else hit much harder than I did, and Breen and Clark took a huge impact."

"Clark… The Australian? Did he…"

Javier shook his head. "He didn't make it. But Ingrid is only here because he wouldn't let the creatures back there keep her. He died getting her out of there. How is she?"

"She has some beautiful puncture wounds which are going to take some time to heal. Did she hit her head at any time?"

"No? Why?"

"Because she was crying uncontrollably, even after she got on board. Not just crying, either, but screaming and punching and kicking out. It didn't seem like the composed and calm young lady I remember. So I wanted to know if she might have suffered a concussion at any time."

Javier shrugged. "She might have suffered just about anything. She got snatched by one of those things and dragged five hundred meters. We all thought she was dead, disemboweled and probably eaten. We didn't even ask her about bumps in the head." He laughed bitterly. "In my opinion, she probably just realized everything that happened to her. Hell, I'd be more worried if she was acting rationally. Can we see her?"

"Well, I've got her under sedation downstairs. She should be asleep for a few hours. I hope she's not as aggressive when she wakes. You can come then."

The doctor wandered off. Javier got the sense that he didn't have too many places to be, and was just wandering the ship trying to find evidence that the last twenty hours or so—what time *was* it, anyway?—had been a bad dream.

Javier faced Natasha. He grinned. "I guess it's just you and me, now."

She blushed. "Yes."

"Are you having regrets?"

"No. None. You?"

"Only that your arm is broken and the doctor has ordered me not to make you do anything strenuous."

"Forget the doctor."

Their lovemaking this time was more measured, less desperate, and when they were done, Natasha fell asleep again.

Javier wanted nothing more than to join her and he found himself exhausted… but unable to sleep. He contented himself with just watching her breathe.

He wondered what this meant… if it meant anything. A small part of him was still convinced that she would come to her senses and realize that whatever she thought she felt for him was just the stress of the past few days. Was she just lost and confused, looking for something, anything, to anchor to?

Then he felt ashamed at the thought. Natasha had been a rock through the whole ordeal, there was no reason to suppose that she would need to cling to some random guy just to get through, with the intention of dropping him like a hot potato when she got out the other end.

Those were his own insecurities speaking.

His entire upbringing had revolved around family values, with the married couple as the axle around which the entire world revolved. His parents had been that way, and the fact that his father worked for the defense ministry offered stability and a respectable framework. They'd only moved once, when he was seven, to the interior of the country, but even that had only meant living in Córdoba for a couple of years—a city of a million people, and not a huge sacrifice by any measure.

But when he'd gotten out of officer school, his first assignment had been in Misiones province, well up in the northern part of the country, and his girlfriend of the time had flatly refused to come with him. On his first leave, he'd returned to Buenos Aires to try to talk her around, but she'd moved on… and told him so in no uncertain terms.

Relationships had come and gone after that, following a similar pattern. No one he was interested in appeared to want a relationship with a man stationed in far-off places, and though the girls in the places he was posted to would have been perfectly content to put that right, he also found that they were much too provincial. Their world tended to be limited to a very small subset of interests, all intensely local, while his own, perhaps privileged, upbringing meant that he found those limits unpalatable.

It was a cycle he'd never managed to break. He cycled through posting after posting and, by the time he returned to Buenos Aires as a major, he'd pretty much believed that he was destined for eternal bachelorhood.

The fact that he was now lying beside a beautiful, successful, smart woman who, if she wanted to, would have his heart wrapped around her little finger when they got back to civilization.

If she wanted…

Hard experience had taught him that she would take one look at his life and decide she wanted no part of it, disappearing to wherever the rest of them had gone off to. And, really, he couldn't blame her. He'd do the same in her position.

Javier plugged his phone into the wall and got a black screen… he didn't even have enough charge to use it while it began to come back to life.

He really wanted that phone working again. Not knowing what time it was had been driving him nuts. He made a mental note to buy a watch—a good one like all the other senior officers wore—as soon as he made it back to Buenos Aires.

The memory of being out on the ice, with that eternal soft sunlight falling on his head made him shudder. It was enough to drive anyone insane.

CHAPTER 20

The *ARA Almirante Irizar* was a wounded beast, and Camila mourned. Torn metal jutted from it in several places, particularly around the upper levels of the command area. She didn't know the names of ship parts, but there was no mistaking the destruction.

Her sadness was tempered with fury. It was becoming more and more obvious to her with every passing moment that the government had known it was sending the lightly-armed *Irizar* and its crew into a dangerous place. *That* was why command of the science project had been assigned to the inadequate Colonel Balzano, and, much more tellingly, that was why there was an American spy along for the ride. It was obvious to anyone with eyes to see.

Still, they hadn't hesitated. In a way, it was no surprise that the neo-fascist government had bent over for the *Yanquis*. They might call themselves centrists, but everyone knew that centrists were just fascists who were too ashamed to admit it. Centrism was for those without conviction.

Look where it had gotten them. Argentina's only icebreaker, a hero ship which was the pride of the nation's navy, torn to pieces by some Monsanto monstrosity.

She knew exactly what had happened: the Americans needed to see what the new monster they'd created could do, so, instead of testing it in the desert in Utah or someplace where it might put American lives at risk, they'd hatched this plan. Of course, getting the Argentine government to agree would have simply been a question of allowing them a loan at a decent interest rate. The government was always short of funds, even though these right-wingers spent most of their time cutting subsidies from the poor families who needed them most.

Of course, one couldn't just send out a couple of warships to test the thing. That would be too obvious; the Americans probably wanted to keep their pet creatures secret. So what to do? She was looking at the answer: neglect to warn an already scheduled mission into the area, complete with civilians, about the danger and then sit back and watch the carnage. Everyone would believe that it had been an unfortunate turn of events—no one would suspect that the crew had been deliberately sacrificed.

But that was because most outside observers didn't know how fascists thought. Camila knew better.

She scanned the decks of the *Irizar*, trying to pick out Javier or his slut. It was difficult. She was hidden from view by some broken pieces of sea ice pushed aside when the ship had come in, so she could watch without risk, but she was nearly a hundred meters away and behind the ship, which made positive identification of the small figures on deck extremely difficult.

She would know as soon as he appeared, though.

What would be the best way to deal with him once she spotted him? Getting aboard the *Irizar* without being noticed would be damn-near impossible, and there was no question of waiting for nightfall. It was obvious that they were trapped in a spirit world into which night would never come again.

However, even this place had rules. The rules of a mad underworld, perhaps, but rules all the same, and she knew that, when the time came, an opportunity would present itself. That was how things worked.

Her knife made her happy. How fitting that she would do away with the agents of the empire with nothing more than a bit of sharpened metal. The tools she needed had fallen to hand, and so would the chance to slip aboard unseen.

The ice below her began to tremble violently, in a way that could only mean one thing. Camila smiled.

Yes, things were falling into place.

***

This time, Javier knew that they were going to be hit even before the sound of tortured metal reverberated across the ship.

"Come on," he said, shaking Natasha. "We need to get out of bed."

"Whaaaa?" her voice trailed off and she tried to turn back around and return to sleep, but he shook her a little more vigorously.

"The monster. It's coming."

That got her attention. "How do you know? I can't hear anything."

He was dressing quickly. "Everything's shaking. The only thing I can think of that might cause that is something big pushing ice away near us. That or an earthquake. Either way, we're going to want to be dressed when it hits."

She grumbled, still half-asleep, but moved to replace her panties and the thick Antarctic-weight pants. Her socks had remained on her feet throughout.

Javier helped her with her boots and then they raced out onto the deck. Men were already running along, towards the front of the ship.

"Stay here," he told Natasha, and ran after them.

About ten steps in, he realized that the infuriating woman had ignored him and was only a few steps behind. She moved well considering her broken wing, but what use she thought a wounded civilian would be in the upcoming fight, he had no idea.

In fact, he was skeptical about how useful he, himself, would be. He was armed only with a Browning pistol. If the big one appeared, the gun would be just as useful as spitting, or, in a pinch, attacking it with his fists.

A patch of ice ahead of the ship lifted, a clawed forepaw the size of a car emerged and, with much groaning and the snapping of ice ringing like rifle shots through the cold air, the creature's head emerged from under cover.

It roared, whether in anger or triumph, Javier didn't know, but the sound shook the ship.

Pandemonium. A sailor ahead of him opened fire. Another, in an inexplicable move, threw himself, screaming, over the rail. All he achieved was to land on the ice a few meters away, yelling in pain, probably from multiple fractures to his legs. Everyone seemed to be running somewhere.

Cooler heads had thrown rope ladders from the front of the *Irizar* and were already climbing down onto the ice to attempt to keep the monster from reaching the icebreaker. A man standing beside the ladder handed Javier a rifle as he disembarked.

Javier turned, caught Natasha's eye and repeated: "Stay here. There's nothing you can do down there. Here, take my phone. If I don't come back and you do, call my parents. Tell them I love them." Then he descended.

It came as little surprise that the attack hadn't caught the American off guard. Breen was directing traffic. He had a FAL in one hand and a bulky bag hanging from his shoulder. Javier gave it a hard look and wondered what weaponry the American was holding back.

But there was little time to think. The men were organizing into three groups, one that would hit the creature on each flank and a third that would try to hold the center and keep it from hitting the *Irizar* again.

If he'd been in command, Javier would definitely have sent someone to attack from the rear… an animal should be easy to confuse if it didn't know where the pain was coming from, but attempting to change the order of battle now would only delay the defense. Any plan would be better than milling around trying to figure out new orders on the fly.

Javier was assigned to the group on the right. There wasn't much staging, they just stood in a nervous clump for an eternal minute, hoping the overscale nothosaur wouldn't decide to strike while they waited. Once everyone was in position they charged over the ice, guns blazing.

For a few seconds there, at the very beginning, Javier was convinced that the charge was actually going to work. The nothosaur roared and reared back. Only its two front legs were out of the water, and these, as it flinched, struggled to get purchase against the colossal weight pulling the creature back.

It scrabbled madly and slipped nearly five meters.

Emboldened by this unexpected success, the mixed group of sailors and soldiers redoubled their advance, closing to within just a few armlengths, emptying magazines into the monster's flanks and head.

The nothosaur suddenly appeared to realize where it was, and the nature of the terrain beneath its forepaws. Claws suddenly drove deep into the ice and its backwards motion was arrested. Its apparently unstoppable slide into the dark water halted and the mountainous animal teetered for a moment, balanced between two colossal forces: gravity and the strength of its own claws.

The claws won.

Inch by inch at first, and then meter by meter, the grey body emerged from the hole in the ice. The entire process took only a few seconds and it looked like a mountain was moving in front of them. The effect stunned the men who, instead of running for cover, stood gaping.

"Retreat!" Javier shouted, but his words—and those of some others also trying to get the men to run back towards the *Irizar*—were lost in the howling wind. No one moved.

Then the nothosaur's rear legs were out and it stood horse-like on the ice with its tail the only member still underwater. Men still stared in awe.

It roared and reared up on its hind legs as it had when attacking the ship earlier. The men nearest, the group on the left across from Javier's position, appeared to realize their danger and attempted to escape, but it was too late. Like a cat pouncing on a favorite toy, the nothosaur jumped onto them.

The world shook. Javier was certain that the crushing weight had to have broken through the ice. But when he looked over again, the monster was still above the surface and the group of men had... vanished. A couple of isolated figures, faster or luckier than the rest were disappearing into the distance, but the majority—once Javier managed to understand what he was looking at—had been corralled by the front legs and crushed to a pulp by the falling weight. In that cluster of uniforms and blood, nothing moved. Thirty people, wiped out in a flash.

The soldiers and sailors stationed in the central formation retreated and the nothosaur attacked them. The pitched battle became a race back to the *Irizar*, with the men barely ahead of the thing from their nightmares.

The rope ladders were their undoing. As men and women milled about under the bow of the icebreaker, the distance closed and then, seconds later, disappeared.

A lucky few of the central group managed to disappear over the railing and into the ship before death reached them but most suffered a fate similar to the first bunch. Javier watched the carnage and wondered how many of the ship's complement were being massacred. Forty? Fifty?

The view was obstructed, but one image stayed with him. The nothosaur's front paw swept the ground and two small rag dolls flew into the air, describing beautiful parabolic arcs dozens of meters high before disappearing behind an ice ridge. Two more men dead, he realized; there was no way a human body could survive the impact at the far end of such a flight.

Javier's own group had scattered. Some ran towards the ship. Others away from the monster out into the wild white wastes. Only two had remained with him, standing together to his right he turned to them.

A young woman looked back at him. The two sailors with FALs were both female.

"What do we do, Colonel?"

She sounded calm and collected in spite of everything they'd just witnessed. Both of the women were dark-haired and dark-skinned with slight builds of medium height. They could very easily have been sisters.

Javier found himself hoping that they weren't, that no set of siblings other than Ingrid and Anna had sailed with them. Losing two sons or daughters was too much for any family to bear… and it looked increasingly likely that anyone who'd embarked with the *Irizar* would be dead before too long.

"Try to find cover. Hopefully someone on board will think to use the 40mm guns. If they do, they might be able to stop it. But for now, all we can do is hope to stay out of sight."

They looked around. The woman who'd spoken climbed onto a low ice block displaced by the big monster's emergence. She looked for a likely spot. "I think there's some kind of cave, a loop in the ice, just over there, maybe fifty meters away. We might be able to hide there."

Javier turned to look in the direction she was pointing and missed what happened next. The first clue he had that anything was amiss came when the side of his face was sprayed with warm liquid.

He absently reached up to wipe his face, still looking for the cave, and only when he realized that the liquid was too thick to be water did he look at his fingers. They were covered with blood and bits of flesh.

He turned stupidly to see a nothosaur, one of the small ones, savaging one of the women. The other girl, the one who'd been pointing, already lay dead, torn to pieces in the initial onslaught.

Javier didn't react consciously. Whatever shred of basic training still survived in him took over and he pressed the trigger and held steady against the recoil. Once again, an entire magazine was spent and one of the small nothosaurs lay dead at his feet.

Full consciousness returned slowly. When he realized what was happening, he was halfway towards the cave, watching three more of the smaller creatures—he was almost certain they were the final survivors of that clutch—advancing into the fray behind him.

He didn't care. As long as the creatures were distracted, they wouldn't bother him.

***

Breen watched the massacre from a slight ridge. He'd been trying to arm one of his two RPGs, but hadn't been quick enough. The stupid gloves had slowed him down, and then he'd had to run to find a better position. By the time he was ready to fire, two of the groups from the ship consisted mostly of mangled bone and torn cloth.

He felt sick. While the Argentine and American governments might have different objectives on this mission, he'd marched to war with these men and the color of their uniforms made no difference. They were fighting the same enemy, and that meant they were brothers in arms… even if the foe was a little unusual.

He'd wanted to save them, thought he could help out. Now, most of them were dead.

But there was still a chance to help the people still on board.

Breen put the launcher on his shoulder and took aim. A trail of smoke showed him the path of the tiny missile. He scored a direct hit on the nothosaur's shoulder.

A large crater appeared in the mottled grey flesh and the creature screamed. This wasn't the deep-throated roar of its rage, this was a shriek of pure animal pain. Blood poured down its side in a cataract.

But, though it reared and bucked, the monster showed no signs of having been mortally wounded. It landed on all fours again with another bellow of pain and turned towards Breen.

The American smiled. Even though, in theory, he was supposed to remain undetected and fight from the shadows, he was used to looking death in the face. He'd smiled in the face of impossible odds in dusty battlefields from Pakistan to South Sudan and in the humid jungles of Nicaragua. This was the way it was supposed to be.

And, unlike most times when operational security broke down and left him face to face with angry enemies bristling with weapons, he had the advantage. The enemy he was fighting could only react instinctively. Its intelligence might be that of a bright dog… but was likely much less. Yes, it had been bred to be a hunter, but it had been bred to hunt underwater. On land, that advantage disappeared.

The main thing—the only thing—the ugly bastard had going for it was its sheer size. That was the only reason it was hard to stop. The small ones were easy targets, falling over after a few well-placed bursts from the FALs. This one would be the same… if it wasn't so fucking big.

Nevertheless, Breen knew he held all the cards. He'd already established to his satisfaction that he could hurt it badly. Now it was just a question of hitting it where it did more damage.

He had the ultimate advantage: nothosaurs had never invented rocket propelled grenades.

The creature's eyes locked on his position, so Breen sprinted up a rise to his right. He had a few seconds before the thing reached the spot where he'd been, and he wanted to be on the highest ground possible to take his shot.

He settled the RPG on his shoulder and was satisfied to see that the nothosaur limped, favoring the place he'd shot it. Any well-prepared fighting force would make mincemeat out of one of these if they caught it.

Hell, if anyone had suspected what they'd be walking into, the Argentines could have made a fortune. They could have sold the ultimate hunt to some billionaire nutjob. They would probably have had to listen to the ecologists forever after that, but it would have been worth it.

Also, this evil thing deserved to die a thousand deaths.

He nearly pressed the activation stud, but held back. It was still too far away… If he missed, or failed to hurt it badly enough, he was dead and so was everyone on the ship.

Steady… Steady.

At thirty meters, he felt his heart racing like a train, and the butterflies were partying in his stomach. But he let it get closer. It was leading with its head. There was no reason to hurry the shot. Nothing could fall on him until it got there, and stung once already, it was moving cautiously.

Twenty meters.

It roared. He smiled and shot it in the mouth.

The grenade flew true, right between the two rows of man-sized teeth. The smoke trail disappeared into the dark throat.

There was an explosion and, half a second later, a shower of foul-smelling gore.

Breen's smile widened. He'd definitely done mortal damage. All that remained now was to hold his ground as the creature fell.

There was no scream. Whatever he'd hit had apparently not been connected to pain-sensitive nerves, but horrendous internal bleeding would drop it in 3… 2… 1…

As the massive jaws closed around him, Breen thought that, had it been a Hollywood movie, the creature would have dropped inches from his feet.

Breen's smile disappeared as he was swallowed to drown in a pool of stomach acid.

CHAPTER 21

The monster dragged itself across the snow towards the hole from which it had emerged, leaving a trail of bright red on the white surface. When it disappeared under the surface, distant cheers could be heard.

Camila watched it for some moments. She'd had an excellent view of the American as he attacked it. While she had nothing but contempt for the imperialist aspirations of the capitalist north, the man, just a working class stiff with a crap job, had been a paragon of bravery. He hadn't even flinched as the monster devoured him.

But like most heroes of the people, he wouldn't be remembered in the history books, written by the oligarchy to glorify their own. He'd likely be remembered by no one other than—if he was lucky enough to have one—his family. For a few years more, he'd live in someone's memory, and then he'd be forever gone.

So Camila sat and thought about him.

She had other things to do, but there was no rush. Time wouldn't begin to flow normally again just because they'd finally managed to hurt the big monster. They were caught here until the end of time. It was the universe giving justice to the unjust, and the person chosen to deliver the blows was Camila herself. It was at once an honor and a privilege to have been selected.

Mourning time over, she stood and stretched. The wind was unrelenting now, and she was chilled to the bone, summer or no summer. But like time itself, that didn't matter either. Eternal cold was just another part of their sentence.

She strode over the snow.

***

Javier couldn't believe what he'd just seen. Breen had sacrificed himself in a blaze of glory to save everyone on board the *Irizar*. Whatever he'd hit with the RPG might not have been enough to kill the monster, but it had proved to be sufficient to remove its desire to keep fighting. The creature crawled away and disappeared. Javier hoped there were sharks down there who might get a scent of its blood in the water. Being torn apart by hungry fish was the way that that thing deserved to die.

He stood in the entrance to the shallow ice cave, some kind of depression in the snow, and looked around. Though the biggest of the nothosaurs was off the board, he knew there were at least three of the smaller ones out and about. Those were just as deadly and, after emptying the clip of the last FAL, Javier was back to his handgun as the only way to defend himself.

Though he searched deep inside, Javier couldn't find the will to move, even after the largest of the creatures was long gone. He looked in the direction of the icebreaker, but all he could really see was the very top of the superstructure, where the antennae and satellite dishes had once perched and which now consisted mainly of jagged and broken metal.

A dark figure in the distance appeared to be heading his way. It was moving slowly, picking its way through the broken ice, still a hundred meters away.

Javier stepped out of the cave to get a closer look. Surely it couldn't be...

He never finished the thought. Something cold made contact with the exposed skin of his neck, the only part of his body other than his face not covered from the elements.

"Don't move," a voice said softly in his ear.

The coldness, he realized with a start, was a knife beside his jugular.

"Good. Now, the first thing I'm going to do is to remove the pistol from this holster. If you so much as twitch, I'll give you a big red smile. Do we understand each other? If we do, don't nod." A strange giggle followed the words.

Javier was in shock. This was a bolt out of the blue, so completely unexpected that he was having trouble processing what was happening. It even took him a few seconds to understand that the person with a knife at his throat was a woman… and that the voice sounded familiar.

"There we are. Now turn around… slowly."

He obeyed. And then smiled.

"Camila! You're all right! We thought they'd gotten you."

Her eyes didn't waver, and neither did the pistol she now held. "You can't get rid of me that easily."

Confusion reigned. "What do you mean? We searched for you but you were nowhere to be found… well, we didn't search the pile of bodies too closely."

"I meant what I said. You can't get rid of me that easily. I can only imagine how happy you were to see I was gone. One less enemy of your kind."

"I don't know…"

"Shut up!" Camila waved the gun in his face. "I have absolutely no interest in listening to your lies. I'm not just some powerless ignorant who will do your bidding. Now get in the cave and kneel down. I don't want anyone stumbling on us before we're done."

Javier said nothing. He didn't know what to say. All he wanted was to get back to the *Irizar*, to see if Natasha was all right. He waited to see what Camila would say next. Hopefully, now that she was back with the crew, and safe, she would calm down.

She seemed surprised to realize that he wasn't going to respond. "Listen to me well Javier *Fucking* Balzano. If you don't play the fool, I'll make it quick, but you need to hear the judgement before we finish."

"Judgement?"

"Of course. Did you really think you could just go through life as an oppressor and nothing would happen to you? Just like that? Well, I'm here to tell you different."

"An oppressor?" he laughed. "Of who?"

"Of the people who give their lives so you can be comfortable atop the pyramid."

"Doesn't God judge those things?" Javier replied. He wasn't a practicing Catholic, but it was as mild an answer as anyone could give in Argentina. Everyone was Catholic, even if no one ever went to church.

"I don't buy into the fiction of the church, either. We live in the 21st century, Javier. The tide has turned, and people like you don't run the world any more. It's time you realized that."

He had to laugh. "People like me? I'm just a guy trying to work his way up through the ranks. I'm about as far from running the world as you can be without actually being on a different planet. If I ran the world, I'd ask them to give me something better than my two-room apartment."

She stamped her foot. "Don't even think about pretending to be poor with me. You don't have the faintest idea what it really means to be powerless. Think of the plight of the real poor, people who know what it's like to be hungry. Have you ever been truly hungry?"

He remembered the survival training and other times out in the field, but he said nothing. It wasn't what she'd meant, and that answer would only enrage her further. He remained silent.

"I thought so. You can't even understand what it means to be poor. But that's just the tip of the iceberg of the people you oppress. What about the native Argentines, the people who were here before we Europeans arrived? Or, even women. Have you stopped to think about the plight of women in our society?" She sneered. "Oh, I almost forgot. You're from the upper classes. Maybe the Opus Dei hasn't mentioned that it's not a great idea to make women have ten or fifteen kids?"

"I don't have any children, Camila."

"That's not what I'm talking about, and you know it!" This last was a screech, and for the first time since he'd realized who his assailant was, Javier wondered if he should rush her. This was a stressful time for everyone, and she might do something stupid before she came to her senses.

The question was whether she would react in time to fire before he could reach her. Normally, he'd have expected a woman to be unable to fire the gun, but the first thing Camila had done when he'd handed it to her was to thumb the safety. She could shoot him if she chose.

Maybe if he dove at her feet she would be caught out. He tensed.

"Are you even listening? You're here to be judged."

"If this is a trial, don't I get to defend myself?"

"Why should you? None of your victims gets to choose to avoid being oppressed by you."

"Why do you insist on that? I have never oppressed anyone. I've spent my entire life protecting my people."

"Correction. You spend your days ordering the people who do the protecting around. If things get tricky, you'll be the one sitting in an office giving instructions, while the sons of the poor do all the dying."

"Listen…"

"Stay where you are. If you move, I'll shoot you."

"All right. Calm down. Just remember that if you shoot me, you'll be the one on trial when we get back."

"We aren't going back. Haven't you noticed? We're not in the world we knew anymore. You might think we're in Antarctica, but we haven't been here since we landed. The sun hasn't set, and it will never set again. We've moved beyond. This isn't the world of men, it's a place of judgement."

For a second he remembered feeling the same thing, out on the ice. For the barest instant, he wondered if she might actually be right. Then he mastered himself. "Don't be silly. It's just the way the sun moves in the summer. You're a scientist, you should understand that."

"So you admit that the fact that you were assigned to lead our expedition was just so the army could control us?"

"What? No. Where did you even get that idea?"

"One sees things a lot more clearly once you accept that you're never going back to your old life."

"Come on, Camila. Let's get you back to the ship." A thought struck him. "When was the last time you ate anything?"

"Don't try to change the subject. You know perfectly well that you left me to die in that concrete box with all the other people who weren't from your class. What did you care about my students? They were just laborer's sons."

"Are you insane? And besides, what is this about my class? As if you weren't just as much a part of my class. Where'd you go to school, anyway?"

She hesitated and Javier knew he'd struck a nerve. There were subtle cues that one could spot in Argentina to tell whether a person came from a well-to-do background. Though Camila never wore designer labels or spoke of her life in any detail, other than the single slip about having sushi once a week, Javier would have bet quite a bit of cash that she was from an upper middle class or upper-class family. He'd never have found any takers for that bet, either. Even the most innocent soldier from way out in the boonies would have spotted her a mile off. Maybe it was the way she stretched her words in what Argentines called the language of the porteños, the people from Buenos Aires, so-called because the city had long been the country's most important seaport. If that wasn't it, there was something else, working below the level of consciousness that was giving him the vibe.

"Where I'm from makes no difference. It's where I choose to be that matters."

"Yeah, eating sushi once a week. I suppose you must be choosing a strange kind of poverty."

She took three steps forward and smashed the gun across his face, breaking his lip.

He cursed himself for being caught by surprise. Not because of the pain—the blow had done no serious damage—but because her attack had been the perfect moment to take the gun away from Camila. He should be able to disarm her with little trouble once she became distracted… but would she become distracted again?

"I've been at every demonstration. I've stood in the rain in front of the house of Congress to pressure the plutocrats inside to remember the people. I've marched against the International Monetary Fund, I've been at all the rallies in favor of legalizing abortion. The fact that these things won't benefit me or my family directly make them more noble, not less."

"More noble than what?"

"Than people like you, who allow the poor to be trodden underfoot."

"What do you know about that? What do you know about me? You know absolutely nothing, other than the fact that I'm in the army and that you're mad at me for leading the expedition."

"Do you really think it's about that? Do you think the entire universe would shut us off for something as silly as a job title? No.

There's so much more here at stake than the fact that your ego was too big to accept having a woman in charge."

Javier just stared at her. How could she possibly be serious? "I had no say in this. I didn't want this assignment. If it had been up to me, I'd be back in Buenos Aires with my friends."

"I already told you. This isn't about you. It's about bigger things, justice on a cosmic scale."

"I have no idea what you're talking about."

She was walking to and fro now as she spoke, waving the gun around in distraction but too far away to lunge at. He wondered if he should try it anyway. How long before she tired of the crazy talk and just shot him?

She suddenly stopped and smiled at him sadly. "No. I suppose you don't. Ironic, isn't it, to die before you've understood… well, anything, really." She shrugged. "But it's not my job to enlighten you, just to judge you."

She turned back to him, gun steady now. She was silhouetted against the mouth of the cave and, fifteen meters behind her…

Natasha.

He stayed perfectly still. Every bone in his body wanted to scream to her that she should run to get help, to save herself from this crazy person. But he knew that to do so would only serve to call Camila's attention to her.

Natasha came closer, apparently unaware of what was happening in the cave and then she stopped. A look of alarm crossed her features and then, without warning, she disappeared off to the side of the cave.

Javier relaxed. She probably wouldn't be in time to bring the crew to save him before things in the cave came to a head—he was tensing for a final suicidal lunge—but she would be safe, and she would be able to tell people what had happened to him. They could track Camila down and arrest her.

The scientist smiled at him. "So I guess this is it. Since you won't be able to understand the deeper nature of your crimes, let me just say this: the powers that hold us here have given me authority to judge you. I've done that, and found you guilty of oppressing the brave and true workers of the world."

She raised the gun and Javier was about to spring out of the way when they heard a noise outside.

"What is that?" Camila asked. She kept the gun trained on him.

"It… It sounds like Metallica," Javier replied. The riff from *Enter Sandman* was easy to identify, even though the bass from whatever speakers here carrying the music was a bit tinny.

Was it a tribute to Breen? After all, that was the same song the American had chosen at the base… but only a few people knew that.

And then it hit him. That song was on his cellphone, and the speakers, the last he'd seen of them, had been in Natasha's pocket. Had she actually set up the system here on the ice? If so, what was she trying to achieve? Even if she succeeded in distracting Camila, which, for the moment, it appeared she had, the woman was armed, and Natasha wasn't. Besides, the battery on his phone wouldn't hold out for long it that was what was powering those speakers.

Camila backed out of the cave slowly, keeping him covered. She emerged and looked around. Left, right. It was clear from her body language that she couldn't find the source of the interruption.

"Show yourself!" she yelled.

Javier decided it was now or never. If she was a good shot, she'd fill him with lead long before he made it near her, but he had to try. He rolled to one side and then, using the impetus from the roll, came to his feet.

His eyes never left the gun. Camila's reflexes were good. As he was standing, she was bringing the Browning to bear. He would never make it unless she missed him completely.

Then the completely unexpected happened. The gun wavered as Camila suddenly pointed it away. Three shots rang out.

He hesitated for a moment then, as he was about to close the gap, something dropped from above the mouth of the cave, eclipsing the wan light for a moment. It landed with a thud atop Camila.

The woman screamed.

For a single second, Javier thought the shape must have been Natasha. She could have climbed around the cave and dropped in when Camila went to investigate the music. That had to be it.

But the figure was much too large to be Natasha. As his eyes came to grip with the scale, the black blob resolved itself into a nothosaur, one of the small ones. The creature gripped Camila with its jaws to the sound of cracking ribs and squelching noises that didn't bode well for her and then bounded into the distance.

Javier emerged and picked up the fallen Browning. There should still be a few bullets in it.

The music had stopped. He hoped that was because Natasha realized it would attract more of the creatures, and not because she'd been crushed between razor-edged teeth.

Concern for her flooded him. "Natasha?" he called.

"Not so loud. Do you want to be lunch for the next one?"

She emerged from the side of the cavern and they embraced. Then she pulled back and gave him a hard look. "You know you're going to have to explain that, don't you? In the middle of all of this, you must have really done something to that girl for her to forget everything that's happening around here and try to kill you."

"Would you believe me if I told you I have no clue what this was about?"

"I might. But what did she say it was about?"

"I really couldn't follow her reasoning. I think she's crazy."

"And now, I don't believe you after all. Every single guy on the planet says the same thing about their ex."

"Ex? I never even met her until we set off."

"So what? A week's plenty of time to get to know someone you're locked on a ship with."

He was about to argue, about to plead his innocence, when he saw her half-smile. Then she laughed at him. "You should have seen your face. It was priceless."

He allowed himself a chuckle. "You're evil, aren't you?"

"Didn't you know? All Russian women are evil. They bring us up that way so we can marry the men who run the oil companies."

He knew she was teasing him again, but she'd put the poker face back on. Flustered, he changed the subject.

"Did you know it would bring one of the monsters? The music, I mean."

She nodded. "We called them from miles away with the subaquatic one. I thought they'd be able to hear this pretty easily, so when I spotted one of them a few meters away, it came to me. By the way, your playlist reads like something my dad would listen to. Don't you have anything new?"

"Hey, it worked, didn't it? I'm just happy you didn't try to take her on yourself."

"With this arm? She would have kicked my ass. If I'd had both hands, I could take her, even if she outweighed me by ten kilos."

"Ten kilos? I don't think..." Javier caught her look and stopped. "Yeah. She was on the plump side, wasn't she?"

"So you did notice?"

"Wait, no fair. I have no way to win."

"I told you. They train us from birth. You'll never win again." She went up on her tiptoes and planted a kiss on his lips. "Just don't forget that and you'll be fine."

She took him by the hand and they headed towards the *Irizar*.

CHAPTER 22

They only made it about thirty meters in the direction of the *Irizar* when Javier spotted two of the small creatures standing in their way. He was always surprised at how his brain refused to scale them correctly on the open ice: if someone had asked him how big they were, he'd have said that they were the size of a large dog or a small pony.

The reality, that they were as long as two cars parked one behind the other if you counted the tail, just didn't register until you came much closer. The creatures were bent over something.

"Ugh. They're eating the bodies," Natasha said.

"That's strange. They usually take the bodies to their nest."

"Maybe they know these are already dead," she replied. "Or perhaps it's just a question of hunger. Our arrival meant that these creatures have been running around and expending a lot of energy. Plus, you have to remember that they need to keep warm in this cold climate. So they need to eat."

"Yeah. I'm more concerned about how to get around them without being seen. We might need to circle over there, and try to get onto the ship from the left."

"Don't they call it the port side?"

He was about to snap at her that it didn't really matter what sailors called the parts of their ship when, once again, he saw her smile. Her sense of humor was going to take a bit of getting used to. "You're enjoying yourself, aren't you?"

"Shouldn't I be? Try to remember that just a couple of days ago I thought I was going to die. I saw a lot of my friends on that boat torn to pieces in front of me. Then I thought you were dead... Now, it almost looks like we're both going to make it out of this alive. Yeah, I'm in a good place."

"We're not out of this yet."

"And they say Russians are gloomy."

He chuckled. "Do you forget who invented tango? Argentines will always give Russians a run for their money when it comes to negativity in the face of near success."

"I always thought tango was sexy."

"Then you need to listen to the words. Back when it started, tango was all about betrayal and sadness. Fitting, I guess, because it was the music of the poor people's brothels."

"Sex. I told you." She caught his look. "All right, I'll behave. We should be safe while they're feeding as long as we don't get between them and their food."

They began to edge around the nothosaurs, describing a wide circle that would eventually lead them to the Irizar's port side.

Javier was tense, pistol in his gloved hand, trying to look in every direction at once. Natasha on the other hand, appeared perfectly relaxed. She walked along beside him like they were strolling through a garden.

In the end, they reached the icebreaker without incident. A guard posted on deck spotted them and, without speaking, tossed a rope ladder over the side. When they came aboard, the man embraced them.

"Welcome back," he said.

"Thanks. How many made it back?"

"We've been picking up stragglers for the last hour or so, but most…"

"I know. I was there."

They headed back towards Natasha's cabin. The ship had never seemed particularly crowded, but now it was positively deserted. Very few sailors or soldiers could be seen scurrying about, and no clumps of friends were smoking beside the railings. Javier wondered how many of the original three hundred-odd passengers and crew were still alive. Fifty? A hundred? It was hard to tell, but the decimation was obvious.

They sat on Natasha's bed. For a moment, she turned serious. "What was that all about? Why did that woman want to kill you?"

"I already told you, I don't know."

"Look into my eyes and tell me again."

"I have no clue. Really and truly. Camila seemed normal. A bit resentful that I was in charge of the science team, but I thought she was normal otherwise."

"You were in charge of the science team?"

"Yes."

"Hmm." She thought about that for a few moments but then shook her head. "No. Though it would make her mad, it's not enough to kill you for. Another scientist, someone who could steal her publication thunder… Yeah, I'd kill them in a heartbeat," she smiled to show that she was joking, "but not some soldier put in charge for admin reasons. That makes no sense. She must have had other reasons."

"You mean apart from being completely insane?"

"But what triggered it?"

"How should I know? My training teaches me how to shoot people when I have problems with them… it said nothing about dealing with psycho ladies."

"Yeah, that would have worked, too."

"If she hadn't caught me by surprise, I would have been happy to shoot her."

"Oh, really?" she cocked her head at him.

He didn't know the right answer to that one. Was she worried that he was some kind of Neanderthal who'd shoot a woman dead? Most women he'd known would have been appalled at the mere mention of the possibility, but somehow, he felt that Natasha might be different. For all the polish that she must have acquired in England, he thought she might be disappointed if he said he'd never shoot a woman. He decided that honesty would be the best idea in the long run.

"Maybe I would have shot her in the leg or something."

She laughed. "I guess I'll just have to live with that."

It felt as if he'd passed a test. He kissed her.

Minutes later, though, Javier began to get the sense that something was going to happen. He couldn't quite put a finger on it, but he felt a sudden urge to get on deck.

"I need to go find out what's going on," he told Natasha.

She pouted, but nodded. "Do what you need to do."

He went belowdecks and found the doctor, who favored him with a sour look. "Why aren't you dead?" the man asked dourly.

"I don't know. One of the lizard things ate me but spat me out. It said to tell the chef that he's fired."

They shared a chuckle. "You wouldn't want to take command of this tin can, would you?"

"I think you outrank me."

"Bullshit. This is a courtesy commission. I'm almost a civilian."

"Lay off it. What have you been doing?"

"I've had the crew assembling the 40mm guns. My problem is that I don't have time to supervise them."

"I really doubt that anyone is goofing off. They know what's at stake."

"Of course. But I'd still feel more comfortable if someone I trust is supervising. Want to guess who just got the assignment?"

"I'll go look."

The sailors had used the ship's undamaged crane to lift the crates containing the guns to the ship's prow. Javier nodded in approval. With only two guns, it was best to keep them concentrated in the most likely place for the creature to attack them again—if it was still alive. That place was the bow, which had the additional advantage of being the largest open space on the ship. The roof of the central structure would have been better, but the cranes were too short… and the roof had buckled under the very first onslaught.

He took a second look at the guns and groaned. They were Bofors 40mm pieces. Antiques. A Swedish design from the 1930s that saw ample use as anti-aircraft defense and then as general purpose guns in naval uses worldwide. It wasn't a modern gun by any means… and he wondered just how effective they would be if the thing had survived an internal strike with an RPG.

He approached the men around the gun. "How's it going, guys?"

"We were waiting for the order to fire some test rounds. Want to do the honors?"

He shrugged. "Sure. What do I need to do?"

"We've filled the autoloader. There are twenty-five rounds in there, but we want to test it with just one. That's the fire mechanism, just pull on that lever there."

Javier sat in the gunner's chair and followed the instructions. He was rewarded by a big bang. The gun absorbed all the recoil and, he assumed, a shell flew off into the middle distance. Even if it might not be enough to kill the big creature, it was a satisfying feeling to have something better than rifles to defend themselves with.

He searched for some evidence of impact in the snow, but saw nothing. The shell was a bit too small for that.

He waited for the other gun to be tested. One of the sailors fired it, and that was successful as well. Javier smiled. He was pretty sure these guys had never put together two disassembled guns so quickly in their lives—the fact that both worked perfectly was a testament to just how critical it was to get this correct.

"Good work, men," Javier said. The sailors, all frantic energy when he arrived, sat down and began passing each other cigarettes. One of them pulled out a mate and a thermos of water.

"Go tell the doctor that his guns are up and running," Javier asked one of the men. "Take the cigarette. Tell him I let you do it."

The guy gave him a mock salute and sauntered off, trailing smoke. The speed with which everyone had relaxed after the latest attack was surprising. Maybe this was the way they dealt with the stress of seeing their shipmates and friends cut down in such numbers. Maybe, like Ingrid, they would react fully in their own time.

The gunner's chair was comfortable enough, and he didn't feel like doing anything productive, so he looked out across the ice and wondered what could have caused Camila to snap.

What he hadn't told Natasha, and probably never would, was that he'd pegged Camila as the resentful type from the first moment. He'd tried to give her the benefit of the doubt and had nearly convinced himself that it was natural for her not to like him after he was named the leader of the expedition she'd dreamed about all her life, but in hindsight, he'd never been too convinced.

Camila had always seemed to him to be the typical exponent of the Argentine middle class: always resentful of the people who had a little more than they did—whether it be better education, better social connections or just more money—and dismissive of everyone worse off. In her case, that dismissiveness appeared to have turned into guilt, which had led to political activism of a very strange kind. Unfortunately, strange didn't mean unusual.

He shrugged. He'd probably never know what had happened to Camila out on the ice. That the horrors she'd encountered had broken something inside her mind was self-evident. It was something he could sympathize with. Being out there where time appeared to stand still while the wind nibbled coldly through your clothes and the nearest civilization appeared to be infinitely far away was enough to break anyone. He'd felt the call of madness himself… and at no time had he been facing death alone.

Screech.

The sound was like nothing he'd ever heard, the tortured cry of a colossus from hell. It vibrated through his bones and made him think, for a fleeting second, that the frozen landscape had spawned yet another monster.

Then the truth hit him. Not another monster… the same monster, come back for more.

They'd been wrong to assume it would come out the same ice hole as before. Nothosaurs were amphibious; this one had apparently remembered that fact and decided to hit them from the water.

The screeches continued for minutes and echoed weirdly through the metal. Some reached them as groans, others as screams that sounded nearly human, but all turned otherworldly when they mingled with the wind blowing across the frozen plains.

Men stopped and exchanged looks. Though not many crew were left aboard, they congregated at the bow. It reminded Javier of photos he'd seen of people waiting for the newspaper on a street corner to receive news of some global catastrophe. Even the cool palette of the deck and backdrop reminded him of dark black and white photographs.

An agony of time later, the noise just… stopped. Silence returned to Antarctica as even the wind died down. Javier was almost loathe to break it, but he was nominally in charge.

"Everyone grab a gun. You and you," he pointed at two random sailors, one male, one female. "Do you know where the American stowed his gear?"

The woman nodded. "At the back, below the heliports."

"Good, get back there and see if he left any more of those rocket launchers. You have my permission to open all of his crates. If you find anyone, tell them to get armed and take position along the railings. If they see the ice breaking, I need to know about it at once."

"Yessir."

They sprinted aft, looks of hopelessness replaced by purpose. Javier knew that, tactically, what he was doing was less than sound—he should get his ass out of the seat and put a decent screen of lookouts around the ship—but he didn't want to give up the gun position. If anyone survived, they could court-martial him later.

Everyone in sight was standing around trying to spot where the attack would begin. He tried to shout orders that might galvanize them into action like the two others, but he couldn't really think of anything to say. Every single FAL on board had already been taken in the earlier attack; most of the men who'd died sported only their regulation sidearms—there hadn't been anywhere near enough rifles for everyone.

It almost came as a relief when cracking sounds arrived from the ice to his right. Everyone turned that way and watched as the creature found a weak spot it could exploit and began to open an exit hole maybe twenty meters from the starboard hull.

It emerged slowly, without a roar, as if the effort of attacking the bottom of the ship and boring through the ice had exhausted it.

Gone was the terrifying monster that appeared able to bend steel into pretzels and pulp anyone who got too close at whim. The thing that struggled to drag itself upright was a figure to inspire pity more than terror. Whatever Breen had done would end up killing it.

Of course, Javier reminded himself, that didn't mean it couldn't take everyone on board with it.

He spun the handle that rotated the gun and saw the other gunner doing the same. Luck—bad luck in this case—had positioned Javier's gun in a spot where he could only see the monster by craning his neck around a piece of superstructure… but the other man was in exactly the right place.

"Wait for it to get closer," Javier shouted.

The monster might have been wounded—likely mortally so—but it still possessed enough strength to pull itself onto all fours. It took a step towards the ship and Javier heard machine gun fire from aft of his position. The beast paid the bullets no heed and struck downwards with its colossal head. Metal groaned and the firing stopped.

It turned aft.

"Quick, shoot it!" Javier shouted, descending from his seat to stand beside the man on the other gun. He would have preferred to wait until they could concentrate their fire on its head, but that was secondary. Getting the monster to move in their direction was critical—only the Bofors stood any chance of stopping it… and it was leaving their field of fire.

The sailor lowered the muzzle a couple of rotations and fired.

A small crater appeared in the creature's rear flank and it screamed.

"Good shot!" Javier exulted, thumping the sailor's back.

Enraged enough to forget its weakness, the reptile stood on its hind legs, balancing with its tail and turned towards its tormentors.

Huge claws raked the superstructure just meters from the gun emplacement. Parts of the ship—some big enough to crush them—rained down.

"Shoot it again! Come on! What are you waiting for?"

But the sailor was paralyzed.

Javier reacted immediately. He pushed the man from the seat and climbed on himself, only half-aware of the sailor running for the dubious cover of the main cabin area.

He played with the wheel and tried to aim for the head. He fired.

And missed.

The nothosaur turned to look towards the noise. The elongated head darted closer, and Javier fired while frantically turning the wheel. The half-second between each thumping recoil of a shell being fired towards it seemed to last an eternity.

He didn't know if anything hit. He was too busy trying to track the creature's head, attempting to do maximum damage.

Huge teeth tore a chunk of railing away and a flick of the serpentine neck sent it flying across the ice. The thing wasn't slowing down.

A spatter and another screech galvanized him. He'd gotten the creature in the neck, and it was thrashing and gushing blood a mere ten meters away. He fired at the same spot again and again.

Suddenly he was face to face with the creature's head, the long snout just a couple of armlengths away from the cannon's muzzle. A huge eye impaled him. There was no question: the creature had seen him and knew exactly who was responsible for its pain. The maw opened.

Javier watched, frozen at the trigger. This was it. They'd given their all, fought the good fight, and now it was time for him to die.

Breen had shot an RPG down its throat, and still this thing refused to roll over. There was nothing they could do.

Breen.

Breen had fought to the last ounce of strength. He'd repulsed the last attack. Javier would do no less than the gringo.

He pulled back on the firing lever.

Thump.

Half-second.

Thump.

Half-second.

Thump.

The creature recoiled slightly and Javier kept pumping foot-long projectiles into it. He felt himself become covered in blood, but he just kept firing.

The monster's head lay on the deck five meters away and Javier kept firing.

Long after the creature was dead, long after he'd completely depleted the auto-loader, Javier's hand pulled on the firing mechanism again and again and again.

The jubilant crew, when they came to celebrate the victory, had to pry his fingers off the trigger.

CHAPTER 23

The bar—or at least its stash of alcohol—had survived. Champagne, whisky and assorted other spirits appeared and were consumed right there on the deck. Javier stood with his arm around Natasha's waist, working on his fifth plastic cup of bubbly.

He was already at that warm sense between having just enough to drink and having had way too much… and Natasha, from all appearances, had already gone over that particular edge, laughing much too hard at his jokes and whispering obscenities in his ear loud enough for everyone to hear them.

No one seemed to care, but the myth of Russians being able to hold their drink better than anyone else on the planet would never convince him again. Never mind that Natasha, like most of the rest, had consumed staggering amounts of the stuff. Javier's own progress through the drink had been hampered by continuous requests for speeches by the hero of the hour.

One of the sailors, a pudgy guy with darkish skin and hair, walked up to Javier and gave him a hug. "I propose a toast… to Colonel Dragonkiller." He held his glass in the air, and everyone saluted Javier again. It was starting to get old, and the only thing Javier really wanted to know was where in the world the guy had gotten a container made of actual glass. From what he'd seen, every piece of glass on the ship—windows, cups, mirrors—was lying on the deck in small, sharp pieces.

Someone got a set of speakers and plugged a phone into them and Javier found himself laughing almost uncontrollably. It didn't occur to him until later that the music might call one of the small creatures.

He turned to Natasha. "I must be drunker than I thought. I swear the deck is tilting." He bent over to give her a kiss.

She pushed him away. "It is. Look."

He couldn't quite discern what it was she was pointing at—the ice, perhaps the horizon?—but one thing was certain: the tilt of the deck wasn't in his mind. An unattended 40 mm shell rolled down the deck and under the railing. Fortunately it managed not to explode and kill everyone, but it was evidence that there was something amiss with the ship's angle.

"Wait. This is important." He tried to think of why an angle to the deck might be significant but came up blank until a sailor who hadn't been part of the festivities rushed into their midst.

"We're sinking! We're taking on water. Abandon ship!"

They exchanged glances and everyone broke out laughing. Once the mirth had passed, they created a game from trying to drop one of the gangplanks onto the ice. Finally, they got it done and paraded off the ship.

From solid ground, or at least solid-ish ice, the angle became much more pronounced.

"He was right. The ship *is* sinking," Natasha remarked. Then she giggled into his jacket.

The *Irizar*, once the pride of the Argentine Navy, was a wounded vessel. It had a noticeable list to one side and Javier would have sworn he could hear the bubbling sound of more water rushing in. Of course, that might just have been the sound of red wine spilling onto the ice beside him from an overturned bottle.

"It doesn't look anything like blood," he told Natasha.

She nodded. "Too purple."

Suddenly, someone rushed down the gangway. His stride was so purposeful that attention immediately focused on him. Fortunately, the cup in his hand identified him as one of them.

"It's the doctor," Javier said loudly.

Everyone raised their drinks to hail the man.

The doctor walked right up to Javier and threw the contents of his cup into the Colonel's face.

Javier sputtered, and felt anger coming over the glow of wellbeing. "What was that for?"

The doctor held his ground. "To get your attention. This ship is sinking, I have two sedated patients in the infirmary and no one seems sober enough to help me get them out. Or rather the three sober sailors I've found have refused to go below decks. They say the ship might go under at any moment. So I came to look for someone who's shown courage verging on idiocy in the face of danger."

"Ingrid?"

"Yeah, and another guy that will survive if we get him out, but not if he drowns first."

"I'll go."

"I know. That's why I wasted my water on you."

Javier handed Natasha his sidearm. "Use this if any of the nothosaurs come around. I think there are still a couple of the small ones out there."

For a second, the Russian biologist seemed almost sober. "I'd much rather capture one alive." Then she giggled. "Can you imagine the faces of people at Oxford? If anyone doubts me when I say I have a prehistoric," she stumbled over that word quite badly, "reptile in captivity, I'll just release it at them and see who runs fastest and who becomes a nest liner. Fun!"

The doctor led him back up the gangplank and down the nearest stairway. The emergency lights below decks were flickering. Some areas were already immersed in the penumbra.

Javier hadn't been below deck at all since he'd boarded the icebreaker. He'd dismissed those areas as service levels, but now realized that many of the crew who didn't rank highly enough to rate a cabin on the superstructure were housed down there. In the end, the joke had been on those who'd gotten the open views above: most of the cabins in the central section of the ship were now scrap, and possessions were strewn all over the ice or sunk in the ocean.

Of course, that was moot as well. With the ship sinking and most of the crew dead, who was going to come crawling in here to recover some old clothes?

"We should get a light," Javier said. His intoxication was disappearing as his adrenal glands reacted to the fact that he'd just chosen to enter the bowels of a sinking ship.

"No time. Look."

The doctor pointed to the deck below the level they were at, where water was rushing down the stairs to the deeper areas.

"That just means that the hole is there. That big one must have had some seriously sharp claws to penetrate the hull of an icebreaker. It will take a long time for that level to fill with water. Everything below it needs to flood first."

"I'm still not going to take the chance. That level is where we set up the infirmary."

Suddenly, the knowledge that he would have to walk through the dark liquid brought the danger of the situation home. "All right. Let's go."

They descended into the next level of the stairwell. The landing was covered with an inch of water. His black boots held it at bay, for now, but the sensation of the liquid slapping against it was extraordinarily unpleasant.

"This way."

The corridor was illuminated by a single flickering light. It blinked on and off rhythmically, appearing to keep time with their footsteps. A single door opened into another room.

The chamber was a small cabin with a single bunk and, thankfully, the lighting was working. The bunk was occupied; Javier could see Ingrid's unmistakable blond hair spilling all the way to the floor.

The doctor strode to a wheeled drip stand beside the bed. He pulled a needle out of his pocket, took a few seconds to prep it and injected the contents into the transparent rubber bag.

Seconds later, the Swedish scientist began to stir. The doctor bent over her, slapped her wrist a few times and, within a couple of minutes had her sitting on the edge of the bed.

At least Javier's head and phone said it had been minutes. Everything else was screaming at him that they had to run, had to get the hell out of there now. The ship was sinking, dammit. *Hurry*!

But the doctor refused to be rushed. He made sure Ingrid was wearing decent boots before he'd let her step into the frigid water. Only when he was satisfied did they trudge off to see to the other man.

Javier tried to fight back the sensation that the water had gotten higher as they went. There was no way it could rise until the decks below flooded. And when that happened, he had a feeling they would sink before he could really begin to analyze everything.

The sailor's room was just around a corner. The hall there was dark, but the doctor knew where they were going. He navigated and entered the room.

It was nearly pitch dark, but both Javier and the doctor had their phones with them. On came the flashlights, almost simultaneously—in Javier's case, that came with a sigh of relief: after so many hours on the ice with a dead battery, having the phone back, complete with its clock and flashlight, made him feel like a citizen of the twenty-first century again.

The sailor was gone.

In his place was a mess of torn and tangled sheets covered in dark black blood.

"Oh, God," Javier said. He suddenly wanted nothing but to be out on the ice where he could see an animal coming from far away and get his shot in before the thing could reach him. "Let's get out of here."

For once the doctor was amenable. They rushed out and headed towards the stairwell.

A roar stopped them dead in their tracks.

"That came from the stairs," Javier said.

"Are you sure? Aren't those things too big for that space?" the doctor said.

"They're big, but only the head is inflexible. If it can squeeze the skull through the opening, the body can follow eventually."

"All right. Let's try to get out some other set of stairs."

They ran back the way they'd come, splashes echoing loudly in the confined space of the corridor. Now that they were moving quickly,

Javier felt the water splash over the top of his boots and seep inside. He suppressed a gasp; he thought he'd become inured to the cold after so much time on ice and snow, but getting water from the Antarctic Sea in your shoes was another level of cold entirely. It was painful to the touch.

There was a stairwell across the ship, on the starboard side. They reached the cross tunnel and traversed it, but the stairs stopped in a tangle of bent metal meters above their heads.

"Crap. I remember this now," Javier said. "The big monster demolished this whole area."

"Then we need to try to get out through the stairs in the stern."

"Damnit."

They ran aft. Javier soon realized that it wasn't his imagination. The water level was definitely getting higher. Maybe it was just because they were nearing the hole in the hull, or maybe…

Javier shut down that line of thought. If there was one thing he didn't want to be thinking about it was alternative explanations to that.

So he thought about how the hell one of the nothosaurs had gotten below decks without anyone noticing. Of course, the crew had had other problems at the time, but it still seemed a fantastic thing to miss.

Another roar brought him back from his reverie. There was a monster somewhere behind them, and it didn't seem the least bit concerned that the ship was sinking.

They sloshed around another corner and came to a stop. Ten meters away, water was gushing into the corridor in a torrent. For three meters, the water frothed at waist level before pouring down to the two-inch high slurry they were wading through.

"We can't go that way!" the doctor exclaimed.

Scratching and snuffing sounds came from behind.

"We're going to have to," Javier responded grimly.

Pulling the stunned Ingrid along, they advanced towards the torrent. It felt like wading against the current in a stream swollen by snowmelt. Despite the danger, the shock of the freezing water was almost too much to bear. Javier wanted to turn back and run the way they'd come. A prehistoric monster would be a small challenge compared to the pain of this water. How long before hypothermia took him?

As they got deeper, Javier felt Ingrid's wet hand beginning to slip, and then she was gone, tumbling along to lie where the water level tapered off.

"Damn," Javier said. He turned back and, letting the torrent push him, he shouldered past the doctor and knelt next to the Swede.

Grunting, he lifted her onto his shoulders in the same fireman's carry he'd used before and began to work against the torrent once again. He was certain that each step would be his last, that razor claws or dagger teeth would tear into him from behind at any moment.

His skin crawled, but he resisted the urge to look behind. He needed all his strength to fight the water, to keep his numb legs from giving out under the weight of the two bodies.

It was like being back in his first officer training camp. He was exhausted, but he knew that he could only succeed if he concentrated on putting one foot in front of the other. The stakes back then had been a career in the military, a respectable position in society and the respect of his family… Now it was life and death, but the fundamentals were the same: keep moving forward, don't give up, don't let anything distract you. Ignore the pain.

That last one was becoming increasingly hard. His legs trembled with each step. But if he fell now, it wasn't just his own life he'd be throwing away, but Ingrid's as well.

They reached the bubbling fountain of water. The strength of the torrent here was almost overwhelming but, with a final groaning push, he made it past.

Now the water was pushing him in the way they needed to go. He put Ingrid on the ground in front of him.

"Can you walk?"

She nodded, eyes wide.

"Good, stay in front of me."

The doctor was waiting for them, an anxious look on his face. "We need to move."

The water on this side of the torrent was pooling higher than the other. Evidently, it wasn't draining as quickly, and reached the top of Javier's boots, above his ankles.

They began to trudge along when suddenly a wave hit them from behind, slamming into the back of Javier's knees and nearly knocking him over. Ingrid did fall, and for a terrifying moment, she disappeared under the surface of the gelid water before her head popped back out, spluttering and cursing.

"Shit," Javier said. He turned back, expecting to see the bubbling brook turned into a raging river.

What he actually saw was even worse. The enormous mass of the nothosaur behind them was standing right in the water's path, diverting a stream in their direction.

"Run!" he cried.

The doctor wasted no time in setting off down the long hall. By the time Javier had dragged Ingrid back to her feet and set off after him, the man had disappeared around a corner.

The Swedish scientist seemed to have been revived by her icy dunking and she shook him off and sprinted.

Javier was certain that the next thing he'd feel would be the slicing open of his back, the feeling of claws that meant death was nigh. Only when he reached the corner did the itching between his shoulder blades die down. He even risked glancing back at the pursuing monster as he turned. It had been made sluggish by the cold water… or something. It appeared to be trying to get its bearings.

Then it roared and Javier decided not to stick around to see how long it would take to react. He closed the gap on Ingrid and they reached the door—unfortunately, it was a flimsy wooden door instead of the more nautically traditional metal hatch.

They still tried to close it behind them, but moving the door through six inches of water proved impossible. Just as well, it wouldn't have slowed the creature down for more than a few seconds.

The ship lurched sickeningly. "We'd better get the hell out of here," the doctor said.

"You're just now realizing that?" Javier replied. He knew he was getting rattled—the sarcasm had mostly been beaten out of him in officer school, to be used only on training exercises and on wiseass enlisted men and junior officers, never in live-fire situations. And this one was about as live-fire as situations got.

A roar behind them apparently signified that the monster had gotten its bearings. If form held, that meant it would come barreling down the hall at any moment.

The aft staircase was only a single broad flight that led into a storage unit on the first level beneath the deck. Piled crates of supplies intended to last for a year in Antarctica teetered precariously on all sides except for directly ahead, where one of the piles had collapsed in the direction of the ship's lean and was blocking their path.

Javier didn't complain: at least there was no water on this level.

He jumped onto the nearest crate and helped Ingrid up. Other boxes, high overhead, loomed over them, held in place by straps tensed to the breaking point.

The nothosaur's head appeared at the top of the stairs. They turned and ran again, heading aft. Javier could see sunlight ahead of them, less than twenty meters away. All three were sprinting at full tilt. He'd never thought he could possibly be grateful for that wan illumination but right then it was the most perfectly beautiful thing he'd ever seen.

The ship lurched again, and it suddenly became extremely difficult to remain upright. Javier had to correct and run to the right for the final few meters, or he would have slammed into the far wall. Crates shifted ominously and a bright red fire extinguisher rolled across the floor and stopped against the wall with a crash.

Behind them—too close for comfort—the nothosaur was having even more trouble than the humans. With a skittering of claws against metal, it lost purchase and slid downwards.

It went down in a tangle of legs, neck, scales and crates.

The respite allowed Javier to burst into the sunlight. He realized that they'd been running through the storage area under the heliport, and had emerged onto the rearmost deck of the ship.

The ice lay only a couple of meters below their position, and the doctor had already jumped over. He was encouraging Ingrid to jump down after him.

"Come on!"

"This is going to hurt," she replied.

"I'll catch you," he said. "And if you miss, I'll stitch you back together. It will be much easier than having to repair teeth marks again."

Javier didn't bother to join the conversation. He slowed just enough as he ran past to put an arm around her and launch both of them from the ship.

They landed on a pile of ground snow which cushioned the impact, but Javier still had the breath knocked out of him. He stood with difficulty and brushed himself off.

The rising wind had blown ice crystals into the air again, infusing the light with a milky glow. For a moment, Javier recalled Camila's assertion that they were stuck in some kind of demonic time loop, forever condemned to live out the single day that stretched to infinity. It almost seemed that way. Kill one monster, another landed on top of you.

What if she was right?

A woman's scream in the distance brought him out of his reverie. Was it Natasha? He didn't stop to find out: ignoring the difficulty in breathing, Javier jumped to his feet and sprinted across the snow as quickly as he could without falling.

CHAPTER 24

Every nightmare scenario flashed through his mind. He saw Natasha disemboweled, two nothosaurs fighting over her entrails. He saw her beheaded. Or maimed and left to bleed out while he could do nothing but watch and hold her hand as she died.

They'd dropped off the tilting icebreaker on the opposite side from where they'd left the knot of sailors and it was impossible to go around the back due to the channel in the ice where the ship had broken its way through. That meant he had to run along the entire length of the *Irizar* and circle around the prow.

Slipping and sliding in his anxiety to get around the corner and see what was going on, Javier ran. It seemed to take forever in this place of diffuse light and non-existent shadows.

He finally reached the prow and desperately searched for the group they'd left there. There was no one to be seen, just the scattered detritus of their party: a couple of bottles of champagne and a discarded jacket.

Javier stopped. "Natasha!" he shouted.

Gunfire erupted just beyond a ridge so he sprinted in that direction. Just below, five sailors and, to his relief, Natasha, were retreating from one of the monsters. For all he knew, it might be the same one that they'd encountered on the *Irizar*, a creature who'd decided to make it its business to terrorize the survivors of the expedition.

The body of a soldier lay in a pool of his own blood a little further back in the direction they'd come from.

The little group was retreating back the way it had come and Javier lay perfectly still at the edge of the ridge. Natasha passed almost within arm's length, but he didn't want to move in case it set the creature off. He didn't dare move, and even tried to breathe into the snow so the condensation from his breath wouldn't be visible.

Suddenly, the nothosaur charged, galloping with that gait that always reminded Javier of horses.

The sailors retreated, walking backward as fast as they could. Natasha brought the gun up and fired once, but she didn't hit anything. The sailor with the FAL was shaking so badly he would have been hard-pressed to hit the ice if he'd been trying to hit it.

The monster would be upon them in seconds. They just didn't seem to have any concept of how to defend themselves. In all fairness, they were probably still more than a little drunk—they'd put away pretty much the entire contents of several cases of spirits that had survived unscathed in storage.

He acted before he had a chance to think. Suddenly, as if of its own accord, his body was airborne, just as the prehistoric horror passed underneath.

He landed on the neck near the head, and grabbed on with both hands. To Javier's relief, his arms closed around the creature's neck. He tried to pull them closed, to cut off its air supply, to strangle it.

There was no way in the world that was ever going to work. It was like trying to squeeze a concrete pillar.

All he could do was to try and hold on for dear life. He closed his eyes and rode out the bucking and jumping. A smell of decomposing flesh and death reached him from the creature's mouth as it tried to tear him off. But he was too close to its head for that to work. The teeth couldn't reach him.

Next, the thing tried to claw him off, but, again, it couldn't quite bend its legs to where he was located. For a second, Javier was thankful that his opponent had a brain the size of a walnut: had it been a little more intelligent, it probably would have realized that Javier could be brought into range by bending its neck.

The thought didn't last long. Javier was busy trying to stay on its neck. He knew that as soon as he hit the ground, death would follow within seconds.

"Javier!" Natasha's voice cut through the cold air like a sword.

Getting his eyes to focus was difficult. He was taking a thorough thrashing. Finally, the beast swung Natasha into view. She was five or six meters away, pointing the gun at the creature.

"Don't shoot!" he shouted.

She shook her head and he realized that she wasn't aiming. She was showing him she had the gun. She wanted to give it to him.

"No! Run away!"

He couldn't hold on much longer, and though the sailors had gotten out of sight, his sacrifice would be for nothing if Natasha was killed.

Trying to time the bucking correctly, Javier let go of the nothosaur's neck. He arced through the air and landed with a crash three meters from Natasha's feet. He tried to stand, but his leg gave out under him. The constant beating from the expedition had finally taken its toll. He got to his knees and awaited the slavering maw.

"Catch!"

Natasha threw his Browning. It landed on the ice in front of him and only lightning reflexes heightened by the immense pain kept it from sliding away. The creature lunged towards him, enraged at the puny creature who'd dared to inconvenience it by jumping on its neck.

Javier was quicker. Up came the muzzle of the gun and he fired. Once again, he found himself emptying a barrel into a nothosaur. He hadn't been counting, but if he killed this one, he was probably the single person most responsible for the re-extinction of the nothosaur. Asteroids had nothing on him.

There were only six shots left in the gun, and for a single agonizing moment he sat there clicking on an empty magazine.

But the monster was dead. It fell to one side.

Javier turned to Natasha and smiled. "I'm sorry. I know you wanted it alive, but…" he shrugged and a wave of pain flew up his leg. The last thing he saw was the cold ice coming up to see him.

***

Javier woke wrapped in a collection of blankets and jackets, and otherwise naked from the waist down. He felt a pressure on his leg, felt the discomfort of not being able to bend it.

"Welcome back to the world of the living, sleeping beauty," the doctor's deep tones said beside him.

"What happened?"

"You broke both the tibia and the fibula on your left leg. Also, you nearly got eaten by a big reptile. That probably didn't help."

"Where did all this come from?" Javier indicated the blanket and the pillow he just realized someone had put under his head. "Someone went back to the *Irizar* just for that?"

"Sadly, that's not possible anymore. Look."

He pointed towards Javier's feet, so the colonel lifted his head to look. The once-proud icebreaker was nowhere to be seen. Only a long furrow in the ice, disappearing into the distance, served as evidence that there had once been a vessel there.

"Damn."

The doctor grinned at him. "Well, at least it took that thing with it."

"I thought the one I killed might have been the one on the boat."

"Nope. I watched the bastard go down with the ship."

"Good." Javier nodded in satisfaction.

"Too bad they're amphibious," the doctor said.

Javier gave him a dark look. "Is there any whisky?"

"Yes. Plenty. But you can't have any. I've already got you on some reasonably heavy painkillers. I immobilized the bones as best I could, but someone is going to have to operate on you when we get back."

"Not you?"

"I don't think my hands will ever stop shaking after this."

Javier smiled. "Thank you, doctor."

"Me? What for?"

"For taking care of us. Of me, of Natasha, of Ingrid."

The doctor laughed. "I can't believe it. The hero of the hour, and he's thanking me. They're talking about renaming the base after you."

Javier shook his head darkly. "What for? It's not like I saved very many people. How many survived? Six? Seven?"

"We've been getting stragglers coming back from the groups that descended to attack the big creature earlier. There are almost forty men and women alive here who are convinced they owe you their lives. Hell, when I told them you needed to get out of your wet clothes, a couple of guys offered to go naked so you wouldn't have to. I told them not to be silly and sent them to the base for blankets. They ran there and back without a single complaint. They also brought the painkillers that are making this conversation possible."

"Where's Natasha?"

"She's talking to Ingrid. Once we convinced her that everything was fine and that there were no more of the monsters, she melted down completely. I had to put her under again, and put Natasha on suicide watch in case she wakes up." He grinned. "That woman is amazing. After everything she's been through, I'd have expected her to be a complete wreck… but all she's been doing is to try to convince some of the troops to accompany her to some cave to get some eggs. Do you have any idea what she's talking about?"

"Yeah, I do. And it might not be a bad idea to get down there. That's where all the bodies are. The people from the base, I mean. We should probably try to recover them for when the rescue comes." Suddenly doubt hit him. "Help *is* coming, isn't it?"

The doctor put a hand on his arm. "There's a Hercules scheduled to land on the strip near the base in an hour or so. At least the sailors insist that they convinced Buenos Aires that the coast is clear. I'm not sure whether to believe it, and none of the officers survived."

"We did."

"Yeah. But that's only because we're senior guys who get to watch the action from well behind the front lines."

That made Javier laugh hard enough for pain to shoot up from his leg, reminding him that all was not well with his body.

"Could you call her over?"

"Who?"

"Don't be a jerk."

The doctor walked away, chuckling to himself, and was replaced within moments by the much more attractive features of a certain Russian zoologist.

She smiled and kissed him, a light brush on the lips. "That was the craziest thing I've ever seen," she said. "Thank you."

He returned the smile. "Just doing my job."

"Your job is to attack prehistoric animals unarmed? Why would you sign up for something like that?" She knelt closer and allowed him to lay his head on her thighs.

"It sounded like fun at the time. Now, I'm not so sure… who would have thought I'd be injured?"

She laughed.

"Seriously, though, has anyone looked to see if there are more of those things out there?"

"If there are, they're not coming for us. The doctor posted sentries who know how to shoot. We have plenty of FALs recovered from the dead, and more ammo than we really need unless there were many more nothosaurs than we originally saw."

"All right." He studied her face. "What are you going to do now? Once we get back to civilization, I mean."

"I'm going to stay with you until you can walk again."

Javier had his reservations about that. Argentina wasn't exactly a fortress. What would happen if the Russians tried to snatch her? Then he relaxed. It would probably become a moot point once the truth of what had happened here reached the international press. Argentina, after all, wasn't a fortress.

"And after that?"

"I'm going to stay next to you until such a time as you become convinced to leave the army and settle down with a girl."

It was the same thing all the rest had wanted. The same thing he'd refused each and every one of them. But this time, it felt different somehow. Perhaps it was Natasha… but more likely it was the realization that his military career had just reached its apex; nothing he could possibly be involved in from here on out—barring an extremely unlikely war—would ever be as exciting or as important as what had happened over the past twenty-four hours.

"All right. We can talk about it."

Natalia cocked her head. "Do you hear that?"

"Hear what?"

"A noise. A plane?"

Now he heard it. "Not a plane. That's a helicopter."

They looked up, and out of the corner of his eye, Javier saw other men looking up as well.

"Could you call the doctor?" he said and, when the man arrived, he asked: "Buenos Aires was going to send a Hercules, weren't they?"

"Yes."

"That sounds like a helicopter. I wish I could see it through this haze, but I think we can be confident that it's not Argentine. How many men do we have with combat training?"

"Four or five."

"All right. Tell them to take a few more guys with FALs to meet the chopper when it lands. If the bird is American, wave at it and have them land as close as possible… then bring me whoever is in charge. If it has no markings, take cover and shoot at whoever emerges. The Russians weren't in a mood for taking prisoners last time around. But tell them to show some restraint; I'm pretty sure it's the Americans."

Ten minutes later he was proved right: an American officer with short, graying hair and bright blue eyes was marched to where Javier was waiting.

"Help me sit," the colonel told the doctor.

"You're in no condition to sit."

"Just do it, will you?"

Javier grimaced, regretting the decision immediately, but left with no option other than to brazen it out unless he wanted to look like a complete wimp in front of the American.

The gringo saluted. "Colonel, they tell me you're in charge."

"That's right, Major."

"Let me get straight to the point. Are we prisoners? I don't have enough men to fight off ten guys with infantry rifles. This was supposed to be a humanitarian mission into friendly territory."

Always to the point, Americans. "No, Major. You're free to go whenever you like, and to look around at anything you wish. The men with guns are just a precaution against other threats. Oh, and insurance against any attempt to take the Russian woman with you."

"What Russian woman? My orders are to find a guy named Breen and fly him back to the *Polar Star* with anyone else he told me to."

"I'm afraid Breen didn't make it."

The guys eyes narrowed. It was natural for someone surrounded by foreigners—even supposedly friendly foreigners—armed to the teeth to be a little suspicious when said foreigners informed him of a compatriot's death. "Can I see the body?"

"Sure. It's inside that big lizard over there."

"What are you talking about?"

"Doctor, can you show the Major the nothosaur's big brother?"

"Of course."

A considerably more polite major returned from the expedition to see the largest of the monsters. "What the hell happened here?" he said, eyes wide.

"Would you believe me if I said that Russians happened?"

"After what I just saw, I'd believe you if you told me it was Martians."

Javier chuckled. "It wasn't Martians. We think it was a Russian project with unintended consequences. Mr. Breen was killed in helping us take down the big one. We lost a lot of our own men as well if that's any comfort to you."

"Can we report this? Do you mind having one of my men look over the entire scene and send some pics back to Washington?"

"Of course. I meant it when I said you weren't prisoners. But I think Washington is already up to speed. Breen told them all about this. He only died a couple of hours ago."

"Well, no one warned me about this."

Javier just raised an eyebrow. The other man chuckled. "Yeah, I know how it goes. Give me a second."

The Major gave the orders over a cell phone and turned back to Javier. "Can you tell me more about this Russian woman we're not supposed to take back with us?"

"That would be me," Natasha said.

"Pleased to meet you. And now I see why the Colonel refuses to let us take you."

"No. The reason I refuse to let the US take her is that no matter what you and the Russians think, people aren't just pawns in your great game."

The man didn't respond to that. Clearly he'd had experience dealing with foreign officers before because he just gave a tight-lipped smile and said, "Like I told you, I don't know anything about that. Hell, I didn't even know what we were flying into."

"All right. You can go if you want."

"I'd feel more comfortable sticking around for a while. At least until I know the people here are going to be able to get out."

"We have a Hercules coming in at any moment."

"I'll stay."

"As an observer?"

"If you want to call it that. I don't think I'll make any friends if I go back home without taking as much information as I can about what happened here. It's probably something Washington is going to want to hear about."

"I don't doubt that at all. And I can't force you to go. Antarctica belongs to the entire world, after all."

The man nodded his thanks—they both knew that the guys with the guns could always ask the other guys to do whatever they ordered—and walked away. Javier wondered if he would be chastised for allowing the Americans to walk around what was a place of Argentine national disaster, but decided he probably wouldn't. Heroes were thin on the ground in Argentina, and it would be nice for the government to be able to parade one around.

Besides, creating a diplomatic incident with the biggest power in the Western Hemisphere would look terrible on his record. It was bad enough when the Navy sank Chinese ships… but China was far away. The US was a more immediate concern.

"Penny for your thoughts?" Natasha said.

"I was just wondering what is going to happen now."

"Well, for one thing, I need to get some of those eggs and take them back to Oxford. If you hadn't insisted on killing every nothosaur who crossed your path, I'd try for a live one, but if any survived, it's going to be a race among governments to secure it, and I suppose Argentina has the most resources nearby, so I'm not going to win that one. But an egg? Surely they'd sell Oxford an egg."

"Sell?"

"Of course. You don't think they'd let something like this get out of their hands for free?"

"I hadn't thought of it that way."

She sighed. "Academia isn't some pure field, morally perfect, inhabited by people with utter honesty. It's just as political and backstabbing as any other field, and made worse by the fact that the kind of people who choose academia as a field tend to be obsessive and emotionally stunted."

"Wow. Such bitterness."

She smiled. "All right. It might not all be like that. I've met some truly wonderful people at Oxford. But sometimes it can become a bit overwhelming."

He knew exactly what she meant. Perhaps the frustrations in each of their professions were similar. Or perhaps not, but he was willing to see what common ground they could find.

Javier had a feeling they would find quite a bit.

The unmistakable sound of four enormous turboprop engines droned overhead. He smiled and took Natasha's hand. It appeared that this place's magic was broken and they'd be leaving after all.

EPILOGUE

Present day – Yekaterinburg, Russia (formerly Sverdlovsk, USSR)

A grey door opened onto a brightly lit grey room. Three men and a woman awaited his presence patiently. They had every reason to be patient. The thing they were observing was something none of them had ever seen before, and something they certainly weren't expecting.

They'd probably been expecting to be consulted on the genetic sequence of some virus or bacteria. After all that was what a visit to Compound 19 normally entailed.

"I'm sorry I'm late," Dr. Park Sun Lee said in broken Russian. "The weather is filthy outside."

The others, three Russians and one researcher from Finland all nodded, trying to disguise their condescension for the man from North Korea who couldn't deal with a little snow. They'd manage, however, if only because all four of them were curious to know what Park had for them this time around.

"I suppose you're wondering what that is." Park pointed at the egg, encased in a transparent box with a combination lock.

"Some kind of modified ostrich egg?"

He quickly spun the lock and removed the contents, then allowed himself a superior smile. His one pleasure was that, even as a foreigner, his position meant that he didn't have to be polite to these people. "Close. You were only off by a hundred million years or so. This is an egg from a Triassic reptile known as nothosaurus."

Surprise flashed across every face. "Do you expect us to believe that you have managed to reverse engineer a dinosaur?"

"Not exactly a dinosaur, and no, we didn't reverse engineer anything." Park gave them a quick outline of how the nothosaurs had survived to reach them, leaving out most of the more recent events in Antarctica.

"And these eggs are viable?"

"We think so, yes. Apparently, they've developed a survival mechanism over the millennia: the fetus matures only when the outside conditions are above a certain temperature. We think that temperature is five degrees Celsius."

They all peered at the egg as if it would suddenly hatch. The room was well above the threshold. "And you've called us in to help you hatch it?" the Finn asked. "That doesn't really make sense. We're all geneticists and molecular biologists… you need a zookeeper."

"Of course not. There are other teams in other installations taking care of that. They think it will be easy. No. We're here for another purpose. There are reasons to believe that, using a certain strand of the anthrax bacillus, we can mutate the embryo inside this egg to create a much more… interesting version of a nothosaur."

"I still don't understand why we're here. Surely, if anthrax strains were available in Russia, you'd have easier access to them than us."

"Don't play coy with me, Juha. You know we've got anthrax in this lab as well as anyone else does. Hell, even Wikipedia knows about this place… although they certainly don't even suspect the real scope. Getting anthrax isn't the problem. The problem is getting the right kind of anthrax. The strain we need is no longer… stored here."

Anna, a sixty-year-old woman from Murmansk, spoke for the first time. "That strain?" she asked, her normally jovial voice flat and dead.

"Yes," Park responded. "That strain."

"What…" Juha began, and then caught himself. "Oh."

They all looked uncomfortable for a second. There was a longstanding tradition that certain things were not discussed in that lab, or in Russian government projects in general. The big one was the Chernobyl accident, but other disasters such as Kyshtym were included. The Sverdlovsk anthrax leak was, if anything, even more taboo than the rest. After all, nuclear power was perfectly acceptable while biological warfare was anathema in the civilized world.

"The strain we need was the strain that… escaped. From what I've been able to piece together from Soviet records, the remaining samples were diluted, put in metal drums and, supposedly, sent somewhere… but the ship carrying them sank near Antarctica."

"And that's how the nothosaur with cold weather adaptation came into contact with it?"

"That's what we think, yes."

"And you have no remaining samples we can cultivate?"

"No. You won't find any," Anna interjected.

"How do you know?"

"Because I was there. Here, I mean. I'd just started as an assistant, but that day… I honestly thought they'd shoot us all. The soldiers were so angry at us. A lot of them had friends who'd been affected. Instead, we got orders from Moscow to pack all the evidence and put it on a truck. I'm surprised you found any documentation."

"This was a duplicate in… another facility."

Anna grimaced. "And here I thought we were special. Of course they'd duplicate everything."

"Yes. Unfortunately, they never duplicated that particular strain, which means we'll have to build it again. Luckily, with the documentation we have here, you should be able to get that done in a few weeks as opposed to the year or more of work I'd need to isolate it through traditional means. After all, we can print DNA strands here, and we have the Anthrax genome pretty much worked out. All you have to do is to build me Anthrax 836 again."

"That was the worst of all the strains. I was relieved that we got it out of here. Well, at least I was relieved once they convinced me they weren't just going to open all the storage cases and leave us in there to die."

"Yes. The extreme virulence is probably what caused the mutation."

"But how did it get into the nothosaurs? I doubt they ate the anthrax."

"We have no idea. Maybe it made its way up the food chain, algae to krill to fish to nothosaur and then into nothosaur sperm. Maybe it fell onto the nothosaur's eggs. We just don't know. The one thing we do know is that once you recreate the strain, our chosen method of injecting it into a fertilized nothosaur egg should make the mutation come to us that much more powerfully."

"I'd think having a nothosaur should be enough for most people. What exactly are we trying to create with this mutation?"

Park thought of the photos he'd been shown, of the hard men telling how they'd never been so frightened in their lives, how they'd barely escaped. Of the sadness he felt when he got news that the largest of the creatures had been killed in Antarctica.

"Something beautiful," he said.

THE END

facebook.com/severedpress
twitter.com/severedpress

CHECK OUT OTHER GREAT DINOSAUR BOOKS

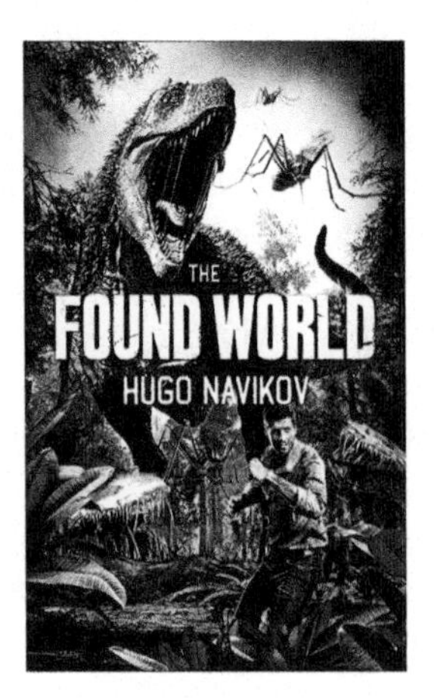

THE FOUND WORLD
by Hugo Navikov

A powerful global cabal wants adventurer Brett Russell to retrieve a superweapon stolen by the scientist who built it. To entice him to travel underneath one of the most dangerous volcanoes on Earth to find the scientist, this shadowy organization will pay him the only thing he cares about: information that will allow him to avenge his family's murder.

But before he can get paid, he and his team must enter an underground hellscape of killer plants, giant insects, terrifying dinosaurs, and an army of other predators never previously seen by man.

At the end of this journey awaits a revelation that could alter the fate of mankind ... if they can make it back from this horrifying found world.

HOUSE OF THE GODS
by Davide Mana

High above the steamy jungle of the Amazon basin, rise the flat plateaus known as the Tepui, the House of the Gods. Lost worlds of unknown beauty, a naturalistic wonder, each an ecology onto itself, shunned by the local tribes for centuries. The House of the Gods was not made for men.

But now, the crew and passengers of a small charter plane are about to find what was hidden for sixty million years.

Lost on an island in the clouds 10.000 feet above the jungle, surrounded by dinosaurs, hunted by mysterious mercenaries, the survivors of Sligo Air flight 001 will quickly learn the only rule of life on Earth: Extinction.

CHECK OUT OTHER GREAT DINOSAUR BOOKS

FLIPSIDE
by JAKE BIBLE

The year is 2046 and dinosaurs are real.

Time bubbles across the world, many as large as one hundred square miles, turn like clockwork, revealing prehistoric landscapes from the Cretaceous Period.

They reveal the Flipside.

Now, thirty years after the first Turn, the clockwork is breaking down as one of the world's powers has decided to exploit the phenomenon for their own gain, possibly destroying everything then and now in the process.

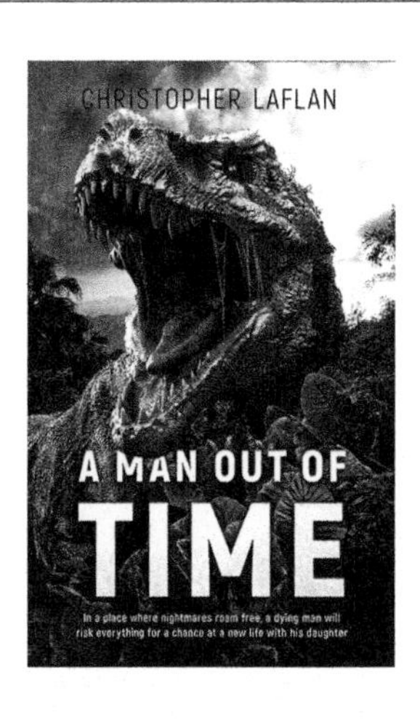

A MAN OUT OF TIME
by Christopher Laflan

Five years after the Chinese Axis detonated an unknown weapon of mass destruction off the southern coast of the United States, Special Ops Sergeant John Crider and the members of Shadow Company have finally captured what they all hope will lead to the end of the war. Unfortunately, the population within the United States is no longer sustainable. In an effort to stabilize the economy, the government enacts the Cryonics Act. One hundred years in suspended animation, all debt forgiven, and a chance at a less crowded future are too good to pass up for John and his young daughter.

Except not everything always goes as planned as Sergeant John Crider finds himself pitted against a land of prehistoric monsters genetically resurrected from the fossil record, murderous inhabitants, and a future he never wanted.

facebook.com/severedpress
twitter.com/severedpress

CHECK OUT OTHER GREAT DINOSAUR BOOKS

PRIMORDIA
by Greig Beck

Ben Cartwright, former soldier, home to mourn the loss of his father stumbles upon cryptic letters from the past between the author, Arthur Conan Doyle and his great, great grandfather who vanished while exploring the Amazon jungle in 1908.

Amazingly, these letters lead Ben to believe that his ancestor's expedition was the basis for Doyle's fantastical tale of a lost world inhabited by long extinct creatures. As Ben digs some more he finds clues to the whereabouts of a lost notebook that might contain a map to a place that is home to creatures that would rewrite everything known about history, biology and evolution.

But other parties now know about the notebook, and will do anything to obtain it. For Ben and his friends, it becomes a race against time and against ruthless rivals.

In the remotest corners of Venezuela, along winding river trails known only to lost tribes, and through near impenetrable jungle, Ben and his novice team find a forbidden place more terrifying and dangerous than anything they could ever have imagined.

PANGAEA EXILES
by Jeff Brackett

Tried and convicted for his crimes, Sean Barrow is sent into temporal exile—banished to a time so far before recorded history that there is no chance that he, or any other criminal sent back, has any chance of altering history.

Now Sean must find a way to survive more than 200 million years in the past, in a world populated by monstrous creatures that would rend him limb from limb if they got the chance. And that's just his fellow prisoners.

The dinosaurs are almost as bad.

Printed in Great Britain
by Amazon